J. L. Haynes is an exciting new author who compels the reader to experience a sense of mystery and adventure. With a keen interest in philosophy, myths, legends and the unexplained, he writes for both young and old, that they may ultimately discover or re-experience that place of wonder buried inside the heart.

To Mum and Dad

J. L. Haynes

ZARA HANSON & THE MYSTERY OF THE PAINTED SYMBOL

AUSTIN MACAULEY PUBLISHERS™

LONDON • CAMBRIDGE • NEW YORK • SHARJAH

A CIP catalogue record for this title is available from the British Library.

ISBN 9781528922869 (Paperback)
ISBN 9781528922876 (Hardback)
ISBN 9781528922883 (Kindle e-book)
ISBN 9781528963930 (ePub e-book)

www.austinmacauley.com

First Published (2019)
Austin Macauley Publishers Ltd
25 Canada Square
Canary Wharf
London
E14 5LQ

Table of Contents

And the hour of man shall come,
To judge them that dwell on the earth,
For whosoever influences the Gods,
Shall be like a God unto themselves.

—Kyubi-K

Chapter One
Planets

In the celestial firmament the seed of infinity is sown in just one bubble in a never-ending cosmic ocean of causality. This great expanse gives way to entire universes and worlds within from which life is born, and from its evolved forms new-universes are shaped. New creations to be watched, but what if they are found wanting—who shall judge them—benevolent or malevolent beings, immortals, deities, the Gods?

An insignificant exo-planet, a water world, orbits a star in the constellation of Lyra. Night-sky stars shine bright over the oceanic depths, reflecting upon the surface of the abyss; still waters mirror a shooting star, a starburst high in the atmosphere but it does not fade. As if sent from the heavens by the very Gods themselves, it descends with such a speed, leaving a shard of light in its wake. Impervious to inertia, it hangs a hairpin turn traversing the surface with phenomenal speed. The plasma orb skims over the hydrosphere, a right-angle turn followed by an abrupt stop above a herd of giant reptilian squid, sheltering from icy currents amidst an aquatic forest of kelp leaves. At rest the orb uncloaks, plasma dissipates as astrionic metalloids morph orb into an autonomous probe. The probe fleets back and forth, scanning the marine life forms, then off it jets, but something odd it processes, reversing back it approaches a mother with a calf. Observing the calf's tentacles' adhesive touch as they delicately re-arrange several luminous molluscs into a pattern on its mother's back, all the while the calf's eyes gazing skywards at a group of stars. At first the probe approaches for a closer look, spinning on its axis to deploy an array of lasers to survey the heavens, mapping the constellations from the calf's viewpoint. Next, the probe projects holograms of star locations, a sequence of animations run, a match found, rotated, resized, and the pinpoint star locations are superimposed over the molluscs. An exact match. The probe's cognitive processes make complex decisions, as if competing in a strategic game, it transmits the message:

SYMBOLS FOUND... DAWN OF INTELLIGENCE

A star-jump, the probe materialises in the system Sol by the Rings of Saturn, minutes later arriving at Earth's lunar companion, the Moon. It disappears into the shadowy depths of a large crater. Soon after, what look like luminescent fish eggs, three luminal shapes ascend from out of the darkness, appearing to phase in and out of space. A flash of light. Now nothing, they are gone.

Into a region far away the luminal objects re-appear, phasing into orbit around Rai, a planet no different to any other except for its Moons. The lights all travel in triangular formation, their trajectory one of the Luna within a group of satellites. Their destination the Eight Heavenly Wonders of Rai, celestial marbles remodelled by advanced civilization. On approach eight Moons focus into sharpness, and around them a myriad of mega-structures. One such construct draws close to reveal giant translucent habitable domes, each one complete with its own ecosystem, correlating to a specific planetary system of origin. Against the empty blackness of space, the geodesic domes reveal their secrets, micro-worlds of ice, water, gas, forests, and varicoloured jewels of life amidst the stars. Appearing as specs of dust against these celestial marvels, the interdimensional vehicles travel onwards.

The journey's end is the last satellite, the Alcazar of the Lords Temporal. An ancient abode for retainers serving the Eyt Ree-Juhns, a group of galaxy-spanning civilisations. Inside the leading vessel holographic glyphs appear, instructions—set linguistics to the modern tongue of Terra, planet Earth. With inquisitiveness, something uttered, "Ru-zhak?"

As the three crafts dock, from the underbelly of the first the outline of a door appears, from which a light-construct morphs into a metallic stairway. A robed being ascends and traverses a walkway, arriving at a doorway over which stands a large effigy of two interlocked triangular sculptures. The being speaks, his facial features partially obscured by a large hood. "It is good to breathe Rai once again, foreseen is my arrival." He kneels, placing a hand on the ground. "Arrival is foreseen!" Of exalted status, the being's prodigious physique is a sight to behold as it unhoods its robe to reveal a golden crown headdress adorned with gold-leaf feathers, inlaid with diamonds and sapphires. For such majesty confirms the arrival of Æther the Golden Ascetic. Stunning to look upon, his rough-hewn features are those of the warrior borne, an elite breed trained to defend the Reydan Monarch's Prime. Greyish in skin tone, his appearance is of a similar height and likeness to a man, except for a rounded head and eyes inset deep into their sockets. His reputation formidable, famed amongst the empire, his reaction times have never been matched—all comers challenged Æther and all were unceremoniously defeated. For Æther embraces an extra sense, at a quantum level—such a sense which allows for the sight of things, shadows in the timeline, a second or two before they occur.

Two giant-size automatons, Master Antariksha and Lady Devanagari, defenders of the Eyt, kneel to receive Æther; their appearance is one of divinity for all that lay eyes on them. It is said the symbiotic life forms were created as a gift to serve life by trans-dimensional entities. A tale believed to be myth, even though none know of their true origin. Both beings have the common form of two arms and two legs, whereas Devanagari's body differs in size, being a tad smaller against the full sixteen cubits height of her partner. Their outer shell, or membrane for a better word, is a weird reflective thing, a transparent anomaly, underneath which lies a constantly morphing panacea. Antariksha's body, his complexion is akin to a mirror of stars and galaxies. His is the image of man. Whereas Devanagari's appearance emulates that of planets, their atmospheres, always changing, never staying the same. Although when serene, her appearance is becoming, a sky-blue thing of beauty with golden beams of light, a heavenly cloudscape. Her body is shapely and curved, in the image of woman.

As always Æther stands in awe to admire the two techno-life forms. Even though Devanagari has no facial features, he stands enchanted by her magnetic allure. "Lady Devanagari, with your beauty nothing can compare—not even the lotus bloom found in the outer clusters." From behind his back, he presents one such flower to the giant automaton. With coy playfulness she waves her hand as if cooling her blushing face, having turned a Jovian red. Then, always in change, her exquisite complexion reverts to its natural sky blue. Reminiscing, Æther muses over the now infamous Axilla Scenario. "The Axilla mission, do you ever think about it? How we retrieved the Ones-and-the-Zeroes from the Red Giant Sect? None thought such a daring ploy possible, to convert their ship the Axilla into a cryo-stasis capsule, inducing hibernation. As they lay comatose, brazen we were as we walked where giants trod. The Ones-and-the-Zeroes retrieved without confrontation, as luck would have it you played a trick most unfair." Devanagari gives an excited nod, upon which Æther raises a finger, "So, you do remember re-routing their star-drive to an uncharted region?" he raises an eyebrow. "Where did you send them?" She gives no response. "You will not say— perhaps it is best not to know." Æther looks up at the heavens, "I often wonder what their reaction will be, when they wake from their coma only to find they are lost within the great void." Devanagari cannot laugh aloud, and yet her form mimics the rhythmic body language of laughter, displaying humanoid emotions. She places a hand over her mouth as if giggling, her shoulders tremble. For Devanagari has a penchant for mischief, as Æther all too well knows. In response Antariksha shakes his head and places a hand on her shoulder to keep her in check. Thereafter he speaks—a non-natural voice echoes—from where it comes none are sure.

"Welcome, Æther. Master Antariksha and Lady Devanagari grant safe passage, the Nei-Kanga awaits."

Antariksha beckons unto Æther with an open hand that he may pass, upon which they both enter a large hallway known as the Hall of Heads. A magnificent hall adorned with a vast array of monuments, the spectacular effigies of the deities, statues of mythological Gods and heroes known as Juhj-iz or Ascetics. Æther stops in his tracks to admire the magnificence of the hall, and the near lifelike perfection of the statues, "Magnificent, is it not, Antariksha? The Harij-ans call it the Valley of the Giants. It is a fitting name." Onto a large conveyor-platform they step and shortly thereafter they arrive at their destination.

THE WHEEL OF THE FIVE PHASES. Æther and Antariksha stand at the outer boundary, in front of them a large pathway encircles an inner disc with five separate paths leading to the heart of the structure. They cross the threshold onto the wheel and head to the centre, where stands a large spherical construction. It is the Citadel of the Sage Lords. Arriving at the inner temple they stop before a megalith, a large stone bed, upon which lies the still body of Lord Kae-Rai. Æther kneels, "Is my Lord well?"

"Thy Lord remains in nano-thermoregulation stasis until bone washing has concluded, nonetheless he shall converse with thee."

The automaton kneels on one leg before the stone bed, placing his colossal-hand over Lord Kae-Rai's head, and lowering his right hand in front of Æther. Its giant hand stretches open to reveal a holographic projection of Lord Kae-Rai, his large, bulbous jet-black eyes gazing upon the Golden Ascetic. He is dressed in in a long white robe, worn only when discussing matters of a serious nature. A noble Solipsi-Rai, his grey skin covered in scars tells a story; in his early life he was one of the legendary Juhj-iz who fought in the time of the great upheaval. Now one of the last elders, honoured by the Eyt as the Nei-Kanga, Supreme Sage Lord. The hologram of Lord Kae-Rai gazes upon Æther; as he speaks the hall echoes his voice.

"Where is everybody? The famed Fermi paradox is something that troubles the Terrans, for the true answer eludes them, as we know," Kae-Rai lifts a finger, "and give life a paradox for being they did, but understood yes or no?"

"Yes, my Lord."

"Then you know this paradox asks that if life truly pervades the cosmos, where are all of the aliens?" Kae-Rai sighs, "To the Terrans the existence of alien life is equally as frightening as its non-existence—they fear loneliness. Yet there are a handful of them who know different. Truth is truth, no matter how you dress it."

"I sense trouble, my Lord." Æther's eyes turn a glint of yellow, seeing the oncoming of misfortune, a time of great trials.

"I asked you to set linguistics to Terra. You will need the practice."

"Practice? The Terran's language… I haven't used it in a long time."

"It has been long, unsuccessful we have been—they have found the pyramid, and the Elb have birthed a new Celestial

Witness. It is no coincidence. They petition for a second trial of strength as we speak, and so we must prepare to defend those who cannot defend themselves," the Sage Lord twirls his finger. "Alas, such things are always in flux."

"The darkness has entered them, my Lord, how can we ever reason with them?"

"They are of the high-evolution, their reasoning is rarely understood. What is life looking for? It is a question that mystifies them so. The Eyt answered this question a long time ago. Life knows itself, this the Elb fail to understand. Now, listen well, for you need to keep the following to thyself. The Eyt, guided by the Ternion Ascended, have taken the decision to help the Terrans once again... to save Earth."

"I see..."

"Do you so?" Kae-Rai taps the corner of his eye with a finger. "If should you fail, the first one of the five will appear, the others always follow. If the five unite, the result is always closure for the species dominant... in this case humankind. If such a fate prevails, in desperation they will use their nuclear deterrent, and with that comes annihilation." He gestures Æther to stand, "You are to contact our friends of the Four Nations of Terra, inform them litigator Ansebe is to visit."

"Our creation will be sent, Lord, the best of the new-beings to come from the unification reserve. He is truly unique."

"One other thing, you are to partner Ansebe with the second one of the three. Bring the two together. The third one, if Kyubi-K was right, will be drawn to them like a moth to the flame."

"How, my Lord? Our retainers have never been able to find him. He is a ghost. It is thought he wears masks, guises, my Lord, to present himself as an absence, an apparition. There are few that can be considered more daring a challenger. Alas, he has given up on everything we follow."

Lord Kae-Rai illumed with amusement, tells a proverb, "Do not discard the snake for having decrepit scales. For who is to say it will not one day shed its skin, and discover an innately pure, brighter layer has formed underneath." Humbled, Æther places a hand on his chest. Lord Kae-Rai adds, "We do not wish to trouble the Eyt with this, until sure we know. Yes or no?"

"Yes, my Lord. Do you believe we can overcome the Elb's Celestial Witness?"

"The Eyt civilisations defer to the three most advanced intelligences in this verse, and yet the Ternion will not—or cannot confront the Elb. It is said the Elb have reached the apex of evolution," he traces a figure-eight with his finger, "who would have thought that to evolve to such a high-level is to go full circle? They no longer understand the unity of life. As such they are lost! Nevertheless, we have the one thing the Elb may have forgotten, Æther."

"We have? What is it, my Lord?"

"The need to evolve, to survive; our instincts may yet save the day. So, let us hope, Æther… let us hope."

EARTH: THE PENTAGON. The present day. An office door within the Pentagon, the Offices of the Secretary of Defence. Without warning the door explodes open from the kick of a Lincoln-style boot. An abrasive scuff of shinola sullies the doors elegant finish as General James Campbell storms out of his office and glances at the door, grumbling, "It's too much— I'm late. So many doors!" He paces an agitated walk, at odds with his slender athletic build. Fingers pressed against his ear, in a low-voice he resumes a hands-free call, "Yes, I understand. I have another agent… you want her specifically? Sure, but she has no experience of—yes, I understand our agreement, I'll get it done." To any onlooker, it would appear James Campbell is talking on handsfree, except no call is connected, nor ever was. He knows well enough that he is conversing with a voice that just announced its presence inside his very own thoughts, his mind. Pacing back and forth, wiping perspiration from his brow, he tries to cool down and returns to his desk. Seated, he loosens his tie and taking a moment to regain his composure, selects a secure telephone line—an unnamed number dialled, the call connects. It is answered silently at the other end, a directive issued from Campbell, "We need to talk, the usual place."

Later, General Campbell stands serene amidst the Pentagon Memorial, paying his respects to the monument he faces. Like all others, it stands poignantly over a shallow pool of water, except this one is special, significant. His thoughts flow with the breeze, reflecting on happier times but dark memories surface with a change in the wind, gnawing at his conscience. He trembles, his resolve reduces to the point of abandonment when a female voice calls out: "James." He turns to see a stylishly dressed lady wearing a classic Parisian design beige trench coat; the belt buckle cutting an elegant figure of sophistication, as if she was a famous actress playing the part of a spy in an old war-time movie.

"James Campbell, my favourite guardian angel."

"Zara Hanson, still in fine shape, alive and kicking, I see." He stands arms open, "So, you managed to get out of the Amazon."

"You know me, James," she shares a hug. "How serious is it?" Campbell hesitates, she pulls away to stare into his eyes, raises an eyebrow.

"Don't give me the look." As always, he feels unsettled by her piercing eyes, the rarity of heterochromia, one eye green, one blue giving her stare a mesmerizing quality.

"It's genetics, I can't help my eyes."

"New hairstyle, I see? What's this one called?"

"It's the short side swept with bangs look, and before you ask it's light-coloured with contrasting highlights," she points a finger, "don't change the subject."

He glances at a steri-strip dressing on the back of her hand, "Hostiles been given a taste of the iron-hand—"

"You know full well it's not called that, now quit stalling and tell me what's got you so troubled."

"Is it that noticeable? Hell… sure it is! This one's on a need to know…" He pauses, stares into nothingness, visibly stressed.

"What's my objective, James—James, are you feeling all right?"

"What… sorry, miles away. We need you to work on a fishing project, it seems work on the underground generator has awakened something that should be respected—fools have no idea what they're playing with!"

"You mean the reports of the pyramid?"

"I never asked for this, I'm usually the one that causes the stress," he wipes his forehead with a handkerchief, "it's just got—hell it's too much." He passes a sealed file, "The report is way out there, the intel you need to study, it's a weird one. God dammit… this duty leaves you with an unbalanced mind."

"James?"

"At home I have a printer in the cellar, not plugged into anything but I'm told to keep paper in it. Anyhow, I'm in there with my grandson and we're building a kit model, McDonnell Phantom fighter jet, and the damn printer just powers up. Prints the report in that file. In front of my grandson, dammit—"

"I have this recurring dream, in which I die thousands of unusual ways, but the real freak-on is I always wake up, still alive in my dream. Then I really wake up! In a cold sweat, heart pounding—you're not alone, James."

"My grandson is more important to me than all of this."

"We do what we do, it's what we're good at."

"Yes, of course…"

"The mission, James?"

"Yes, the mission. Our friends from the stars sent us info, coupled with our own observations, it confirms our worst fears. Just outside the Oort cloud, we've picked up unusual activity. They say it's imperative you don't know all the variables."

"A dark mission?"

"See your file for more info. Our friends believe that work on the pyramid involves an unlimited power source, which may have attracted the attention of intra-dimensional entities."

"Intra-dimensional what?"

"Their think-tank believes we're going to use the pyramid to tap into extra-dimensions—putting humanity in danger," his tone changes, "we need to close this project down."

"This operation seems different, James."

"Your partner is still tying up loose ends with the NASA fallout, from the last debacle. We need your skill-set to get to the bottom of this, time is of the essence. So, no matter how long you think it'll take, do it in half the time."

"Our friends must have a hold on this, after all they protect us… don't they?"

"That's the goddamned joke, this one's even got them spooked, so much so they're sending one of their own, a so-called new-being, someone, something, with a particular skillset."

"A new-being," Zara smiles, "they're really sending one?"

"Tomorrow or the day after, you'll get to work with your first contact or being. I don't envy you on this, just make sure you're on your top game—they're preparing a Dodecahedron as we speak, just in case we screw up."

"A Dodecahedron?" she frowns a nonplussed expression.

"You heard right—it's an Ark just like the one from the book of Genesis."

"James, I believe my partner should accompany me on this mission, our combined talents may be better qualified—"

"No! They specifically requested you and no one else."

"They really want me, no one else?" Zara asks, with an inquisitive smile.

"You can out-think and out-fight our best, anyone who comes up against you will be wishing they didn't. I believe in you. I guess they must believe in you, or you play a special part in their plans. Now get out of here," he hugs her, "I know you've got this, God be with you."

"Thanks, James, I'll take all the help I can get."

"Just make sure you take your shots, I don't want any contagion scares on my watch… and be careful out there."

"I will." She walks away smiling, and whispers to herself, "Finally."

Zara's stateside base of operations, an everyday café in Washington, a low-key outlet, one you'd pass if you aren't looking for it. An area where no one takes notice, a see no evil, speak no evil neighbourhood. *Not followed, good.* Hardly any sunlight cuts under the shop's awning, shading the seated area. She takes a seat, waves the waitress, places her sunglasses over her head.

Two girls sitting, no threatening body language, all normal. A guy on his own, looking at me.

The waitress brings her usual. Espresso, two sugars. "Thank you, Ling."

"Please enjoy, it is safe to do so."

"I will."

Ling runs the base of operations, has her back. Assured all is well, Zara takes out of the envelope holding the mission directives, and from it a strip of medication. Dreamland anti-viral vaccine. She sugars her coffee, sips down two pills. The anti-viral meds dissipate—a second sip—a sharp reaction. She coughs, gaining the attention of the handsome guy at the opposite table. "You okay?" he asks.

"I'm fine, thank you," they share a smile.

"So, now I'm immune to all sorts of chills and fever," she whispers, "well, almost." With nothing else of concern and reassured it's safe, she slips the mission papers between the morning pages of the Washington Post, reading the mission codename. "The Painted Symbol… they like their names." On paper the name of the new-being, she smiles, says the name to herself, "Ansebe… what are you?" The mission papers name the rendezvous: Rendlesham Forest, England. Insertion method— skydiving. "An air-drop? I hate parachutes." Zara sighs, then quickly types a message on her mobile: Painted Symbol Received. But an odd feeling of indecision overcomes her, should she send the text? Holding a coin in her hand she briefly looks at it, then spins it on the table. Time seems to slow— closing her eyes she positions her forefinger above the spinning coin and taps down, stopping it upright mid-spin. Opening her eyes she exhales slowly and carefully lifts her finger, leaving the coin balanced on its edge. "I don't think I'll need any travel insurance," she says smiling as she sends the text.

Chapter Two
US Air Force Cargo Transportation

The next day airborne in a special cargo transporter, a passenger on a long-haul flight with the US Air Force. Approaching Rendlesham. "The C5 is a special cargo transporter, a tall order for transferring an individual asset," shouts a stout airman over the background noise as he and another escort Zara from the upper decks to the cargo bay. "Nice suit," he adds, his eyes drawn to her unusual all-in-one black body suit, designed with thin white strips running down each arm; complete with seamless utilities-belt and inbuilt comms devices. On her chest, an added touch of her own, a patch with the letter Z in white.

"What's the mission?" he adds, probing for info.

"Stick to protocol and we'll get along just fine."

"What's your deal, you got a name?"

"Zara… Zara Hanson."

"Yeh, that must be what this Z stands for," he says, prodding her chest.

"It might stand for zero tolerance," she replies, slapping his arm away.

"Indeed, I believe it might. Okay, nearing the drop zone, cargo doors opening." Both airmen smirk, to which she returns a piercing stare. "Something on your minds?" she asks, only to be received with silence. The airmen share a calculating glance, then the stout one speaks, "Okay Zara, best get ready." Her sixth sense tingles like crazy, as a silent tenseness is shared in everyone's body language, then she notices the taller airman—a bead of sweat on his forehead, and yet they are too high, too cold, something's not right. He speaks, "Okay Zara, I have some good news and some bad-news. The bad news, it's going to drop below zero tonight—so suit up, approaching drop zone."

Zara takes hold of the parachute, running through the pre-checks she asks, "What was the good news?" He moves closer, "The good news is that you won't notice the temperature—you'll be dead!"

In one split second he delivers a punishing hook kick to her back, just as the cargo doors open. Aircraft noise overwhelms her senses, but she avoids the kick by rolling forwards to stand several feet away. The stout airman charges, swings a high kick at her head, she ducks and moves to one side, grabbing his collar, spinning him around, adding to his momentum. He loses his footing, tilts perilously close the edge of the cargo door, desperately trying to retain balance. Zara makes up two metres in an instant, to let loose a powerful front push kick. "Raise up, wing-nut!" she snarls, as the kick sends him stumbling out of the aircraft, arms flailing, desperate to hold onto something as he falls to his certain end. She turns to face the taller airman, gun held firmly he takes aim. Trying to buy some time, she wisecracks, "Has your man gone to ground?"

The airman throws her chute out of the door in a frantic bid that it might reach his counterpart. "Who sent you?" she shouts. He smirks, aims his pistol, firing several shots—one misses by inches.

Training kicks in, Zara calculates the variables, distance, time, worst-case scenario. She counts.

"One one-thousand," a second later,

"Two one-thousand," the distance to the taller airman cannot be closed, "Three one-thousand," shots fired, she hears a voice inside her head…

"Move."

A bullet grazes her shoulder… *That voice, is someone is looking after me?*

No time to think—action becomes reaction, only one way out! "Four one-thousand," she jumps outside.

"Five one-thousand," diving in a fast fall posture.

"Six one-thousand," air blusters in all directions, her thoughts focus on the available remaining descent time. She glances at her watch, 65 seconds of free fall. Precious seconds tick away. *No, can't see—nothing!*

Overwhelmed with panic, fear grips her stomach. She squeezes her eyes shut and at that moment from everywhere, voices echo with the wind.

"Zara, why do you believe thyself only a mortal—when the universe is a part of you? Look inside thyself and see!"

So real, is it in her head? The words hit hard, enthusing courage, she calms, becomes empty, no longer afraid. A blast of wind triggers her survival instinct, returns her to the present moment.

She scans the area below. Seconds flash by, she sees the parachute then from the corner of her eye, the airman approaching.

"Ten one-thousand," she falls fast, but both have the same goal. The airman grabs the chute first, trying to thread one arm through the strap.

"Fifteen one-thousand," she manages to grab his arm, spinning out of control they tussle downwards, punching and kicking. An eternity passes in her mind. An opportunity presents as she slides an arm inside the harness—suppleness is her ally, and lifting a leg into the hip attachment, she elbows her assailant in the eye. As he winces in pain, she clips on the rig.

A wild mid-air fight follows with kicking, gouging and scratching, but in the mayhem her hand finds the ripcord. The chute opens with a roar—sudden G forces combine with the might of her legs, kicking the agent away. A surreal second shared as they stare at each other, briefly experiencing a moment in time. The canopy opens, instant deceleration forces their parting. His free fall is rapid, but his eyes frozen—realizing the end—are seared into her memory.

"Time to meet your maker," she says calmly, as the cold killer instinct in her comes to the fore. A coping mechanism. Then out of nowhere a strong gust of wind cuts across her path, almost twisting the canopy lines. She quickly gains control and checks her watch as the minute hand ticks past fifty seconds, she nods in a self-assured manner. Steering down to the ground, she checks for the agent, it's unthinkable that he may have survived. On landing she quickly discards the parachute but sees in the air another canopy gliding down to land several hundred metres away, amidst the setting Sun. The other one, an asset sent to kill her. "Where are you from, who sent you?" she says, and with little time to spare she sprints towards his location. The mission requires unarmed engagement, no guns, this could be bad. Her last contact-assignment was called off following the detection of an agent's sidearm. If her assassin is heavily armed, her mission may be over before it's even begun, and this mission is of dire consequence.

She spies the agent landing in a clearing, the forest in her line of sight. A quick calculation, the polymath in her plans the best approximation, the most favourable odds for a desired outcome. Decided, she launches into action—as bait—sprinting rapidly at a cross angle into the forest, allowing the agent to see her. He gives chase, she knows he won't shoot, not until he has a clear shot, so she sprints into the woods and while running jumps several feet into the air, catching a branch, and with the dexterity of cat she hastily climbs a tree. The skill of parkour—her abilities are extraordinary—she darts atop the trees, amidst the foliage. From high up she scans the forest, spies an outcropped area below, and hastily assembles items from her utility belt. The assembled device is carefully thrown onto the outcrop, then with both hands shaped around mouth, she voices a cry of pain in the direction of her hunter. Blending to the side of a large tree bough like a chameleon imperceptible to its prey, she waits. The agent tracks the direction of her scream, as he gets close, her breath stills on hearing his light footsteps brushing against the undergrowth. Then the agent stands still, listens carefully, looking around, yet there is nothing to be seen or heard. The natural noise of the forest breeze breaks the tense silence. The agent does not take any chances, he slowly retreats—something is not right—he hears movement, pauses in his tracks. A buzzing noise, from the forest floor, a sounder fast-tracks to rapid pulses, it's about to go south. Zara dismounts the tree, she attacks, kicking her would-be assassin whilst he is off-guard. He break-rolls and turns to face her with gun in hand. Zara defiantly shows a hand-held remote, presses her thumb down. The agent grimaces, his lips silently mouth, "Mother…" too late, the improvised explosive device detonates—PETN—plastic explosive. It explodes from the inside out, waves of power tear into deadly shards of force, blasting her adversary sideways, leaving debris littered in all directions.

The agent lies dead, she stands still as leaves set free from the blast descend, turned a mottled red from stains of blood. She picks a leaf free from the air, and looking at it speaks to herself, "Red-stained leaves from an autumn forest floor, death comes a knocking at our door." Tears roll down her face and her hands begin tremble from the realization of cheating death. A sombre mood takes over, she kneels and with a gentle touch wipes the agent's eyelids closed. A moment of grief for the loss of life, her body shakes but she slaps her face to snap out of it. Back to the mission. She drags the agent to the undergrowth, checking him for any personal effects or identification, none. Her thoughts mull over. Who are you, who do you work for? Then several feet away the metallic glimmer of a dog tag catches her eye, she picks it up. An assassin with identification, unusual. Holding it against the light, she reads the engraving, no personal information, no blood type, nothing except for a code-name. "Majik—Team 11… damn!" She quickly wipes the dog tag clean, leaving it beside the lifeless body, removes the bullets from the assassin's gun and throws it away. Zara continues onwards into the forest, but as she walks old memories surface, old ghosts follow her.

Chapter Three
Memories

Zara checks the inbuilt navigator on her wrist-watch, only a short hike to her destination. Unsettled by the two kills, she thinks back on happier times, a flashback to her late teens. It was a hot, humid day in Beijing, her beloved mentor Master Wang was giving tutelage on the martial arts, "Zara, you will stand in the horse stance until there is evidence of your work!" By this Master Wang meant beads of sweat on her forehead, although oftentimes she would try to cheat by wearing a beanie hat, but whenever Wang caught her doing this he would confiscate the hat. There she stood, still, upright with arms outstretched, standing. A training process of the Ultimate Salvation School, a mysterious sect of unknown origin, proficient in the ancient ways of the martial arts and internal alchemy—the Neijia. It was the famed courtyard of her godfather's lodgings, Master Wang and Zara had been standing in horse posture for over an hour. "You may now you commence your formal routines, start with monkey grasps dragon's tail." Master Wang was a hard taskmaster and often continued with chores, sweeping the courtyard while she practiced her Gong Fu, such was the training regime at the home of the Wang family. On this occasion she practiced the form, an entering step, then turning with a cutting motion to her rear. "Why do you not get it right? It is a simple movement, flank opponent, turn and strike to the back of their neck. Try again!" Once more she tried. "And again," Master Wang ordered, but no sooner had she completed the move, he would shout, "Again." Whole training sessions were often spent mastering just the one movement, such was Wang's insistence on perfection.

From this residence, she was home-schooled in multiple academia and physical education, including inside the door teaching of the Wang family martial arts and induction into the higher levels of the Ultimate Salvation School and its teachings.

The daughter of a British diplomat for the embassy in Beijing, Zara spent her early childhood in China. Tragically, her father met with an untimely death when she was very young. Her father's bodyguard Master Wang stepped in to bring up Zara as his own with his wife Meizhen, fulfilling her father's dying wish. She had never known her mother, who had passed in childbirth, but was always told that she was a Javanese lady of considerable status and that her name was Zaidee. She always carried a photo of her, resplendent in traditional Javanese garb. Even though she saw Meizhen as a mother, the picture always used to fascinate her, which she would oftentimes look at last thing at night. Wang was a mysterious character, a renowned master, although mild in stature he was very athletic—unfortunately, his reputation often preceded him, and he received many impromptu challenges.

On one such day, Zara was training in the standing post posture and Master Wang was sweeping the courtyard when a Russian man of extreme athletic build and height arrived unannounced. "Where is your master?" he asked in a brusque tone. Master Wang continued to sweep the floor, but the Russian shouted, "I have travelled far to test your master, where is he?"

Master Wang stopped sweeping the yard, "I am he," he said softly.

The Russian gave Wang a disdainful look and promptly announced, "I have studied a mixed field of the martial arts and understand that you may be able to teach me the error of my ways?" Master Wang smiled and asked the man his name to which he replied, "I am great Russian wrestler, Oleg the Bear!" Oleg clenched his fists, which shook with power as he sneered at Master Wang, then he mocked, "In my eyes, Chinese Wushu resembles something comparable to gymnastics, having little value in actual fights. I have never met anyone to disprove this opinion, can you?" This did not vex Master Wang, who smiled, but then Oleg said, "I hear many believe you are great master, but you have only little girl for student—maybe you are a fake?" Oleg seemed very happy he was dealing with someone of slight build. He then challenged Wang, "I would win without fail, should we both wish to compare skill."

Hearing this Master Wang's expression changed, his eyes became piercing, "This middle-aged gentleman stands before you, ready to take on any rivals, including those guests coming from foreign countries, if you please..." Wang invited his challenger to the centre of the courtyard, "Oleg the Bear please step forward, I am ready, if you wish us to test our skills?"

Oleg, who loved fighting, was eager for the duel to start. He began at first circling his opponent, then pacing forward and back, taunting Wang with shadow-boxing. Without any hesitation Wang stepped forward with arms held wide apart in the invitation posture. Oleg launched a sudden attack at Wang's head. At the same time, Wang parried Oleg's elbow with a downward chop, cutting into the elbow crease, stealing Oleg's balance. With Oleg's footing lost, he teetered forward, off-balance, desperately trying to regain stability. Wang's other hand remained high, then suddenly cut down as he screamed aloud, "Fali!" His arm cut through the air, like an axe cutting at the back of Oleg's neck, at the very same moment the wrestler went to stand. In a transitory state of martial perfection, Oleg was knocked to the ground. There he laid motionless before Master Wang; the skirmish had lasted all but a few seconds. Zara smiles to herself, recalling the vacant look on Oleg's face when he was revived with a bucket of water.

Continuing through the forest, her mind wanders to when she graduated university, she was so happy. A memory, when Master Wang began teaching level one of his system, when she was first introduced to the inner teachings of the Ultimate Salvation. It was a freezing winter evening; a full moon floodlit a blanket of snow, a serene glow of white. Master Wang was practicing seated meditation in traditional wushu attire, but worried her teacher would catch a chill, she brought out his coat and gloves. This touched Master Wang, who decided there and then that Zara would be the successor of the teachings of his lineage, all knowledge passed down from master to disciple. Master Wang's eyes glazed over, "Zara, that was most kind of you, but do not worry, I am not cold. One does not need an outer garment to keep warm when the unification, circulation and control of one's vital-energy is achieved." He smiled, and went on to say, "Once in a lifetime, and only once, a successor is chosen, a disciple to inherit the inner teachings of the Ultimate Salvation. This is to be you."

"The Ultimate Salvation," she frowned, "I thought I've been learning your system?"

"So far, I have only given you a foundation, a stage to play on."

"There's no mention of this system in your library, in your wushu literature."

"My system is one of the most secretive and mysterious schools of the Neijia, which was rumoured to be founded by the Heavenly Sage—the legendary Monkey King."

A miffed look from Zara, "Isn't the Monkey King a myth? Not real?"

He smiled, "The Monkey King in our story is most definitely a real being."

"Really, the same one of myth that fought the Gods?"

"Not quite, the legends of our lineage are wild and speculative, alas our ancestors often embellished such stories of his feats, an in-joke with some disciples who would often impersonate him. In truth, the founder of our system comes from a faraway world, often assumed to be the Monkey King of legend, because he would descend to earth in a trail of smoke and mist."

"Have you seen him at all?"

"His spirit talks to me, but I assure you he's real," he scooped up snow, "as tangible as these snowflakes," and made a snowball, throwing it at the moon, "as animated as the moonlit sky," he turned to face Zara, "and as real or as you or I."

"Shall I ever meet him?" Master Wang held a finger high, "Ours is a school of mystery, from which devotees—if found worthy—are taught by the very spirits themselves. Do you wish to partake on this journey? If you do, you must believe in our system, unquestionably and without doubt."

"I believe with all my heart," she said.

"It is decided then, listen carefully to the first incantation." Master Wang began to recite from his school's canon. He spoke in a sombre tone, "Positive and negative, yin and yang, the polarity of the sphere is derived from rotational ability—" just as Master Wang was to continue speaking, from the corner of their eyes they noticed in the sky three bright multi-coloured lights travelling in silence at amazing speed. He whispered, "Look Zara, a sign from the heavens. You believe!" Zara was mesmerized, even the more so when the lights stopped and hovered above them. She stood rooted on the spot, marvelling at the sky and then glanced at Master Wang, who seemed to be in an enchanted trance, following which he bowed deeply. As if in acknowledgement the lights revolved in a semi-circular path and departed. Then as if nothing peculiar had just occurred, Master Wang continued with the incantation,

"There are hidden depths within this method,

"Sixty-four levels of ultimate realization,

"Seventy-two levels of infinite potential,

"We learn to control our mind in the three-dimensional and the biological,

"Regulate the parallel and the perpendicular,

"If we wish to make our body imperceptible, we become a suggestion,

"If we wish to travel in stillness, we shall ascend to the astral plane,

"In movement, we descend into cosmic clarity,

"If we wish to break the confines of the negative, we shall compress the positive,

"Once this is achieved, force and matter are simply experienced as energy."

A snap, a broken twig on the forest floor, separates Zara from her memories, bringing her back to the present moment. A quick check of the coordinates on her navigator, not far now. The hike ends with the navigation device beeping. Zara kneels, carries out a recon of the area—now is the moment more than ever she feels unerringly nervous. For she's about to meet a friend and contact of the Four Nations. His name is Ansebe.

Chapter Four
Meditation

Remote viewing was never Zara's specialty, but the mission requires a remote view of her current coordinates—to transmit her location using conscious thought. Uncertain, having never tried this method for real, she breathes deeply and prepares. Sitting in the lotus posture, she begins to meditate, intent on her current location; assisted by two photographs, she lays them on the ground—one of earth, the other a satellite picture of the forest. A mental image learned, imprinted. She closes her eyes and begins by softly whispering to herself:

"The realm of consciousness is common to all beings throughout the universe,

"The light of the body is the eye—let my eye be single, let it be full of light."

Zara stills her mind, transcends to a state of heightened consciousness—visualizes herself as meditating but as an invisible spirit body that covers all of the forest. From the top of her head, a vision of a beam of white light shooting skywards. An irrelevant thought distracts her meditation. The moment goes awry. *No, no thoughts, must have no mind, believe in the method.* Time stands still, what seems like minutes has been over an hour, then without any prompting her eyes open as if awakening from a dream state. *It hasn't worked!* A deflated silence, then in the setting dusk something illuminated, encased in brilliant white plasma, an ethereal silhouette appears. At first it hovers, then descends silently down through the forest canopy, whereby trees bend as if being moved by an invisible hand brushing corn in a field. She looks on, tries to appear as non-threatening as possible. *What on earth... this is crazy!*

Although highly trained and educated in the sciences, the arts and philosophy, nothing ever prepared Zara for this. She stands rooted to the ground, unable or not wanting to move, when a shaft of light emits downward and an audible hum fills the air, which begins to pulse. Scintillations of diamond-hard light beam brightly, sparkling like a thousand stars, but it does not affect her sight. Reaching out Zara touches the translucent light, in response the beam as if alive pushes and pulls against her arm, then it emits an aurora, a spectral hue of colours. The light has substance, it affects her senses, "Are you communicating… talking?" The light fades to reveal the profile of the being called Ansebe standing in front of the interstellar craft, which remains cloaked in plasma. As he approaches his physique comes into focus; his appearance, and characteristics leave Zara thunderstruck. "What the hell? Stay calm…" she tells herself. Her apprehension turns to curiosity as she gazes upon the beings amazing golden skin. *His skin, it changes colour… like a cuttlefish.*

Before her stands a striking figure at least six feet tall, in a magnificent robe with strange hieroglyphs woven into the fabric. His eyes seem to gaze upon her very soul, her mind, her thoughts. An unusual face, but around his head two large wrap-around ears; they twitch and as they do a smaller set of ears briefly descends. Zara steps to one side to get a better look, glimpsing a third set of ears behind the large ones, pointing backwards. All moving independently from each other, sensing the minutest of sounds, changes in the air with pinpoint accuracy. *Whoa… he's got six wolf-like ears!* A shallow nose connects to smaller nasal cavities under his eyes, hardly noticeable—unusual but not ugly, on the contrary a fetching figure with an aura of splendour stands before her. He nods, and as if in-tune with Zara's exhilaration, his skin shimmers a rainbow of colours. Her eyes follow the patterns, as if under a hypnotic trance, but she snaps out of it on noticing unusual metallic points under his skin all linked together with luminescent meridian lines. *An acupuncture chart, he's a freaking glowing acupuncture chart!* "Oh man," she says, smiling, "bio-augmentation of the meridians?" With a steely glare he nods. There they stand looking at each other; she can't help but stand still on the spot, captivated, mesmerized. He leans his head from side to side and smiles. Likewise, she smiles as both share amusement coupled with curiosity. The traveller then stands to attention, lifts a hand up, points his four fingers skywards then slowly closes them. He gestures her to do the same. As she raises her hand he says, "Unity," and nods.

"Unity," Zara replies.

"We try. I am Ansebe… I am new, we consummate now?"

Taken aback, unsure she heard right, she replies, "I'm married… marriage, wedlock, do you understand?" Ansebe tilts his head to one side, then realizes the misinterpretation.

"Translation, meaning… we partner, team up for mission. Interpretation implant still in calibration, verse soon be improved. We try."

Zara bites her lip, tries to subdue a nervous giggle, "Yes… of course, will your calibration take long?"

"Upgrade ongoing, recalibration to Terran language English," he places a finger to his forehead and concentrates. "We try, again we try." A mild moment of amusement shared, Ansebe smiles, he gestures, "Come please sit… sit. We try, I am translation ready." They sit, "My appearance, your expression, you were surprised. We try, Ansebe introduce us, in your tongue we are known as Artificial Nano Synthetic Electrochemical Biological Entity," he smiles, "Ansebe for short—you say."

"Ansebe," Zara smiles, "nice name."

"Yes, this name we use on Terra at first some time ago, now we use always."

"What exactly are you and how does your biology work, your implants?"

"I am vessel made to simulate many of your species' genetic characteristics, eel, fish, wolf and bat, I am of these—made to perform well on Terra, a new-being from the unification reserve, the first of us were created long ago, in the age of genetics."

"The age of genetics?" Zara's raises an eyebrow, her interest piqued.

"There are many ages in which a civilization passes through to progress, most start at stone age—further ages follow—the age of electricity, the ages of gravity, genetics, time and the most unknown of all ages—the age of evolution."

"Wow, what age has your civilization reached?"

"Ansebe cannot say, this not allowed."

Zara tries another question. "The age of evolution—an unknown age, how is it unknown?"

"Ansebe can tell you that few reach the age of evolution, our race has not reached that stage for it is very rare, but we do know it exists," he gazes at Zara's hands, neck. "You have been in fight—you are in pain."

"I have so much to ask you!"

"We will answer what we can, but first you rest." Ansebe's forehead furrows with concern.

"I'm fine, I'll live."

"Then let us sit comfortably, I have much to tell."

"Go on."

"First eat, let us how you say… break bread," he rubs his belly, "we share a feast fit for kings."

Zara looks puzzled, "Um… I have some flapjacks." Ansebe laughs, and gently brushes his arm upon which hieroglyphic symbols glow under his skin. He taps the symbols, and pulls two small cubes from his belt, like dice but covered in glyphs. He places them on the ground, moving his finger above them in three small circles. They begin to spin slow at first, then faster, and as they do lasers beam outward, creating a strobe effect—faster still, then too fast for the eye when a three-dimensional holographic fire appears.

"Wow, a fire… it's warm," Zara smiles, as she warms her hands in front of the holographic camp fire. As the night time chill takes hold the fire has a calming effect, imbuing her with an odd but overwhelming feeling of safety.

"We must eat, create hyphae orbs—you'll see." He pulls a cannister from his belt, opens it, stirs the contents with a circular wand, smiles and gently blows into the wand, forming a foam of bubbles which float into the holographic fire.

"This is manna," he smiles, "food, good food for long voyage," he points, "watch, look reconstruction." The manna bubbles inside the hologram lose their translucence and morph into dough balloons, inflating they rise out of the fire. "We try. It is good to try." He picks some of the floating manna and passes it to Zara, "Eat, eat—it is good for pain, good for health."

"Mmm… tastes good," touching fingers to her thumb she kisses her fingertips, Ansebe looks on puzzled. "It's a sign of perfection."

He mimics her actions, kisses his fingertips, "It does not make it taste any better. Here, manna can feed many," he passes her more to eat. "It is microbiomorphology, we give as a gift to your leaders once. Alas, they never use."

"They never used it? That figures."

"It would have ended world hunger—please explain, what it tastes… what is it you feel eating manna?"

"Mmm… sweet, ambrosial."

"What is ambrosial?"

"Fragrant, delicious." Zara recalls an earlier comment, "Your name Ansebe, the A is for artificial?"

"Yes, you could say I am of an artificial nature but with a soul."

"No offence, but how can you have a soul, being artificial?" Ansebe nods at the question. "Also what does we try mean, and what's with the remote transmission stuff?"

His skin shimmers silver then blue, "Questions, questions," he pauses, closes his eyes. "We shall illuminate, you ask if I, if we, have a soul? Ansebe most certainly feels he has a soul. You tell me, what is the soul?"

"Oh, that's simple, it's what goes to heaven if you believe in God."

"How do you know the body only holds one soul, it could hold tens of thousands."

"Really?"

"My body is container for thought history of another. Although we do not recognize any separateness, we can work on same problem—two for the price of one, as you humans say."

"And you believe this—why?"

"You ask if Ansebe has a soul—perhaps artificial is just a name—not what you believe artificial to be. No human could ever create life without a seed, yet I was made from just an egg, and a little knowhow. To answer questions of the soul, we ask, do we exist, are we real?"

"Well," Zara smirks, "doesn't a punch in the face answer this?"

"Only if you accept it as real, we should ask what isn't real," he smiles, holds his hand up, upon which it turns invisible, "that which is not, can you define it?" Zara grasps the air, catching hold of his hand, upon which it turns visible, "Whoa… how'd you do that?"

"Simple, watch, I do slowly," pigments change in his hand, mirroring the surrounding area, "you see now?"

"I see, but humans can't understand the fundamental nature of reality, what's real—what's not, our senses are too limited… they just are."

Ansebe nods, "Such is nature, allow me to illuminate an alternative view. Have you ever understood what gives life to a body? What do you find with the dead? Body is there, it is existent to you and to your senses, alas the individual you knew is not there, and yet there is no change in the atoms which make up a living or a dead body."

"I've seen my share of dead bodies."

"Ahh, but did you? There is more to a body than the shell that we occupy—maybe we exist because we are simply telling ourselves that we do." He touches a finger to Zara's forehead, "Our minds are nothing more than matter arranged in a complex pattern, this pattern maintains our frequency in space time and from this coherent thought is borne. This process projects our hologram—that which we see as reality."

"I see, I think."

"Stop being a thought!"

"A thought?"

"What if we stop all thought, cease all concepts—become a nonentity whereby our reality fades to nothing. It is not real."

"I feel real enough."

"Because you do not accept. All is emptiness, all matter is an intricate weave of illusion—when we agree to such a possibility—we can say that we are the imagination of ourselves, a quantum fluctuation."

Zara leans forward, her face lit up from the holographic fire, "So, do we ever wake up from this imagination dream world of yours?"

"What if there are two universes—a dream one, and a real one—in a never-ending ballet of causality?"

"I'll take your word for it," she answers in an unconvinced tone, one eyebrow raised. "Tell me, what's with the meditating? How'd you find me?"

"Rai technology can find your frequency in space time—when you meditate you create a signature—with it we can plot a line between two spaces and navigate through the causal-ocean to your exact location."

"Why here, this forest?"

"Because here began or begins the search for humanity. This is of great significance. Alas we cannot talk of this for it would be unwise."

"Okay I get it, you're sightseeing—what about the mission?"

"The mission?" Ansebe's ears twitch, his skin turns from red to a light shade of blue, "It begins with the tell."

Chapter Five
Equations

"Zara, your leaders believe your world is unique. It is not. I am here on behalf of a group of ancient and powerful civilizations, some of which are many millions of your Earth-years old. They watch your world."

"How long have they been watching us?"

"Terra has been watched for a very, very long time."

"Tell me about these civilizations."

"They are called the Eyt, a group of civilizations which safeguards your planet. Terra benefits from a reservation status, not unlike your people's conservation attempts to protect endangered species," he passes her more manna.

"Thank you… why the interest in us?"

"The Eyt have an unwavering interest in the evolution of all life, which like a virus expands throughout the stars—for such a long time—until a secondary variation touches it, when there is effect, a merge occurs then continuation. All life searches for life. This is evolution on a cosmic scale. Alas, the problem with new civilizations is their life span, many only exist as a brief spark, and become extinct before they realize any potential. This is usually at the age of the atom," he waves a hand, whereby the holographic fire mimics a nuclear mushroom cloud, "a form of natural selection where many destroy their planets with nuclear destruction. It the first great filter, a filter from which was borne an equation, not unlike your drake equation which arrives at the number of estimated empires within the Milky Way."

He waves his hand once more, a hologram of the solar system appears, "We call this equation the Painted Symbol. Its variables are complex and require data such as the make-up of a species, their planets ecosystem and the type of solar system they inhabit." Another wave of his hand, a hologram of a probe exploring a planet, "The data for this equation is obtained by interstellar probes, sent to all parts of the galaxy, searching for life. From this equation, we can prophesize the expected moment in time a civilization becomes capable of harnessing the energy radiated by its own star."

"How is this data collected… probes you say?" Zara asks, her eyes ablaze with curiosity.

"These probes seek out species which leave signs of a developing intelligence," he points at the hologram, a probe exploring a cave system. "When a species starts to express their environment by way of cave paintings, or carvings or any other medium—these are the symbols. Once these are discovered, the Painted Symbol equation calculates the expected time when civilizations become technological. A timetable for return to witness and study a species' first interstellar steps—your own Moon landings, for example."

"Wait a minute…" Zara exclaims, eyes wide open, "are you saying you witnessed Neil Armstrong's first steps?"

"Everything is true. The Eyt were there as were the Others, watching."

"Who are the Others?"

"Not so much who, but what. The Terrans are not the only ones to experience unidentified aerial phenomena."

"Hold on, what did you say?" Zara's mouth drops.

"There are things supernatural to the Eyt… the Terrans do not have the monopoly on ghostly phenomena."

"What? You see UFOs as well? You're the ones supposed to be inside the damn things—not trip-out seeing them."

"Indeed, there will always be unexplained mysteries. Now, back to the tell," he raises a finger, "and the history of your organization, the Four Nations. It began with crashed interstellar vehicles, retrieved by your government. A bounty of unlimited technology to work on, whereby your leaders deemed it fit to create a shadow government of individuals to deal with such matters. This group you know as Majik, a mere twelve persons deciding matters on behalf of humanity. We soon discovered Majik were planning to use our own tech for evil. This was when the Eyt secretly formed the Four Nations, a clandestine administration operating in England, Russia, China and the USA. We recruited key individuals, formed a covert agency to act as ambassadors to the Eyt. From these few good people of Terra a legacy was inherited—"

"Hold on... a legacy? Meaning something handed down from a predecessor?"

"Yes, we have worked in the background throughout your history, nevertheless, it was time to be done again."

Zara looks miffed, "How come I don't know about this?"

"One must be lowered gently into the rabbit hole, for it is deep," his tone changes, "and darker than you could imagine."

Zara squeezes her fists with anticipation, "How dark?"

Ansebe draws a sharp breath, his eyes narrow, "A long time ago a project was carried out by the Maitra to send hyper-luminal probes to far-reaching corners of the verse, to run the Painted Symbol. To search for new life, new universes, new Gods. At that time, hyper-luminal travel was not restricted to our galaxy— it should have been. What was found was that which exists outside the furthest reaches of knowledge, they are what you may call Gods, we call them the bringers of light. They are the Elb!"

"Wait, it's possible to travel to the realm of the Gods? You have to explain."

"We try. My craft is a vimana, named the Newara, a talisman of the Siṃha clan of the Nirayana. It has five modes of travel. In mode one, it travels by creating a warp bubble. This way of travel was suitable for eons, until the Maitra developed hyper-luminal engines which far surpassed warp-drive technology."

"Hyper-luminal, that's faster than light. How's it work?"

"If physical mass can be represented as a complex something in mass space, then objects in that space may be able to spin to new orientations along real and imaginary coordinate axes. The Maitra discovered how to make a craft's mass imaginary, to take it off the real-line in a complex space and onto an imaginary-line. When it is so, we become tachyons and can travel anywhere in the multiverse. The trouble is which doors to use—infinite doors, infinite possibilities." Ansebe waves his hand, a hologram of the universe appears where the fire was, "These Elb I mentioned, it is said they can make an entire universe imaginary," the hologram morphs into two duplicate universes. "We first learned of them when the Maitra's hyper-luminal probes returned, with them an ominous message from the Elb."

"What kind of message?"

"The worst kind. The Elb said they are validating the races of our universe, said there were instances where some races' technology had advanced too fast—faster than their spiritual abilities—like leaving a child in charge of a hydrogen bomb. Such races are periodically judged by the Elb, by their Celestial Witness." Ansebe stands, paces a circle, "Many are eliminated from existence… the Terrans may well soon be judged," his skin turns dark, "and found wanting!"

Zara's mind races, "We can't be no threat to these Elb. Why us? Why?"

Ansebe shakes his head, "You may ask this of those who visited Terra a long time past, the An-Nuakai. The ones who modified humankind's genetic code. Alas, after this modification, your intelligence evolved fast, so fast that men would achieve the age of the atom before losing their instinct for war. This the Elb noticed."

"How'd they even know about us?"

Ansebe's eyes narrow, "The An-Nuakai leave on all planets they visit a satellite, to monitor the fruits of their endeavours. These satellites act as a beacon to the Elb."

"What… how can we be judged for something beyond our control?"

"They care not about your excuses. They are highly evolved light beings infected with a trans-dimensional intelligence. There is usually one Elb in orbit around a system, when three appear, it is bad," Ansebe sighs, "but when five arrive, they merge into one—so that they may pass judgment."

"So, how does this affect our mission?"

"We believe the Elb are coming."

"What kind of mission is this, and what do you expect me to about it? I'm only human."

Ansebe places a hand on her shoulder, "We need humanity, a fresh set of eyes, to see if we are missing anything. Maybe you're far more capable than you realize."

"But why earth, why us?"

"As I have said, life is a virus, constant throughout the cosmos, it continues merging, continually finding new contact, there is always eternal change. With an ever-changing force, there is always the potential for destructive failure—"

"And we have demonstrated we are less than capable of building for peace."

"When your race discovered the wonders of technology, you expected to build for peace. Sadly… when technology evolves faster than a race's spirituality, dreadful things happen, such as the nuclear terrors unleashed on Japan. This did not go unnoticed. Shortly thereafter the Elb held the first trial of strength, to judge humanity. The Eyt guided by the Ternion, won an adjournment, these normally last some millennia, but not this time, the Elb are back. We believe your black-ops work on the underground pyramid in Alaska has vexed the Elb. You should have never entered the crypt of the Gods! As a result, the Elb are running in judgement mode, currently deciding what you are—a destructive failure or a race with peace-building potential."

"You can't be serious…" Zara bites her lip, her eyes glaze over, "tell me we can stop this."

"We try… we pass, we fail, tell you I cannot. We can only investigate and play their game. Do not worry, child, it is foretold the Terrans may overcome several future extinction events, the failure rate is always in flux."

"Nice to know. Maybe we can flux things up for the Elb."

"We shall try our best to alter the outcome. Now, eat and rest, we take advantage of the calm before the storm."

Chapter Six
The Newara

"Sub-Rohza, uncloak please," Ansebe says, upon which it unveils, metallic contours shimmer as if visually distorted by heat waves. Its chromium splendour visible one second, the next it turns dark depths of black.

"The shell, it looks alive…" Zara stands awestruck, admiring the seamless shape of the gravity-defying vessel. "Classic flying saucer look, no seams, as if it was moulded into shape," she touches the shell, it recoils away from her hand, "it feels alive."

A metallic voice sounds, reverberating around the vessel. A feminine voice.

"Assertion. I am alive and right here in front of you—who pray tell are you?" It ends with an irritated metallic hum.

"What the hell, is your space ship unhappy with me?" Zara asks, her brow knitted with a frown.

"Be kind, Rohza," Ansebe says, placing his hand on the craft, "meet Zara, we'll be working with her, I want you both to get on. We try."

"Lady, if you put my boss in danger—it's on like kazzi-zam!"

Arms crossed Zara drums her fingers in response, "Okay—I'm impressed with the talking ship with an attitude, but we need to concentrate on the mission directive."

"And we will." Without warning Ansebe places a hypodermic gun to her neck, the contents inject in an instant. Zara suddenly spins around, striking his wrist and snatching away the gun, "What the hell, no one's ever caught me off guard!"

"Zara trust me, calm yourself." The dosage acts fast, a sudden bitter chemical taste hits the back of her throat, senses dull, "What's in this… oh-crap, feel strange."

"Breathe, child," Ansebe holds her up, "allow the polymorphic-nano to go into your mind."

"Polymorph…" unable to speak Zara quickly loses consciousness.

Thereafter Zara awakes, to find herself seated within the Newara. "This is a momentous time for you," Ansebe says, "in your mind grows a pattern, a sea of biosensors. You must accept that these are inside you, creating a mirror image of your mind." Zara puckers her forehead trying to keep her half-closed eyes open—when she suddenly jolts forward wide awake.

"Magnetic resonance mapping," says Sub-Rohza.

Ansebe kneels, facing Zara, "Billions of your neural pathways are being mapped inside your mind, Rohza is uploading these as we speak to her infinite memory, creating a white matter interface. Let's try a mind-link conversation—Rohza if you please."

"< He means telepathy. >"

Zara hears it inside her head, a shiver runs down her spine. Intense feelings of euphoria combine with a sensation of pins and needles all over her body and as the feeling subsides, a vibrant awareness seizes her senses, her third-eye awakens. Sub-Rohza announces, "System online." Zara regains a steely composure, just as the voice inside her head sounds again.

"< Zara, I'm almost done mapping your mind-link. Aeronautic interface uploaded, we are flight ready—you are ready to guide the Newara. >" A sudden panic attack. Zara loses her breath as her sensory capacity is pushed to the limit.

"< Please remain calm, or the haptic interface will really unsettle you. >" With a slow breath taken panic subsides, Zara's natural thought pattern returns.

"< Sub-Rohza can you hear me? >"

Sub-Rohza responds inside her mind, "< Don't think so loud, of course I can. We can! >" Zara gives a wry smile, briefly disconnecting from the mind-link.

"So, now I'm an astral-intellectual."

"< I detect sarcasm. >" Eager for more, Zara tries again.

"< What's next, you said I can guide your ship? >"

Ansebe joins the mind-link, "< And you shall, Rohza please upload Zara's interface. >"

"< Interface is ready, locked and loaded. >" Ansebe begins teaching.

"< Okay Zara… let's try an atmospheric ascent, to the thermosphere. >"

"< I'm not sure how high you mean? >" she shakes her head, unsure.

"< Height is meaningless, feel for an expansion, find the feeling and expand. >" The ship appears to react, a slight tremor.

"< Zara you've ascended just above the forest canopy, try again. Remember, if you try to make certainty from uncertainty, the result will still be uncertainty. There is a connection we call the spirit of the wind. The wise know what we see through our eyes is never— >"

Zara breaks mind-link, "Let me try!"

Ansebe inhales deeply, an incredible aura exudes as he concentrates on boosting her interface, and as he does waves of green and purple run over his skin in alignment with his psychic abilities. Zara calms, concentrates. A mysterious spring-like elastic force combines her thoughts with a simple compulsion, a notion of expansion.

"< Up, Newara. Show me, ascend us high. >"

Ansebe smiles, "< Zara, open your eyes, let all your senses take in the glory of the infinite. Rohza deploy the uni-screen. >"

"< Instruction. Uni-screen activated. >"

"The spirit of the wind, I can feel it!" Zara opens her eyes, "No, it's so much more than a feeling, it's one of our senses."

Ansebe nods, "Yes, one of the many senses humans were originally gifted with. Now my protégé, open your mind's eye, open it wide."

An odd feeling felt, as Zara opens her third eye, "Whoa, where'd the ship go?" Her head darts left to right, up and down, "Aim for the stars he says… we're in orbit." Zara's eyes widen, spellbound at the view. The Newara having turned transparent shows off the beauty of space, all that separates them seems to be an invisible lattice-like construct. Zara looks to Ansebe, her eyes sparkle with fascination.

"< Where's the framework, the shell? >"

"< The ship is still here, the uni-screen simply paints the image of all that surrounds us onto the walls. >" Zara takes charge and with the simple thought of down, the ship moves at unbelievable speed, to return from whence it came, hovering above the trees.

"< Wait a minute, I can feel something different, the power, the ship feels less powerful. I can feel a restriction in the Earth's atmosphere, a dampener on the speed output. Hold on, how do I know that I know this? >"

Sub-Rohza responds. "< She learns fast boss, interface is calibrating at a record rate. >"

"As we predicted, we chose well." Ansebe says, disconnecting from mind-link.

"You did?" Zara asks.

"We did," he nods, smiles. "Why the restriction you ask, it is because of gravity, when we travel in space we create a warp-bubble and inside this magnetic sphere we don't feel the effects of gravity or inertia—"

With a thought Zara completes his sentence,

"< So we don't pulp our inner organs into mush. >"

"< Sub-Rohza does not allow this, this unit manages the inertia dampeners. >"

"< Does the Sub-Rohza always chatter so much? >"

"< Boss, this one acts like she hung the moon and stars! >"

Ansebe places a finger to his lips, requesting silence from his two companions. "I say this aloud. When we traverse a planetary system with a sizable g-force, an inertia dampener allows us to safely transit from basic gravity propulsion fields into a warp field." Ansebe gazes into Zara's eyes to make a point.

"This is one of the lower forms of flight, it is not trans-dimensional—"

"Wait-a-minute, trans-dimensional? You have to explain that."

"Travelling as thought. It is like comparing hand-held binoculars to your Hubble telescope, do not read too much into the meaning of that statement. For now, know this vessel can arrive at Jupiter in next to no time at all." He waves a hand, opens a holographic control panel, adjusting it like a rear view mirror. "This panel displays our point in space time, it is rarely used by accomplished pilots, but still, it is useful for beginners."

"So, you travel light years but still need help with reverse parking."

"< Emotive. She's being facetious, boss. All calibrations complete—her neural oscillations are too strong, a slight theta imbalance affecting her reaction times. Over-calibrated, too precise. >"

A thought from Ansebe. "< The rhythm-fix then. >" He looks at Zara, smiles, "< Please recall some music of your choice. >"

"You want me to learn to fly an interplanetary craft listening to music?"

Ansebe leans over from his seat, "If you can't think of any music, then we shall pick some for you."

Zara pauses for thought, decided she couples a hand to her ear, listens for her choice: What the World Needs Now is Love. No sooner does she think of the song when subtle tones of treble and bass fill the craft as the classic melody begins. Ansebe's ears twitch to the opening notes. Looking at him, Zara bites her lip, trying not to smirk at the sight of his lupine ears, all six of them swaying in tune to the easy swing jazz classic. In appreciation, he waves his hands, draws patterns as if conducting—in a musical trance. Ansebe draws a long, deep breath, closes his eyes, "An excellent choice! We try."

Chapter Seven
Empathy Is a Quick-Change Artist

"I know nothing, you know nothing, we know nothing." The eerie voice of a captive extra-terrestrial biological entity, it answers repeated questioning. Named Ebe, the being is classified as a voluntary guest, albeit under detainment. Located in a classified underground military base in Nevada, USA. Above top secret, an unacknowledged project known only to a few, and on this day, voices reverberate off the walls of a dimly lit chamber. In one corner sits a dolphin-skinned being, its large black oval eyes blinking, ill at ease with the desktop lighting— exhausted it tries to steady its oversized head.

"Ebe, we need to see what you know, now let's try again— are you with me?" The interrogator frowns, his demeanour unrelenting, his questioning untiring, as it has been for many hours. The Ebe replies in a hoarse tone, unclear but comprehensible.

"I… know… nothing."

"Ebe, why don't you tell us more on the zero-point energy field?" The interrogator continues, "Ebe, the zero-point field?" but the Ebe stays silent.

"Dammit, Ebe," he slams his fist on the table, "I can't protect you from them," he sighs. "God only knows what things they'll do to you." The Ebe looks away, indicating it will only converse with its one and only friend Sergeant Rogers, an empath trained by specialist covert divisions within the military. The interrogator speaks into a desktop intercom.

"Sir, I believe the Ebe is distressed, perhaps a session with Sergeant Rogers is required, for the Ebe to open up." Director General Abner Bullock, a stocky overweight man, observes the questioning from behind a two-way mirror. He picks up a wall mounted phone and replies.

"Okay son, let's do it, but I want every second of this session monitored, nothing left to chance," he turns to his staff. "Get me Sergeant Rogers."

"He's on leave, sir."

"Then recall him now, get him to report for duty, dammit!"

It is sometime later, when Sergeant Rogers arrives.

"Sir, Sergeant Rogers," he salutes Bullock, "reporting for duty, sir."

"Son, we called you hours ago—why the delay?"

A faint smirk from Rogers follows with an odd squint of his left eye.

"Sir, Sergeant Rogers is sick, sir."

Bullock faces Rogers, stares into his eyes, "Son, I suggest you make a remarkable recovery," he cups his ear, "I can't hear you!"

"Sir, yes sir. Sergeant Rogers is making a remarkable recovery."

"Are you feeling up to the task Rogers, are you with us?"

"Sir, yes sir."

"At ease son, now as usual the Ebe will only talk to you, it's this connection thing you two have. I need you to get on top of this, son. I don't like this one bit, but the powers that be need information, as of yesterday—do you understand?"

"Yes sir, I will not let you down, sir!" Rogers answers in a firm tone.

"Are you okay, son?"

"Sir, I believe the connection I have with the Ebe will out the truth."

Director Bullock takes a deep breath, "Son, I hope you're right."

Rogers enters the holding cell and sits opposite the Ebe, "Ebe, we need some information. I know you don't like it here, let's give them something, stop their edgy paranoia and all their fear—so much fear." The Ebe gazes at Rogers, then at the others, it waves to request their removal. A wry grin from Rogers follows with a facial tic, hardly noticeable, but it does not go unnoticed by the Ebe as it shifts its head slightly to the side in an inquisitive manner. Rogers concentrates, places two fingers to his temple. "The Ebe is distressed, needs some one on one time, to open up… can't communicate fully with others present," Rogers looks to the others, "only then will the Ebe co-operate." Director Bullock places both hands on the desk in the monitoring room, looks down, considering the request, he claps his hands.

"Okay people, let's give Sergeant Rogers and the Ebe some alone time."

In silence, Sergeant Rogers and the Ebe stare into each other's eyes, then the Ebe sniffs the air as if detecting a stranger's scent, which is met with a smile from Rogers, knowing the Ebe's sense of smell is so acute it can identify health problems in people.

Rogers taps his fingers, nothing quite says impatience more than the sound of fingers tapping, except that this is no normal finger tapping. He traces a V on the desk with his forefinger, it is a cypher, a secret code. His fingers tap on the table, a rapid combination of taps and shapes follow and from this simple code a universal language arrives. Moving his fingers with the dexterity of a master pianist, he codes several questions.

The Ebe speaks, "I speak Rai fluently."

Rogers smiles, replies in Rai, "Did you know on Terra, American POWs in the Vietnam War were prevented from speaking, so the prisoners had to invent a way of talking if only to keep their sanity." Rogers closes his fingers together and touches his forehead, opening them wide, "Kaboom! They came up with the tap-code, by tapping on a simple five by five grid, assigned to the letters of the alphabet—the prisoners prevented from speaking were able to talk in code."

A maniacal smirk from Rogers on seeing the Ebe's reactions, he goes on to say, "In feudal Japan, the Shogun's concubines dare not speak aloud without permission, so they came up with an intricate sign language—dozens of signals conveyed by the opening, closing and fluttering of a fan in relation to where it was held against the body."

The Ebe scowls, "Your point is?"

"Secrets, my point is secrets," Rogers sways his hand from side to side imitating a cobra, "secretive languages for things that others should not know!"

"Enough with games, this charade!" shouts the Ebe. They gaze into each other's eyes, then the Ebe cusses in Ergot, a long-forgotten language, the language of the ancients, "Venomous harem-skarem, what have you done with Sergeant Rogers?"

But Rogers interprets, "Ergot, the language of the few, surprised that a harem-skarem would know the lingo."

The Ebe half-frowns, taken aback.

"Is he alive?"

"A look of concern for the human, worry not for your friend—he lives—or at least he was alive when I left him." From behind the two-way glass, Bullock shouts.

"What the hell… what is this? What language are they talking in?"

"Director," a scientist answers, "they've established a telepathic rapport, even though they're speaking in tongues, this situation is covered in our protocols."

"Do we proceed… do we proceed? Answer me, dammit!"

"Sir, I believe we should."

Inside in the cell the Ebe looks at Sergeant Rogers, his alien expression is one of disdain that even a human could recognize amid the unfamiliar facial scowls. It snarls at Rogers.

"You're Fez-Pyan, the serpent with a thousand faces?"

Fez smirks, "Incognito!"

The Ebe's jaw drops, then it regains composure as if accepting fate, "One created to assist the humans, turned renegade—a loose cannon!" Fez's eyes glare a sociopathic glint, his face begins to twitch. He takes a deep breath, then to avoid any suspicion he smiles, trying to retain the jovial appearance of Rogers. The Ebe adds, "It is said you are talented, one of the best—alas, nothing but a common assassin, there is no art in taking a life with your own hands."

"How so?" An amused look from Fez. "What would your kind know of art when all you know is the way of manipulation. Mine is creativity, to be at one with the task at hand, with emotion, fluidity, with my own hands art I create."

"The psychopathic traits of the artist," a tear wells up in the corner of the Ebe's eye, "I wish you… salvation."

"Now, to business," Fez sighs, his eyes also glaze over, "have you gifted them any information, such that they are not ready for?"

"Worry not, they do not yet know our secrets."

"Bravo, you have held out—you know the Ergot's rules when a captive is at risk of disclosing the secrets of their covenant."

"I do. I know the charge and the sentence," a serene look from the Ebe, "a new container awaits me in the next dimension."

Fez-Pyan clears his throat, visibly upset, "Are you sure you can make the transfer? This base uses low level electronics to jam the signal."

"The transition can be accomplished, if you can assist with the fading of this shell."

"I give you my word that Sergeant Rogers shall live on without any pain of this incident. You ready to go?"

The Ebe takes a moment to reflect, it replies bravely. "I am ready…" Fate being decided the Ebe shuts both eyes, scans Fez-Pyan with its empathic senses, finding a reading.

"You are scared?" the Ebe asks.

"Only of living, the void does not arouse any fear in my soul."

"And when you gaze long into the darkness?"

"It also gazes into me, and it is awestruck!"

"You have become one with what it is you seek to destroy, leaving a part of you spent, empty."

"My art-form fills the emptiness."

"The way of the assassin, an art which requires you to spend a part of yourself in order to participate. The concept is flawed."

A moment of respect sweeps over Fez-Pyan, "Dammit! I take no satisfaction from this—needs must—for the good of the many, so that they may stay on the path." He takes a deep breath and rolling his tongue over, lays a pin-sized object between his teeth. His personality becomes that of a cold executioner. "Well then," he talks through his teeth, "there's nothing more to say except ciao, bon voyage, sayonara." Without warning Fez draws a short deep breath and exhales, his bloated cheeks rapidly compressing as if spitting venom.

"P h s s s s . . . t t t t!"

A carefully concealed nano-dart shoots out from his mouth, the miniscule object finds its mark and quickly dissolves on contact with the Ebe's neck, once inside fast-acting toxins attack the central nervous system. The Ebe stills then drops. "Ta-da!"

Fez exclaims, in a soft tone. An ECG monitoring the Ebe's vital signs signals the alarm, upon which Fez reverts to Roger's persona, he screams, "Medics!" The medical team rush in and ready a defibrillator in a frantic attempt at resuscitation. In the melee, a stack of papers is knocked on the floor, photographic evidence of UFOs. Fez-Pyan's eyes fixate on one of the prints, his eyes widen, he's never one to be shocked but this time is different—haunting memories in front of him. Is this destiny, fate? He looks at the image, and speaks to himself, "The Newara!"

"Sergeant Rogers, please stand back." A medic desperately tries to revive the Ebe, but to no avail; after several failed attempts at resuscitation, the medics call the time of death.

Later, he reports to Director Bullock. A wry grin from the disguised Fez-Pyan at the satisfaction of having completed another near impossible hit. He walks into Bullock's office, salutes. Bullock sits in his revolving chair, his back to him. He spins around to face Rogers, the look on his face is one of disappointment and frustration.

"Sergeant Rogers, sir."

"What the hell went on in that room?"

"Sir, I had no idea the Ebe was going to die, our empathic connection was fine. There were absolutely no signs—"

"No signs?" a heated look from Bullock. "Dammit, Rogers you were talking in an unknown language, the team believe it sounded like Sanskrit, hell I never even heard Sanskrit till today."

"Sir, I believe I was talking at all times in English, perhaps if I could review the footage I might be able to help?"

"Sergeant Rogers," a long sigh from Bullock, "you'll be processed in full, you won't be going anywhere until we get a hold on this. At ease sergeant, report to medical." A full interrogation of Rogers follows, several hours later he's given the all clear to leave the base.

Later Fez-Pyan arrives at the apartment of the real Sergeant Rogers, lets himself in, pours out a whiskey and goes upstairs, where Rogers lies tied up on his bed.

"Hey," he looks at the bed confused, "you've wrapped yourself in curtain?" He swigs some more whiskey, "Oh yeh... I remember." Sergeant Rogers sleeps rolled up in the living room curtain, still under the effect of drugs which should have long worn off.

"You're pretending to sleep, aren't you?" Fez sits beside him, like a sociopath he feels no shame in his actions, "Life, you never realize how precious it is until you hold it in your fingertips." Nano-med dispenser in hand he breathes in a dosage of meds, "Keep the voices in check," then changes the setting, administering the antidote to rouse his captive from unconsciousness. He rolls Rogers onto the floor, who wakes slowly, to see his captor untying his hands and legs. With a dark wit known only to himself, he tells Rogers, "So, I told the voices inside my head that I question my sanity, and they said we're one-hundred-percent with you on this, even though it's completely irrational," he taps his head, "I thought I was crazy but I'm not the only one in here." Sergeant Rogers comes around to see the odd sight of Fez-Pyan sitting on the edge of his bed, smoking a cigar and gently tugging at his hair, which falls away in large tufts in his hand. Rogers gawks, dismayed at seeing a bald double of himself, a lifeless reflection of his own face. Fez warns, "Don't think about going for the gun taped under the cabinet, no matter how fast you think you are, I'm faster." Rogers although drained, begins to recall a muddled series of events from the previous day. He was attacked and bound, but more astounding is his recollection of being effortlessly disabled with inhuman skills by his captor. He plucks up the nerve to speak.

"What are you?"

"I'm a whirlwind, a hurricane, a freakin' force of nature. Or an alien," he winces in pain, "hey, want to see something odd?" A surreal transformation occurs, his facial structure begins to rearrange, as if a mudded cosmetic face pack had hardened. He scratches the surface, which crumbles away to reveal a chromium metallic face-plate, no nose, no ears as such, only eyes, mouth and strange engraved patterns where his eyebrows should be.

"Are… are you okay?"

"What do you care?" Fez snarls, breathes in some more nano-meds. "No, that was rude of me," he adds, no longer in pain.

"I can help is all—what's your name, sir?" Rogers tries to create a rapport with his captor.

"Sir?" Fez shrugs, "Dude, it's Master," he ponders a name, "Master of the Nine Deadly Venoms. Hell yeh!"

"Master, what are you—"

"It's Master of the Nine Deadly Venoms!"

"Master of the Nine Deadly Venoms, what are you going to do with me?"

"Nothing—I just want to tell you a story."

"A story?" Rogers looks confused.

"Master of the Nine Deadly Venoms, will you tell me a story," Fez nods, "you say it."

"Ah… Master of the Nine Deadly Venoms, will you tell me a story?"

"Sure, I'll tell you a story hot-shot, you only had to ask," he passes Rogers the bottle of whiskey. "It's a story about three saviours born of an earth woman, created to show the light, to bring warmth to the iciest of lands. Where there was no hope, the three pure ones would bring balance, in times of war they would show others the essence of peace. All were educated to a zenith few would achieve, trained in the sacred arts of combat. And so, the prophecy of the three pure ones came to be.

"Soothsayers named them individually Heaven, Man and Earth. Man was a woman, but let's not confuse things." Fez goes awry, taps his head as if trying to remember, "Oh yeh… Heaven and Earth the two brothers were the pinnacle of molecular biology, new-beings from the unification reserve. Let's call them rich man, poor man… well, not yet but we're leading up to that bit. The woman was hidden at birth, she's the still point of the three, a key to gain access to hidden knowledge some say.

"One day a glitch was discovered in the genetic mapping of the one named Earth. At first the creators believed they could address the problem with nano-meds, but this just triggered a runaway effect in his genome sequencing. It all started to go south big time," Fez sighs, shakes his head, "you see the three pure ones were all designed with two minds imprinted onto one. Two for the price of one—ya feel me? Duplex neuro-mapping improved their efficiency that they may run faster, jump higher and perform stronger in both body and mind.

"Alas, the problem with Earth's genetic code worsened rapidly, his duplex mindset started to splinter—there was no stopping this. Some say he was going quite mad, insane, an unknown mental-phenomena, forget schizophrenia hot-shot, we're talking kilophrenia for this unfortunate soul." Fez pauses, holds his head rocking back and forth, "I said, let me finish," he says, talking to himself. "Sorry about that."

"That's okay," says Rogers.

"Where were we?"

"You said Earth was going mad, insane."

"How'd you know that?" Fez's eyes narrow, he clenches a fist.

"You just said so."

"Oh yeh… I did?" He lets out a maniacal laugh. "So, Earth was insane, a problem they believed they should end, and so they planned his demise. One of the creators, a father-figure protested this action, to no avail. And so, Earth's mind was broken, but when he found out about such plans his heart was torn apart! One night, in a rage he bit the hands that created him, leaving a trail of annihilation in their midst. Of course, his creators didn't like this, they didn't like it one bit. So much so that they sent a crack team of mercenaries to capture him, but such was the love of Heaven for Earth that he pleaded with the powers that be to save him. Alas, to save him it was resolved that he would be banished to the planet of his name, to serve the rest of his life there—never to fulfil his destiny. And thus, Earth became a poor man, whereas his brother continued to receive all the glory of his name, and his adventures were painted as legendary exploits throughout the stars—he's the rich man, you'll catch on." Fez goes silent, waiting for a response but his captive just gazes back at him, both afraid and mystified.

"Well?" he asks, opening both his hands. "What do you think?"

"It's a great story!" Rogers praises Fez, trying to befriend him.

"I knew it, I just knew it—you figure out who Earth is?"

"Ahh… is it you?"

"I'm saying nothing," he points his thumb at his chest, "say would you like to know how I defeated the Zihna clan of the Nirayana?"

"Who are they?"

"Why they're the Twelve Twisted Celestial Assassins!"

An alarm sounds on Fez's watch, he sighs, "Damn—party's over! Hey, should I erase your memory?" Rogers shakes his head, "Rogers, it's been emotionless," he knocks out Rogers with a shot of nano-meds, "till next time." He then walks to the window, looks at three vehicles parked outside, "Spooks!" he says as a team of black suited men prepare to raid Rogers' apartment. A quick tap on his forearm, and his military uniform transmutes into a black nano-weave, a uniform of alien origin adorned with strange hieroglyphs. He is ready for action. More on this later.

Chapter Eight
Beyond Visual Range

We return to our airborne team who, unbeknown to themselves, are surfing into the unwritten lore of history. Zara smiles at Ansebe as she pilots the Newara, thrilled at her progress.

"A natural," Ansebe says, "why don't you try opening her up, see what you can do?"

"Hold on, she's proficient in Parkour," Rohza says, "I've cross-referenced the haptic interface with her subconscious, so that the Newara may mimic such agility."

"Parkour?" Ansebe asks.

"Boss, Parkour is the activity of moving rapidly through a built-up urban environment."

"Master Wang sent me to France when I was in my teens. Our French friends trained me to excel in Parkour, to specialize in fast-track deployment and retrieval—received tutelage from the world's best." Zara stops talking, looks down. Ansebe snaps his fingers twice, "It is dangerous to recall memories in the Newara, you could trigger other modes, upgrades the Newara is fitted with." With a subtle shake of her head she brings her attention back to the mission at hand.

"Good," Ansebe nods, "Rohza, create a training session."

"Writing code boss."

"Now Zara," Ansebe instructs, "reach inwards, visualize the feeling of moving in line with your trajectory, that's it! All-out forward momentum if you please." Zara becomes one with her senses, one with the spirit of the wind. As if from the outside looking in a restructuring occurs, the vessel's outer shell morphs as internal aesthetics rearrange.

Rohza calls out over via mind-link. "< Vector mode now! >" A three-dimensional construct appears in Zara's mind, mirroring the outer environment. The chessboard of her mind merges with the uni-screen, creating an extra sense of the surrounding space outside the Newara. As an unravelling of her sub-conscious takes hold, her mouth drops, she looks to Ansebe, "Earth's atmosphere, I can feel it talking to me… allowing safe passage."

"< Gaia has accepted you, Mach speed now—kick it! >" Ansebe replies via mind-link.

From zero to Mach speed in an instant, the Newara skims over the Himalayas at break-neck speed. "Now Rohza," Ansebe yells, "those mountains." The virtual construct in Zara's mind reveals an interlaced roadway through the mountains, a route of extreme complexity.

"< Quickly Zara! Follow the route, avoid the obstacles. >" Zara concentrates, suddenly the Newara swoops down at terminal velocity heading for valleys, sidestepping and back-dropping with phenomenal agility, avoiding 3-D constructs which pop up both inside her mind and on the uni-screen.

Rohza warns, "< Stepping up complexity. >" A mountain range appears without warning.

"That's no 3-D construct!" Zara yells, only just avoiding the mountain as the Newara applies an automated evasive manoeuvre.

Ansebe places a finger to Zara's temple, "Oust the ego from your sensory awareness, simply witness the now." Zara mind-melds with the Newara and as she does the craft spins in a corkscrew motion, and accelerates, Mach one, Mach four, incredible speeds—the haptic interface hums with her every thought. "Excellent Zara," Ansebe smiles. The saucer passes the Himalayas, slaloms through China and onwards to Japan, then it stops abruptly—levitating at a forty-five-degree angle over Tokyo tower.

A smile from Zara, as the Newara swoops down like a swallow in front of crowds of sightseers. Many of whom start to video or photo the incident. "That's one for the sceptics," says Zara, with a wry smile.

Ansebe shakes his head, "We would have to land outside the Whitehouse, and even that they would try to debunk."

"< Warning. Play time's over boss, we need to leave this place. Scalar tracking technology detected. Re-routing to Alaska via Hawaii, avoiding known hot spots. >"

Seen or unseen, the hypervelocity departure of the Newara leaves no doubt, like a meteoroid it leaves a trail of plasma in its wake. Once out of sight, many onlookers prefer to disbelieve their senses, deciding they saw an advertising stunt by way of a hologram.

Our team soar over the Pacific Ocean, not realizing they are about to become the stuff of legend. Having left Japan's shores, they head off in the direction of Hawaii, silently buffering the clouds at hyper-sonic speed when a weird sensation overwhelms Zara's senses. "Strange, I just thought, no I felt a swarm of locusts. They seemed so real."

Her shoulders shudder, on seeing this Ansebe becomes tense, alert, "It was calculated we would have more time, this is not good—Rohza, logistics report."

"< Several sorties scrambled boss, looks like half the US Air Force are coming down on us, a few minutes to critical distance. Picking up comms. Oh dear, their goal is to shoot us down with extreme prejudice. >"

Ansebe shouts, "Deploy shields, apply pre-collision damper, let the skies be our stage! Let us give them a short but not forgotten lesson—switching to dual piloting." He stays calm, despite the severity of the situation.

"< Boss, just detected a team of Raptors in stealth mode. >"

The Newara's vector mode displays on the uni-screen but a paranormal vision appears inside Zara's mind, "Six Raptors approaching," she whispers, then closes her eyes, "from the south at Mach speed."

"< Oh my. Zara is right! >" Rohza calculates, "< Warning. Sophisticated avionics applied by two naval destroyers, missiles locked on the Newara. We have incoming, front, rear and side escape routes blocked, six seconds, five seconds… >"

"< Wait for it… >" Ansebe holds up a finger, < go! >"

Missiles explode, encasing the sky in a sea of fire, but the saucer has already corkscrewed into an evasive manoeuvre, climbing up to fourteen thousand feet in a second. It hangs a hairpin turn into a north-westerly direction, temporarily losing the Raptors, but seconds later they all turn in pursuit, locked onto the Newara with advanced avionics they do not require visual sight of their target.

"< Sub-Rohza, would you play Ravel's Boléro, if you please.>"

"< On it boss, playing philharmonic version. >"

A raised eyebrow from Zara, as the classical melody begins. It is an odd sensation as the Newara appears to dance along to the ostinato rhythm of snare drum and flute, setting the tone for what follows. A second blanket of missiles explodes in their path, this time the Newara responds with a ten-thousand-foot back-drop. To the disbelief of the Raptor pilots, one reports, "Bogie just descended, repeat bogie just descended."

Inside the Newara, the sound of snare drums echo, as a serene ballet of stealth plays out. Then as bassoon, horns and trumpets all sound, the Newara spirals upward into a three-hundred-and-sixty-degree spin, releasing nano-flares with every whirl. The Raptors evade. "Flares," yells the leading pilot, "I'm a dot!" He hangs an evasive turn, yet these are no normal flares. In a millisecond one after another draws energy from the clouds, designed to turn the full ferocity of nature against man. Unsuspecting pilots find themselves caught-up in the field of burning flares, then from the clouds multiple bolts of lightning— anvil crawlers—a horrendous tree-like electrostatic discharge. The eerie plasma tentacles disable an entire sortie of Raptors with their touch. "Punch out, punch out!" the pilots yell as one by one the Raptors drop out of the sky, leaving a trail of ejector seats. In response the US Air Force up their game.

"< Boss, fourteen more Raptors approaching for close-range combat, suggest the graphonine netting. >"

"< No… >" Ansebe shakes his head, closes his eyes, "< we wait. >"

Their pursuers advance. "Eyeball, bogie in range… closing," the lead pilot takes the initiative, "six-aside, let's flank this bogie, I want two hawks staying above the fight." Integrated-avionics assist with the formation of a pincer movement, but the Newara counters, shooting upwards in the blink of an eye. All the pilots cross-talk over comms, "Heads up, bogie got through!"

"Give me a visual."

"No joy, don't see it."

"Contact—got a magnetic bearing on the bogie."

"I've got a bullseye."

"Take the kill, take the kill," orders the lead pilot.

Inside the Newara the classical sound of the soprano saxophone plays. Outside an onslaught of firepower is heading their way, but the Newara side-winds and releases more nano-flares, "Abort, abort!" the lead pilot calls off the chase. They retreat out of the dog-fight, just in time avoiding the onslaught of the flares. Departing with breakneck speed, the Newara heads off towards the West Coast, California. As they approach the coastline a third team of Raptors intercept them, not unlike a gaggle of geese the Newara stands flanked, but they kick-it, leaving the fighters behind to arrive seconds later at Los Angeles.

"We use the city skyscrapers against them, as booby trap or snare," yells Ansebe.

The pursuit swings low, their flight path weaves to and fro between the skyscrapers, then as the Newara cuts a near right angle, the jets unable to track bank off. Only to be replaced by three unmanned Predator drones which swoop down, in pursuit.

"Rohza," Zara asks, "are there any tunnels nearby? Any we can go through?"

"On it. Schematics. Found one, internal diameter of tubes no problem."

"Ansebe?" Zara looks to Ansebe, who nods.

"We try! Go!" The saucer hugs the highway, a bottleneck of traffic below them and in front of them a tunnel. To the astonishment of the drivers caught up in rush-hour traffic, a flying saucer skims past them, chased by the three drones. Ansebe raises his hand, starts to countdown, "Five, four, three—now," he claps his hands, "deploy shields." The craft juts into the tunnel, buffering from side to side trying to stabilize, the pressure of the electromagnetic shields cracking windscreens of the vehicles below. Two of the Predator drones veer off, narrowly avoiding the passageway but a smaller stealth drone enters the shaft in pursuit, but once inside it loses its signal and ploughs into the traffic, losing its wings. It is a miracle none are hurt.

In no time at all the Newara exits the underpass and ascends five thousand feet, there it hovers in analysis mode—seconds pass—two more sorties of Raptors appear on the holographic overlay. Sub-Rohza hacks the Raptors' communications, broadcasting aloud the fighter pilots' instructions, "Bogie is bottlenecked, bullseye AMRAMS locked on."

"We're about to be clam-baked!" yells Zara.

"< Defensive nullifiers actioned, boss. >" Sub-Rohza boosts the power output. Hell is unleashed as guided missiles are fired from the Raptors in unison—advanced medium-range air-to-air missiles track the Newara, but Rohza responds by firing a scattergun shot of dense fog. Hidden within the mist are thousands of tiny orbs which all explode in unison, releasing minute nano-strings of extreme density. The tiny threads net together, forming an unbreakable web, ensnaring the missiles. Once snared in the invisible web, a static-surge disables the payload, whereupon the missiles drop out of the sky. The US Air Force can only watch.

Their counter-defence pays off, allowing the Newara to sashay into a corridor of free airspace. Inside the saucer Bolero's concerto plays on, vector mode harmonics whirr with uncanny symmetry to the music.

Outside, once again the fighter aircraft break off from the pursuit.

Inside the Newara the sound of flutes, oboes, clarinets and piccolo sing, but as the violins sound Rohza speaks aloud, "Boss, the Raptors have fixed their lasers on us, sending our co-ordinates to a supersonic aircraft equipped with HEL tech, an airborne laser."

"Its power, its range?" Ansebe asks.

"The high-energy laser has a vaporizing range of ninety miles!"

"I know what to do—"

"Get us out of here!" Zara shouts.

The HEL weapon locks on target, its laser discharges. Ansebe smiles wryly, "Behold HEL hath not found its mark." The laser misses by some five-hundred yards. Zara sighs, looks at Ansebe, waving his hands in tune with Ravel's composition. "We still have some tricks up our sleeves—" he stops mid-sentence, receiving analysis via mind-link. "< Not good! >" His thoughts betray his calm demeanour.

All becomes clear as the three-dimensional array shows three craft tracking at phenomenal speed and manoeuvrability. A concerned frown from Ansebe.

"Boss, I've detected two tetragravimana and one vimana."

"Tetragravi what?" Zara raises an eyebrow.

"Flying Triangles," Rohza replies, "if it's circular it's a vimana, if it's biological it's a tetraporphyrin—"

"Rohza," Ansebe cuts in, "identification."

"Yes boss, only one true interstellar, its glyphs indicate it to be of Dries origin, the other two tetragravimana appear to be reverse-engineered. Oh, how odd… they've accessed the shunt program on the Dries vehicle—tractor shunt."

"Is that anything like a tractor beam?" Zara asks.

"Yes, it is. Any ideas, boss?"

Ansebe raises a hand and as he does the music stops, "We capitulate for the time being. They will try to shepherd us to the Nellis Range, to Area 51," he claps his hands, "time to play our masterstroke—release the oblong!" A jet-black oblong-shaped box with a marble-like texture phases from out of the flight console floor.

"Rohza, hide inside the oblong."

Bursts of static electricity buzz from the jet-black box. An oddity follows, a small circular ball of plasma drops from the ceiling of the Newara, for some reason Zara goes to catch it in her hands, "Whoa," she juggles it, thinking it's hot, but it's cool to touch. The orb levitates up to face her.

"Hi Zara."

"Rohza?"

"In the flesh."

"Holy moley! You're a real life will-o'-the-wisp." Zara says, her face lit up from Rohza's flickering light.

"I have to hide, good luck." And with that the technological wonder dives into the oblong, phasing into its jet-black surface.

"So, what now?" Zara asks.

"Remain calm and follow my lead."

As the two flying triangles and the saucer flank the Newara, the craft succumbs to the gravitational tug. Ansebe closes the virtual interface and sits in a meditative posture, holding the oblong on his lap.

Decelerating, the triangles flank them as they land, holding the Newara in place. The tractor field releases, and the Newara drops to the ground. Upon impact, advanced metalloids compress like a basketball, rebounding the craft until it settles still. The three vessels hover above the Newara, their gravitational fields triangulate, making take-off for the Newara impossible. A Mexican standoff takes place, then the quite noise of the desert is disrupted by the disturbance of tumbleweed hailing the arrival of two Black Hawk helicopters, their blades thrashing up a sandstorm as they land. A quick reaction force sprints to the Newara and attaches explosive EMP devices to the craft's shell, but the magnetic devices slide off like air hockey pucks. The soldiers leave the devices in the sand and retreat, sprinting back to a safe distance they stand ready, aiming their rifles at the craft. Once the explosives are in situ, the Dries vessel and the two triangles leave the area.

Then an older gentleman exits one of the helicopters, megaphone in hand, "This is Director Bullock," he says with a Texan twang, "I represent certain parties within our government, tasked with the capture, retrieval and control of unauthorized extra-terrestrial craft in our airspace. We know you have a female with you, first call—hand her over."

Ansebe shakes his head, looks to Zara, "Do not worry."

Bullock continues, "Now the devices we just deployed, if detonated could cause your vehicle to malfunction, failed life support and all—we can make this uncomplicated, or real hard, your call!"

"What are we going to do?" Zara asks.

"I have a plan."

"What's the plan?"

"How you say… we release the chains that bind the Kraken."

"That's not the saying," she smiles, "but it's close enough."

"We release the chains then. Watch. We try."

"Watch?" she takes a deep breath, sighs, "I'm watching."

Ansebe smiles, looks down at the oblong sitting on his legs. He waves a hand over it, glyphs glow under the skin of his wrist. Seconds pass, a jar-sized vial elevates out from the jet-black surface. He holds the vial in his hand, "Don't move!" he says, carefully unscrewing the lid to reveal a light viscous fluid, filled with hundreds of tiny critters. He whispers to the vial.

"Synthesize." Seconds pass, the tiny creatures begin to morph into metallic nano-shreds. "Hatch!" From out of the shreds tiny winged critters crawl.

"Behold, spirit-mites!"

Zara looks on in awe as all the tiny nano-critters fly out of the fluid, with the unerring appearance of mosquitos. The floor behind the cockpit litters with the tiny devices. Ansebe smiles at Zara, "Once outside, do not speak, just watch." They exit the Newara. Outside the craft vibrates, its metallic shell transmutes, opening a doorway.

One of the soldiers takes aim, awestruck he says, "Un-freaking-believable!"

"Hey, check out the newbie," one of the them calls out, to laughter from the team. They shout out to their captives, "Kneel, do it! Get your hands on your heads!"

Advancing with firearms aimed, the team leader screams, "Goddammit, I will blow your ugly extra-terrestrial brains all over this desert floor, stop looking at me!" He stands over Ansebe, "What's this?" he kicks the oblong out of his lap. "Oooh, it's a baby monolith," the leader says leaning over it, to sniggers from his men.

A wry smile from Ansebe, he whispers, "Five, four, three, two, one," then shouts, "DASNA." At the exact same moment, their would-be abductors all drop unconscious.

"The wind… stings," Ansebe says.

Zara looks at him astonished. "What the hell, how'd that come about?"

"The bite of the spirit-louse, it releases a potent cocktail."

"Good, let's fly the hell out of here."

"No, explosive devices are rigged to blast at the slightest movement. Besides, it may prove useful to have the Newara impounded," Ansebe smirks, "for the time being at least."

"So, we pilot one of the Black Hawks?"

"No, that is not the plan."

"Well Mister Know-it-All, what is the plan?"

"They're going to take us captive, transport us back to area fifty-one for interrogation."

"What? No way, no freaking way!"

"To all intent and purposes, they'll have us held captive, but we won't be." Ansebe picks up the oblong, sits with it and proceeds to operate the unit.

"When I revive them, it is important to keep still, do not speak."

"Sure, it can't get any worse."

Ansebe completes his programming of the arcane technology and with a wave of his hand, the task-force all regain consciousness and stand. Seconds pass, one of the soldiers speaks, "What the…" but before he can complete his sentence, Ansebe claps his hands, upon which all standing switch to an altered state of awareness.

The team leader speaks over comms, "This is team alpha-wolf, targets tagged and bagged, returning to base." The Black Hawks lift off, stirring the desert air, minutes later they are a dot on the horizon.

Chapter Nine
Cold Is the Desert

Ansebe gazes at the horizon, his far-reaching eyes able to see for miles. Arcane senses detect the direction they need to head off in, "We go this way."

"So, that was an experience," Zara says, "just in case you haven't noticed, we're in the middle of the freakin' desert. How we going to get out of here without water?"

"We're going to glide out of here."

"Glide he says!" Zara paces back and forth hands on hips, "How?"

"Hover—yes that is a better description." He steadies the oblong above the ground, it sits in mid-air, defying gravity.

"A skateboard? Now we're onto skateboards," she places a hand to her brow, "you only have one board."

A wry smile from Ansebe, "Not for long!" He pulls one of the quantum dice from his belt, places it on the oblong. The six faces of the dice all separate to reveal a pearl-like object. Ansebe holds it in his fingers, "Rohza, you can come out now."

Sub-Rohza jumps out of the jet-black box, flickering like a candle as she talks, "Hi boss, I've calculated the best route out of here, we should leave at once."

Ansebe holds the pearl up, "This is an egg, the oblong is a half-alive entity, a supreme merger of electronics and bacteria, now watch this…" Ansebe drops it on the jet-black surface. It slowly sinks out of sight, then the oblong begins to hum—the quantum dice levitates above it and begins to spin. Seconds later from the jet-black box an audible harmonic builds up to a crescendo. The oblong shudders from side to side, then separates—like a cell dividing—leaving a white mist in the air. The haze evaporates, to reveal two oblongs.

"Oh!" Zara raises both eyebrows, her mouth drops, "Amazing... bacteria can do that?"

"Not any bacteria, they are microorganisms fused with nano-chemistry and quantum-electronica—a processor—the ultimate calculator."

"A calculation device," Zara smirks, "so how do bacteria differentiate multiplication from division?"

Ansebe's ears twitch, "I see... bacteria divide and multiply," he pauses for a second, then laughs.

Then an odd reaction from Sub-Rohza, one of laughter, "Ha! Ha! Ha! Ha! Very funny!" The sound of laughter acts as a tonic, settling tension.

Ansebe's skin lights up a bright-blue hue, his ears twitch as he speaks excitedly. "It cannot be? Surely... it can't be."

"Can't what?" Zara asks.

"It is said that the key to the wisdom of Kyubi-K shall be found within the laughter of a sub-quantum."

"Who's Kyubi-K?" Ansebe does not answer, he turns to Sub-Rohza.

"Quickly, query your index bank, tell me the code which triggered your laughter."

"On it, boss."

"What code, what's going on?" Zara asks, none the wiser.

"It is written that only a pure one may cause a sub-quantum to laugh, to open its logic gates. It is my destiny to find the key."

"The key? The key to what?" A puzzled look from Zara.

"Boss, code is encrypted," Rohza lights up a green-hue, "running de-encryption it may take some time," she turns amber. "Need to leave this place."

"Later then," glyphs glow on Ansebe's wrist, he waves a hand over them. On doing so, the two oblongs begin to transmute, from the front of each oblong grow two feelers, like ski-poles, except with orbs in place of handles.

Then a mask rises out of one of the oblongs, a copy of Zara's face, "What! How?" she asks.

"The oblong has created a mask for you," Ansebe says, "try it on." Gingerly holding the mask against her face, it makes contact, and as if alive, it wraps around her ears. Ansebe steps onto his oblong, "How to drive," he looks at Zara, "step on, hold the poles, pull to accelerate, push to break. Lean sideways to bank, there is a haptic interface working in unison with the controls. We try."

"Okay, let's see," she steps on. "Oh… it's growing around my feet."

"Yes, for safety," Ansebe says, "Rohza, go with Zara."

"Yes, boss." Sub-Rohza lands on her shoulder, "Let's go Zara."

Ansebe looks on, she finds balancing cumbersome at first, "Whoa… how fast do these things go?"

"Watch me!" In the blink of any eye Ansebe accelerates at phenomenal speed.

"We need to go, Zara, I can autopilot if you—"

"No thanks, I'm good," she holds the controls, shifts her weight, the vehicle glides some several yards. "Okeydokey, now let's try this… whoa!" The oblong skims the desert floor at break neck speed, but Zara learns fast and quickly gains control of the makeshift vehicle. As the night air chills, she begins to shiver. "What this?" Zara looks down as the oblong begins to weave a protective cocoon, rising at first over her legs, then covering her entire body. "What's the oblong doing, Rohza?"

"The desert can experience extremely low temperatures when dusk falls. I have instructed the oblong to weave a shell so that you retain your body heat."

"Oh… thanks." They catch up with Ansebe, riding alongside him. Zara looks to her shoulder, a question pops up from earlier, "Rohza, what's a tetraporphyrin?"

"It's a biological interstellar lifeform with hyper-luminal capabilities, they usually have a symbiotic relationship with lifeforms from their birth planet. They're not unlike your marsupials—they have a pouch or chamber in which they create breathable atmospheres and liquid sustenance for lifeforms that may travel in them. They're not unlike a horse or a dolphin, except, of course, they're far more intelligent. And well-known for their inclination to help your kind. It is a privilege to be accepted as 'the one of the fish.'"

"One of the fish?"

"Yes, to be the one of the whale, or one that travels with the whale or big fish. The story of Jonah tells of this, are you familiar with this?"

"The Biblical story of Jonah and the whale?"

71

"Historic interpretations describe a variety of categories, from a big fish or whale of unspecified species to that of a special creation, sent by God."

"The stories of unidentified submerged sea objects seen by mariners, so they're real?"

"They are."

"Wow! I wish I could see one."

"Be careful in what you wish for, you may get your wish sooner than you think."

"How so?"

"We're heading for California, to the Santa Monica Bay, in order to retrieve a tetraporphyrin from the tetraequestrian stables of the House of Pyan."

Chapter Ten
The Legend of Poison Finger Hands

In the meantime, we return to Sergeant Rogers' abode. Fez-Pyan sneaks a look from a window, ponders what is his next course of action. "Spooks!" His eyes narrow, "A test of skill awaits, should I go, or should I stay?" His fingers roll out a beat on the windowsill, "Go looking for the Newara or risk everything on a challenge?" Decided he punches the wall, turns, and creeps downstairs to the kitchen. With a quick glance he evaluates the battle-ground, his mind plays out a multitude of combat scenarios, then with a triumphant smirk he pulls up a chair to the centre of the kitchen and awaits the agents' offensive.

Seconds pass when a dull thud echoes, announcing the entrance of the covert team. Fez lights a Cuban cigar and with a self-assured demeanour, sits on a chair, raising both legs into the full lotus position. He sits both meditating and smoking his cigar, chanting, "Aum…" with the cigar hanging from the corner of his mouth. Smoke fills the air, the white-mist reflects against his metallic face, which turns a gold-plated hue. He shines, so very bright, like a golden statue. The game of stealth is won by the spooks, who silently surround Fez-Pyan.

He opens his eyes, "Bravo!" he says, blowing smoke rings. "An excellent approach, you have me at a disadvantage, am I in someone's bad books?" He looks behind, and at either side at the men flanking him, "Forgive me, Master Fez-Pyan at your service." The stealth team stand awestruck, staring at the faceless metallic curiosity before them. "Do you like it?" Fez strokes his chin, "It's the ultimate in nano-synthetics." His metallic eyes narrow, then open wide, and with that his chromium features morph into a piercing expression, one that strikes fear into his captors. Their leader, a dark, powerful-looking man speaks.

"Well, well. The infamous Fez-Pyan."

"The man in charge, I presume?"

"There's no escape, one move and we'll open fire, live rounds Mr Pyan, live rounds."

"And you are?"

"Agent Orange."

"Well Mr Orange, your rules of engagement prohibit the assassination of us space-invader types, so your only option is to tag and bag Mr Orange, tag and bag. Alas, you'll know from my prior encounters with your sort, you've no chance of taking me in, unless of course, I wish it so. Therefore, you're playing for time Mr Orange, waiting for back-up."

"You forget," he lets out a half-smile, "for you we'll make an exception, and we do have you at a disadvantage, right in between changing faces. Inorganic single crystalline semiconductors? Is that it, Mr Pyan? Is that how it's done?"

"Ooh! Ya, got me!" Fez holds his hands up, "I guess I'd best reveal my evil intentions. So here goes—I can leave whenever I wish. I can disarm you whenever I wish. I can leave you with life-changing injuries if I so wish—in fact, you'll soon be wishing that this is not my wish," he blows smoke from his cigar, "which is why your detail will have instructed you to build a rapport with me."

"You have my respect Mr Pyan, and I'm too long in the tooth not to recognize one shouldn't start a fight they can't win, and I don't think either of us can win this one. You're free to leave whenever you want to."

"Free to leave? Just walk out the door?"

"Without question," he raises a hand to his men, "stand down," and places his piece on the floor, then moving to one side shows the way out, "free to leave, like I said." As Fez goes to leave, he adds, "Listen—I wasn't sent here to capture you, hell no! We want to recruit you. We'd like you to head up your own team, run your own department."

"How intriguing," Fez takes a coin out of his pocket, flicks it, it turns up heads. "Oh!" He gazes at the coin in his hand, shakes his head, "I want to believe. It's a great poster, got a flying saucer on it!" He pauses for thought, placing two fingers to his forehead, "I think I'm going to turn down your offer," his eyes blaze with a maniacal quality, "you see, I'm the one that does the headhunting, not you." Agent Orange steps back, and drawing a second gun, takes aim. "Who the hell do you think you are?"

"I don't know!" As he speaks the strange decorative engravings above his eyes morph into serpentine scales, glimmering like jewels.

"You can't win, you're just a lone wolf, a snake spreading its poison, trying to thwart the rise of a new world order... one which protects us all from your kind!" Fez draws a deep breath through his cigar, "As I inhale these toxic fumes," he coughs, holds the cigar up, "it slowly burns—watching the cigar burn is such an uncivilized process, it's devoid of conscience—as is the rise of your new world order, formed from the burnt ashes of humanity."

"You're wrong," Orange trains his gun at Fez's head, "it's a righteous cause, with honour we serve."

"It's a causal thing, I suppose," Fez says, blowing smoke at Orange, "a righteous indignation, one which requires honour from its minions, but at the top—at the top, honour is non-existent."

"You're crazy, half-cooked!" Orange nods at his men, they ready themselves.

A wry smirk from Fez, he holds the cigar high, "It's rolled in sun-grown wrappers," he sniffs the cigar's skin, "the tobaccos are aged seven years which gives it a strong, distinctive punch. It's an experience. And yet it's already half-smoked and I'm half-done, alas the experience is fleeting, like relationships, at first pleasant, satisfying, but when inhaled too much, too fast, the breath is stolen and escape from one's pains are easily undone."

"Your point is?" Orange replies.

"My point? The globalist elite you serve can't understand the bright light that is consciousness, and that is their undoing. In trying to take away the basic freedoms from people, to adore anything and everything that's good or bad for them, ignites something inside. We call this the glow."

"The glow? There is no glow, it's all fantasy."

"Really? The wood is consumed by fire and yet the fire passes on, and no one knows where it ends, this is the legacy of your new world—it is called the awakening."

"Enough!" Agent Orange's patience runs out. "Time to take you down."

"Wait—this kitchen is a place of no reason." Fez holds his hands up and winces.

"Too late for smart talk, Mr Pyan," he nods to his men, "bag him." The agents grab his arms and restrain him. A smug smile from Orange, "If he so much as moves, unload a clip in his ass."

"No reason…" Fez whispers, his eyes narrow. Without warning, he thrusts his elbows out and up, uprooting two agents throwing them back with such a force that they lose their footing. Then moving with near mystical speed towards his adversary, his arm uncoils like a cobra, five fingers dart outward releasing the legendary frozen heart punch. It hits at first like a gentle prod with the fingers—then the palm finds its mark. There agent Orange stands, in shock, shaking, paralyzed. Fez snatches the gun out of his hand, turns, throwing it like a knife, hitting an agent square between the eyes knocking him out cold. The remaining agents open fire. A bullet hits Fez in his face, but the silver meta-plating absorbs the bullet, sending it on a wild ricochet. As they duck, he attacks like a cobra, and as he does his fingertips transmute to a toughened nano-shell, not unlike hardened steel. A millisecond is all it takes, with the force of a whirlwind, he unleashes hell. A second or two later, all lay unconscious, broken, all except for one. Fez turns to face him, placing a hand on his shoulder.

"Take a deep breath, Mr Orange, breathe, that's it slowly does it."

"What the hell," a look of panic from Orange, "why can't I move?"

"No reason…"

"What?"

"I told you this kitchen is a place of no reason—hell abuses the human capacity to reason," he whispers in Orange's ear, "and I only took you into the dark woods, we didn't get anywhere near the underworld." Fez then rests his would-be-captor on the floor, back against the wall, and sits in front of him, legs crossed.

Orange glances at his downed operatives, "What are you going to do with me?" he asks, fearful for his life.

"I guess I'll have to explain these," he shows his metallic fingertips, "I was going to tell you the story of poison finger hands and then do-the-do. But you wouldn't wait. I usually tell the story and then do the business. Oh well… would you like to hear the story anyway?"

Orange looks on in disbelief and bartering for time, he nods.

"Excellent, we begin. In the Sorus constellation there once was a master of the poison-finger-tips method," Fez imitates a snake with his hand, "named the Bitter Sage, a tall white alien hybrid, to whom a young protégé was assigned.

"His young student had heard the legends about his abilities, and that only the worthy were ever taught the technique. Alas, the technique was not freely given, and only to those who persevered. And so, the student, not the patient type I might add, started spying on his master's secret practice. He spied at every opportunity, night and day, and studied the ancient texts of the art, but to no avail, he just couldn't get the technique. Nevertheless, he concluded the fingers required an external primer to change them," Fez waves a finger, "which was at odds with his master's advice," he tenses his fists, "being that strength was not involved nor needed, but such reasoning was irrational to the student.

"One day the master found his student training in secret the methods he had spied upon, but was not impressed. The master advised his student, 'The poison finger hand is not developed by excessive conditioning, instead one simply places the mind inside the hand.' He then demonstrated to the student, 'Here, feel,' said the master as he prodded the student lightly, but it felt like a missile hitting his chest.

"So, the student studied harder and came to the opinion that he should walk everywhere, do everything with his fingers pointed. In time he made progress, his fingers became living weapons. Hubris led to the student taking on all comers, he took many a challenge and defeated all. Proud of this he returned to his master, seeking his approval and demanding the higher level be unveiled to him. The Bitter Sage asked the student to walk with him, to a large tree. Now this tree was known for producing a hardwood used by the finest woodworkers. The master then asked his student to demonstrate, upon which the student struck with speed and his fingertips imbedded into the tree," Fez shoots his fingers outwards, "but the Bitter Sage just laughed and said, 'The student has seen with his eyes, but only noticed the hand.

Sense what I do—what I show,' and show the master did. He placed his hand against the tree and drilled his fingers into it. The masters entire body appeared to glow as his hand sank into the tree bough! The student was miffed, he grabbed his master's hand to investigate, and said, 'There are no marks on your hand, how can this be?'

"The master then said, 'Hand and mind become one, at this instant there is energy. A oneness includes that which is touched, hand, tree, mind and universe all entwine and at this instant there is only the spin of things, and this spin is subject to the will.'"

Fez gazes at Orange, waiting, "Well?"

"Well, what?" Orange replies.

"Did the student ever master the poison-finger-hands method?"

"Nice story," he laughs nervously. "You're the student, aren't you?"

"Indeed, I am. You've just sparred with the seventy-seventh generation master of the Nine Deadly Venoms and lived." With that said he leaves but on the way out, Fez turns his head and says, "It must be your lucky day."

Chapter Eleven
There Are Dark Depths

The next day, having arrived at their destination, Zara, Ansebe and Sub-Rohza set sail. Zara gazes out at the horizon, standing at the helm of the Alliance II, a skipper she procured from Santa Monica.

"How far out to Sea, Ansebe?"

"The destination is not precise, out of sight out of mind. We try."

"What? Out of sight… talk straight, you're not making any sense."

"We sail out of sight, from observers."

"I see. So, tell me about the tetraequestrian stables of the House of Pyan."

"The House of Pyan was inherited from my father, Kyubi-K. Our house holds the honour of high office within the Eyt Ree-Juhns," he sighs, "I wish he was still alive, he left us all with too many questions."

"I'm sorry. What was he like?"

"He was… extraordinary. A maverick."

"You said he left you with many questions."

"They are of the prophesy he left, it is one of prophetic riddle."

"Omigod—riddles! I'm quite good at them."

"I have been unable to solve the prophesy of Kyubi-K. What chance have you?"

"Tell it to me," she bites her lip, "go on, what's the word?"

A lopsided smirk from Ansebe, he shakes his head. "Rohza, please recite the first riddle."

"I can be found on you and in you,

"Written by design,

"And by design I am written."

Zara raises an eyebrow, "Found on me and in me, by design—how odd," she ponders, "found on me and in me?"

"The riddle it is not easy. We have tried."

"That's it! Easy as pie," she smiles, looks at Ansebe, "it's DNA."

"It cannot be… that simple."

"It's the double helix, our genetic code, what's the matter, cat got your tongue?"

A look of shock from Ansebe, his mouth drops, such a simple solution; why had he not figured it out? "Rohza, please review your logic," his eyes narrow, "I suspect causal factors are at play, perhaps even those of a metaphysical nature."

"On it, boss. Oh my, there's a trace of a code that blocked my processing of the riddle. How peculiar, I was unaware of an answer to the riddle, albeit the answer is now readily available. Affected process located, gateway opened—accessing. Boss, the code was uploaded by Kyubi-K the day before his departure."

"It would appear Kyubi-K is still pulling our strings from the grave," Ansebe closes his eyes, "nevertheless, we have more pressing concerns to attend to."

The Alliance II sails on cutting through the surf, when Ansebe's ears twitch, he sniffs the air, raises his hand, "This is the location—release the anchor!"

"Aye, aye, captain," with a nonchalant salute Zara proceeds to lower the anchor. Ansebe walks to the rear of the skipper. He stands so very still, and closing his eyes he opens his arms wide, his robe and large wrap-around ears flail behind him, meeting the sea breeze head on. He shouts out over the wind:

"The House of Pyan owns claim to the Catalina area of the Pacific Ocean."

"The government might just argue that with you."

"They might. Nonetheless, as litigator for the Eyt Ree-Juhns, I argue ownership."

"So, whose planet is it? Ours or the Eyt's?"

Ansebe faces Zara, his skin turns a lighter shade of sea-green merging with the oceanic view, "The lion is king of the jungle, and yet it remains unaware of the reservation—it is time." The sea turns an eerie calm, Ansebe places a finger to his lips, "Shhh," he whispers, "Rohza, broadcast the harmonics."

Sub-Rohza floats to the front of the boat, fires a beam of light into the ocean, "On it, boss. No reading, you're going to have to make the call."

"The call it is," Ansebe replies, as he sits, and placing the oblong on his lap, waves a hand over it in a circle. As he does it morphs into the shape of a drum. He begins to play with his palms a calypso-style beat. The sound resonates, echoes over the calm waters.

Something in the sea catches Zara's eyes, her mouth drops on seeing waves skimming away from them at breakneck speed, "Wow!" A mysterious glow appears from below, moving to and fro in the dark depths, anxiety leads to fascination. "Ansebe, there's something circling us in the deep…"

"Do not worry, child. Which one is it, Rohza?"

"It's the tetraporphyrin prime boss. It's Por-Pyan!"

Still waters turn to swirling waves, as something from the abyss causes the boat to lean to one side. Ansebe changes the drum roll, and with it the waters calm to reveal a brightness illuminating the sea an emerald green. The water glistens as the marine behemoth soars upwards from fathoms below—its size creating a sudden bulge of water, rolling the boat to one side. With a self-righting movement the Alliance II regains stability, and with that a sound heard from the water, an angelic song which ends with a clicking noise. All goes quiet.

At that moment it begins to emerge, a shimmer of skin breaks the surface—deceptive at first glance—an odd-looking silvery-green, but this is only the head of the beast. Its submerged neck leads to a large emerald shadow. A feeling of excitement fills Zara's lungs as she stares into the blue depths, trying to see what lies beneath the white surf. "Arise!" At the sound of Ansebe's voice, the waters break to reveal its true size. With deft silence the leviathan levitates above the skipper, its large triangular-shaped body dwarfing the boat, its large fins swaying delicately in the wind. Once again, the tetraporphyrin sings in whistles, clicks and hums, and as it does its skin changes colour from green to azure blue. It sways in front of them, from side to side. At first the tetra rotates slightly, then moves forward, tilting its large translucent head down to examine the Alliance II. From inside its bulbous head, two eyes move inside their sockets to get a closer look. They glow bright blue. It turns to gaze at Zara, then with a sideways sway it confronts her head on. Ansebe whispers, "Zara, do not move… allow Por-Pyan to touch his head against yours."

"It's a big ghost-fish with wings! Why would I want to move?" Por-Pyan moves forward to greet her, its huge size at odds with its precision as it inches in to touch. Zara stands still with baited breath, not knowing what to expect. They make contact. A static buzz of energy tingles her forehead, her heart skips a beat as the giant creature triggers a lovable reaction from Zara—one that's impossible to resist—she reaches out to touch the beast. "You're cute as a bug's ear," she says, then instinctively whistles softly. It reacts with a harmonic click, cycling fast at first then slowing to an audible tone. A form of coherent communication.

"Zzz…ar… Zzzarah."

"Yes, my name is Zara, and you are?"

"P…P…Por-Pyan."

"Well Por-Pyan, it's very nice to meet you," she looks to Ansebe, for guidance. The creature's empathic abilities pickup on this, it phases several metres to face him. Zara gives a double-take, having just seen two visions of Por-Pyan. Then one. The first vision now a fading wraithlike outline in the mist.

"No way! No freakin' way! Did it just phase in and out of space?"

"It did. A few metres here or there—a few light years here or there—this is the way of the tetraporphyrin." Ansebe pats the tetra, "It's been too long Por-Pyan, you look well. Is the herd keeping well?" the leviathan nods. "Has anything changed on Gaia recently?" Por-Pyan's entire body gives a shiver, as if disturbed. "What is it? What worries you so?"

The tetra speaks. Its vocalization echoes, sounding an eerie tone. "T…T…Tetragrammaton… doorway."

Ansebe's mouth drops, his lupine ears twitch then slump, "The doorway to that which is above all—where is the doorway?" Por-Pyan moves its head as if gazing northwards, upon which Ansebe draws a shape with his two hands, to represent the pattern of a landmass, a coastline. "Is this the land?" Por-Pyan nods in agreement. Ansebe draws a pyramid, "Above or below ground?" the tetra nods downwards several times. "Underground?" Por-Pyan nods again. "It is decided then. We wait not one second further—we go to Alaska."

Por-Pyan hovers above the Alliance II, descends as close to the rear of the boat as possible. Ansebe walks under the tetra, and taps her belly, upon which a pouch opens and stretches downwards, to the deck. He beckons Zara, who follows with Rohza on her shoulder, "Get on, be careful not to step onto the seam—it is a biological seal and should not be contaminated." Once inside the pouch seals closed, whereupon the leviathan begins to glisten brightly. A sight to behold as it makes a one-hundred-and-eighty-degree turn, glides from side to side, then sinks backward like a sprinter readying to power off the mark. The air seems to tremor, flash lightening lights up the air. Then from the tetraporphyrin rises a high decibel tone, it begins to phase and in the blink of an eye it is gone!

Chapter Twelve
Family

A lone man stands on a deserted beach, viewing on a hand-held device a live feed of overhead images. It is Fez-Pyan, he speaks to himself, "It's them! The concave lens does not lie." He smiles, for the tech has worked, giving him the undetected covert surveillance of the tetraporphyrin and speaking through a comms implant, he calls out. "Gnash-Byte, did you record the calling?" An electronic dog-like gruffle replies, after which a recording of the calypso rhythm plays. "Well done, Gnash! Bring it to me, come to Fez…" He lets out a high-pitched whistle and watches the sky for the return of his techno-morphing pet, a Rai-xylographitet.

Awaiting the return of the hi-tech device, his thoughts wander back to his early years marooned on Earth, Terra. With a shake of his head a facial tic follows, his hands begin to tremble. Such sour memories. He had lived undetected on Terra for some time until one ill-fated mission which went south big time. The day the intelligence services became aware of his presence. The day he came know to the black suits. He had avoided them for over a year, but it took them just one day to find his hideout, but when raided he wasn't there, so they left a calling card—shooting his pet bulldog, leaving it for dead. His only link to reality, sanity. Fez snarls to himself, "They shot my dog… they shot my Gnash-Byte!" A tear wells, running like mercury down his silver face-plate as he recalls the moment he sacrificed his one ticket off Terra. It had taken him months to track down a buried xylographitet in the Antarctic region— advanced technology of the Rai which transcends even that of an oblong. It was his one ticket off Terra, its techno-organic parameters could have been set to morph, to grow into a spacecraft. A ticket he sacrificed in a heartbeat, to save his pet dog as it lay dying, shot in the leg and chest.

He remembers how his fingers trembled so. How he activated the xylographitet's astral interface, instructing the unit to absorb the memory, consciousness and intelligence of his beloved dog. Heartwrenching memories—interrupted by a whistle and gruffling noise from on high. He looks up. "That's my Gnash-Byte, down here boy." He slaps his legs as the arcane technology scampers from on high back to him, crashing down at breakneck speed. Sand sprays high into the air, as the robotic oddity scuttles across the beach, stops and jumps high into the air, only to dive under the sand. A faint whir and a click is heard as nano-carbonite transforms, then like a mole it burrows at incredible speed to its master, jumping out of the sand to land in his arms. Its size that of a bowling ball, with two large electronic eyes, happy to return, it wags its multiple tentacle-like appendages. Strange the thing is, a metallic sea anemone with techno-morphing abilities—its appearance never the same. A sentient lifeform which would have transmuted into a gravity-defying vessel, one able to navigate the stars. Alas, such growth is forever stunted, while it retains the consciousness of his beloved pet. The xylographitet runs a circle, wanting to play.

"Sit—I said sit!" Fez commands. It scampers in a circle, growling, "Grr… grup," until he points a finger—its darkly-bright eyes dart from side to side as it sits still, waiting. "Now, did you find them?" It replies with a growl. "Good, play the calling, play it Gnash." A recording plays, it is a recording of the calypso beat played by Ansebe earlier. Fez talks to himself, "Well brother, it's time to settle our differences. How long I have waited for this day, and yet it does not feel as good as I thought it would. Nevertheless, settled our difference will be. Today shall be mine."

Meanwhile, Por-Pyan has ascended high into the upper atmosphere, piloted by Sub-Rohza. Zara explores their new mode of transport, "How do we know where we're going?" The tetra responds directly, painting a mirror image of the outer surroundings onto her underbelly. Zara looks down mesmerized, "Oh… now that's just wrong," she stands speechless as the view morphs to show the sea, then re-arranges to show a deserted beach.

"That's odd," Ansebe says, "Rohza, an analysis of our trajectory please."

"We have changed direction boss, it appears we are re-tracing our tracks, returning to where we just came from."

"Impossible, only a calling could—" Ansebe kneels, placing his fingers outstretched on the floor, "Por-Pyan, turn back. I said turn back…" The biological vessel vibrates, then nothing, "It's no good, I cannot reign her in!" The tetra continues onwards to an undetermined destination, one that they have no control over. Ansebe stands, and placing a finger to his temple, closes his eyes, "She is reacting to another, one more is calling, we have been compromised."

"Well, that's just zippy," Zara's eyes widen, "you're saying someone else knows how to whisper to your sea horse?"

"It would appear so," Ansebe says softly.

"Sorry, I couldn't hear you?"

"It would appear so! Rohza, how low are your bio-levels?"

"At level thirty boss, should I switch to defensive condition? I may evaporate?"

"Switch to defensive condition. We are in danger."

"Wait, what happens to Rohza if she evaporates?" Zara asks.

"I cease to be, no longer capable of quantum fluctuation."

"You're happy to command this, Ansebe? To risk her life?"

"Enough, far more may be at stake than we have foreseen. We are all dispensable."

"She's a sentient life form," Zara yells, "I get dispensing of the enemy, but there must be some other way? One where we don't have to sacrifice her?"

Ansebe turns away, his eyes glaze over. He clears his throat to speak, "Sub-Rohza is artificial. As a Rai litigator, I have set rules to follow."

"That's a clam-bake call, and you know it is."

Rohza settles the dispute, "Zara, your concern for this model's functions are appreciated, please know my code has agreed to the possible outcome, my will is free, and my logic gates are set. Worry not, this module only needs to retain the lowest percentage of energy to remain. And there are many ways I can replenish my energy."

"Such as?"

"Submerging into an active volcano, absorbing the electrical power of a cumulus cloud or syphoning the kinetic energy of a tornado."

"Sounds dangerous!"

"Not really, this module can access these power sources safely—approaching our destination, detecting two life-forms. How interesting! Readings of elevated techno-intelligence." Seconds pass, more data follows. "Boss, one of the lifeforms appears to be a xylographitet. How odd! Reading multiple fault codes; oh my, its coding is in a sorry state. Further analysis required."

Ansebe's mouth drops, "A xylographitet with multiple fault codes? Impossible!"

"Boss, we're landing on an isolated beach. The two subjects appear to be awaiting our arrival. Ahh, clarity. It appears the xylographitet is playing a recording of the calling."

Ansebe weighs up what to do, "Follow my lead, until we ascertain what forces are at play."

The tetra opens its pouch, allowing the crew to disembark to confront the two life-forms waiting on the beach. As they exit the living vessel, a voice calls out to them: "It appears a melting glacier has unleashed a devastating torrent before you!"

Ansebe's ears twitch, it is his brother's voice. He looks at him, then to the shoreline at the low waves of an ebbing tide retreating from the sand. "The torrent is nothing when it meets the sea," he replies, then turns away, hands clasped behind his back.

Zara mind-links, "< What's going on, guys? Who is this, do you know him? >"

To her astonishment, Fez joins the mind-link, "< Yes woman, he does. Don't you, brother? >"

Ansebe shouts, "Sub-Rohza, pause the mind-link now," and turns to face his brother. There they stand staring at each other.

"What's going on?" Zara whispers.

Rohza levitates to her shoulder, "Its Ansebe's brother, Fez-Pyan. I think he wants a duel, that he may regain high office within the Eyt Ree-Juhns."

"Are you ready, brother?" Fez shouts.

"I am," Ansebe's eyes narrow, "you know the rules, should you be unable to test my mettle I am obliged to take your life, and so, I must refuse your challenge. I relinquish my house to you, brother…"

Fez stamps on the floor, punches his fist to palm, "That is a non-eventuality that I can assure you shall not occur!"

"Oh, how so?" Ansebe tries to reason.

"The human you have with you, if you don't comply, I shall instruct my pet to attack her, to deploy its mecho-maws. How do you like that, brother? Once bitten, twice shy, or so they say— do we have terms?"

Ansebe clenches his hand, a visible shaking occurs. Fez smirks, his metalloid mask shifts in structure and over his eyes red lenses descend like eyelids, leaving a reddish demonic afterglow.

"Do you like the look?" Fez-Pyan raises his hands, "Let the trial begin."

Ansebe responds by standing so very still, one hand held above his head, the other low. He calls out, "Brother, we do not have time for your antics, do you wish to withdraw?"

"I do not. We try!"

A reluctant reply from Ansebe, "We try."

Without warning, Fez springs forward like a cobra, his fingers darting towards his brother's chest, when just prior to meeting Ansebe turns, slapping his brother on the shoulder, sending him off balance. His centre of gravity compromised— a throw setup! A normal fighter would be thrown hard. These are no normal fighters. Fez avoids the throw by swooping down only to explode upwards from a low hurdle posture, striking Ansebe in the ribs with his shoulder. His whole body a battering ram. He shouts, "Hah!" as the technique hits home, but Ansebe yields, absorbing the body blow with a subtle twist.

As he turns he extends out his elbow, which hits Fez's jaw with such a force that a loud crack is heard. Ansebe asks, "How do you like that?"

His brother steps back reeling from the strike, but still manages to let out a maniacal laugh, even though his jaw hangs to one side, dislocated. He leans forward and slaps the back of his neck upon which his jawline snaps back into place. "Been practicing huh?" Fez says, and once more squares up to his brother, ready for another round. This time he clicks his fingers, whereupon a spark of electrical energy exudes from his fingertips. A look of shock from Ansebe.

"The magus ability… but you don't have any bio-augmentation."

"I stole it! I suggest that you use yours."

Ansebe's skin tone changes, matching that of the sand. He touches his wrist, glyphs glow, meeting points along his artificial meridian lines light up. Both brothers up their game. Fez sneers then points to his chin, pulling a face goading his brother, then he attacks kicking a clump of sand into the air, aimed at Ansebe's eyes. A fast break attack follows. Ansebe turns avoiding the sand but falls into a trap. Fez moves like a cheetah after its prey. He stomps the rear of Ansebe's knee, and like a cat climbing a tree, goes in for the kill. Ansebe counters, simultaneously whirling his arm in an upward arc knocking his brother off balance. Seizing the moment, Ansebe turns and grabbing his brother's leg, does a shoulder throw. Fez hits the ground pole-axed. Ansebe quips, "When the eagle spreads its wings, the snake fears its shadow."

His brother slaps the sand, frustrated, and goes to get up but collapses on the floor, writhing in pain, "Aargh, my back!" Ansebe steps forward concerned for his brother, but it is an injury feigned. As he comes within range Fez attacks, back-rolling into a handspring, kicking his brother in the stomach. He hits hard, but Ansebe breathes in with the kick then exhales, pushing his belly out, along with a step forward—a catapult effect unleashed. The recoil is hard. Arms buckle but Fez avoids hitting his head by turning, rolling on his shoulder. He quickly cartwheels onto his feet, brushes the sand away and pulls a wow-face, one of derision. "The fearful snake finds out it has legs…" Fez says, taunting Ansebe with several snap-sidekicks.

Ansebe sighs, realizing his brother won't stop. "This game stops now!" From his belt he draws out his quantum dice, throwing them. They spin, shooting out nano-strands, which bind, trap, and ensnare whatever they touch. But Fez is too quick, he dives out of the way, back-flipping to safety. "Gnash-Byte go crunch, bite-em." The xylographitet obeys its master, shooting across the beach with phenomenal speed it catches the dice in its mecho-maws, snapping the nano-strands. Straining hard, the metalloid marvel glows red as it tries to crunch the dice, but cannot, it tries harder, harder still—a loud cracking noise heard, then it spits out the broken dice to a stunned look from Ansebe.

"Did you see that? Did you see that?" Fez smirks, "Who's the master? Who's the best, who puts the rest to the test?" He performs an odd shuffle, then adds, "Oh! Looks like someone re-coded a xylographitet, whoops."

Ansebe walks up to retrieve his dice, "Your pet has broken that which is unbreakable!" The two brothers erupt into laughter, they lock arms, patting each other on the back.

"It's been too long, brother," Fez says, "your skill is very fine indeed."

"Only very fine?"

"You're not a Nei-Kanga, not yet brother, not yet."

"I am waiting for that rank—the Hall of Heads awaits."

"I have no time for that place, statues built in one's honour—unless one has the chance to decline such an honour. Besides, I've won my honour, disabled the infamous quantum dice."

"It appears you have."

"I know I have!" As if directed by a divine force, Fez looks to Zara, both feel an odd sensation, a strange feeling of déjà vu. "My daemon," Fez says, "now there's a sign if ever there was one; can you feel the magus effect, brother? I suspect freakin' weird science at work." He walks to Zara, kneels on one knee. Zara looks to Ansebe, shrugs her shoulders.

"Fez is rendering courtesy, touch his head—like so."

Ansebe demonstrates, places his thumb to pinkie to form a circle, with the remaining fingers pointing. Likewise, she places her fingers upon Fez's head, but as they touch a discharge of electrical energy runs up her arm. An odd sensation follows, a change, hidden within her, dormant nano-mites unlock a chain-reaction at the cellular level. Fez also feels the change; chemicals unleash within his mind, triggering a strong impulse. He jumps up, an instinctual reaction—as if recalling a past life.

"Brother, get over here," he grabs Zara's arm, "look, watch…"

"What the hell? My arm feels like it's on fire!"

"It cannot be, can it?" Ansebe says.

"What can't be? What's going on?" Zara asks, looking at her arm as it turns a fluorescent shimmer, then from nowhere glyphs form on her wrist, not unlike tattoos—except these are of a different nature.

"I know this work," Ansebe says, "it is designed by Kyubi-K." The glyphs take on a glowing quality, as they transform into symbols. Ansebe reads the symbols aloud as they morph into view.

"I am the primer, and the cypher,

"The one which unites the three."

Ansebe's jaw drops, his mind races to process the information.

"I know that look! What is it?" Fez asks.

Ansebe looks at him, then at Zara, "Sister, we have a sister. She is human," her wrist shows a complex bar-code, "the cypher Kyubi-K… Rohza quick…"

Sub-Rohza scans the code, she lets out a giggle, "We try family. The third one is revealed. Ha! Ha! Ha!" Her logic gates trigger humour, just like before. The metallic laughter lasts for a few seconds, then an odd reaction from Rohza as she freezes, then as if rebooting she reports.

"Unencrypting. Data retrieved, hidden code unlocked."

"What does it say?"

"Oh my! It's another riddle, boss."

"Go on…" Rohza shines bright blue and swaying to and fro, she tells the riddle.

"When the celestial witness rises,

"Use the cypher to unlock code which is hidden within,

"Find the Painted Symbol."

"Interesting," Ansebe raises an eyebrow, "a cypher that tells of another cypher?"

"Boss," Sub-Rohza glows red, "we need to leave; we're being watched."

Chapter Thirteen
Watchers

The sky broods, clouds swirl high above into dark streaks like arteries of flowing energy. All is not as it should be. Ansebe looks to his brother, who looks back at him, for once with a serious face. His uncanny senses respond to invisible changes in the ultraviolet spectrum, causing a fluorescent shimmer to run through his skin, he looks up, detecting an otherworldly presence.

"We are being watched…"

"I can feel them also," Fez places two fingers to his temple, "my higher-self has just spoken to me."

Ansebe shakes his head, he knows his brother has good intentions, but the voices that occupy his head are many. He waves a hand for the others to sit, then says to himself, "The question is which is it that watches, the Ternion or the Elb?"

As they sit, Fez looks to Zara placing a finger to his lips, "Shhhh."

In front of them Ansebe sits in the lotus posture, calming his mind, and as he does his skin tone blends with the sand. Behind, Fez notices his brother's left arm turning a golden gleam of yellow and looks skywards in a leftward direction, catching sight of two golden orbs on the horizon. A deceptive apparition, beautiful at first but then his mouth drops. He nudges Zara, "Frak, the Elb are watching, don't look at 'em… a little bit of celestial voodoo is about to go down," his tone turns solemn, "I don't like the rabbit hole—I don't like it one bit."

Zara averts her gaze, but on seeing Ansebe's right arm turning a moon-glow shade of blue, her heart skips a beat for she also senses something to the right of them. Ansebe able to see what the others cannot, calls out: "We know you are there. We are well-intentioned, your blessing will be a boon to us. Is our fate worthy of your guidance? Humble are we in your shining light. Grant us an audience, oh great Ascended Ones." There is no response. Ansebe continues. "We know you are there—"

Fez interrupts, his madcap reasoning unable to resist, "Hey, show your selves! I said show your selves!"

Ansebe closes his eyes, shaking his head and with a sharp exhale turns to confront his brother, who just shrugs. "What is wrong with you? They are gone, gone I say."

His brother does not reply, instead he leans to one side, looking behind Ansebe. On his chromium face reflects an iridescence of white and blue radiance. Ansebe's eyes widen on seeing his brother's reaction, his ears twitching as he turns around to look. In front of them an interspatial glitch within the very fabric of space-time. The brightness fades to reveal a large bubble upon which reflects rainbow hues of light, it is the unconventional form of a wormhole. From within appears a trail of endless reflections of three silhouetted life-forms, of what is three living creatures, surrounded by a plasma through which pervades an assortment of shades.

"Omigosh…" Zara's mouth drops, "it's like a colour-changing sapphire."

"I knew it, knew they'd show," Fez whispers to himself, "they tried to abduct me once. Sure they did! Nothing at all to do with your visiting that shaman in Peru."

The two brothers gaze on awestruck, then look to each other, aware that the appearance of these beings usually has a sole purpose—that of revelation or divine intervention. The mood becomes solemn. Then from out of nowhere, a sudden rapture of sound explodes everywhere with such a force that the very sand vibrates, then all goes silent. A warning it could be, from the space Gods to one another. The sound of seagulls roused by the uproar fills the air, when from out of the wormhole a tetracube is thrown by a tentacled appendage, landing in front of Ansebe. It clicks and whirrs as the chambers of the cell slowly open. Ansebe raises an eyebrow as his shattered quantum dice begin to tremble, whereupon they shoot into the tetracube. As it closes, the cube glows a neon blue and from it a strange mist exudes as it begins to dissolve before their very eyes, leaving behind in the sand two new quantum dice. Ansebe opens out his hand, upon which the dice bounce onto his palm, he grasps them tight, and in doing so a powerful energy releases—spiralling throughout his entire body. His third eye point glows bright as if being enlightened to a higher level.

"The shamanic mind has been bestowed upon me. The legends… it is real!" Ansebe bows in gratitude, whereupon the wormhole shudders and implodes into nothingness, leaving a short air-burst. "The Ternion have departed," Ansebe closes his eyes, "I sense, no wait… I know! A greater game is being played in this reality. Our fishing expedition has brought the attention of those who watch. A most serious business is at hand—I fear the bringing together of the family Pyan is neither a coincidental act nor that of serendipity."

"You haven't got the shamanic mind," Fez says, "the ability to call on the Akashic records, to instinctively make the right choice. It's a myth."

"I fear it is not," Ansebe's ears twitch, "I can feel it… the Ternion have allowed my mind unfettered access to the higher-awareness. What we sow in consciousness we reap. This is a universal law. Alas, this is no longer applicable to one-that-can-see."

"Then tell me brother, what do you see?"

"Allow me to—by the stars! I don't know how I know this—the Ternion are trying to hide us from the Elb. Or more specifically from one Elb, one that preys, kills. The Malignant Elb."

While Fez rarely stresses, on this one occasion he freaks, "Hell no. I've enjoyed living—the Malignant Elb after us? I heard about a guy crossing the road in Russia—there one second, gone the next, like absorbed gone—it was the Malignant one's doing." Fez paces a circle, while Zara, not realizing the severity of the situation, calls for calm.

"Look, there's a reason we've all been brought together, and the way I see it there's nothing we can do about it. So, let's all tough up and get the job done, come hell or high water!" Zara looks Fez in the eyes, "Agreed?"

He shrugs, "What's with you? I was just jibber-jabbing. Nice pep-talk though, it's all cool. The Ternion can mask us from it, sure they can." Zara glares an unamused look at Fez, who holds both arms open in a what'd-I-do mannerism. "Okay," he says, "we should go."

"He's coming with us?" Zara asks, looking at Ansebe.

"Try keeping me away."

Ansebe places a hand on his brother's shoulder, "Perhaps this may be good for all of us."

They all turn to embark Por-Pyan, only to find the leviathan sitting side by side with Gnash-Byte, looking at the sand in front of them. As they get closer, all stand still in their tracks. "What the frak is this?" Fez exclaims. For burned into the sand are glyphs spelling the names of Zar-Pyan and Fez-Pyan, behind which artefacts, gifts from the Ternion, lay on a pile of pebbles. Beside one name sits an unusual metallic artefact coiled like a sleeping snake on top of a satchel, and by the other name one half of the jaw-bone of an ass, laid on what appears to be part of a ram's fleece. The fleece, finely sewn with golden brocade into a short shoulder cape, sparkles golden against the sunlight.

Fez rushes to the artefacts left in his name, he picks up the donkey's jaw-bone. "Hey, this feels weird, the weight is unbalanced as you move it. What do I want with an old jaw-bone? Useless!" He throws the jaw-bone over his shoulder, but when it lands several feet behind them, the ground shudders and a sudden shockwave surges through the sand, like ripples in water. He turns to see in front of him a round ditch and at the bottom the jaw-bone. With a somersault he jumps into the pit to retrieve the artefact and picks it up, holding it high. "That's handy. I have an ass that bites, I'm gonna to call it my ass-bone!"

Having tucked the bone into his belt, he holds up the fleece, "Now what do we have here? Hey, it's covered in golden dust." He dons the garb, locking the buckles together over his chest, "It just doesn't suit me, it just doesn't." He stands pensive, waiting to see what power the fleece imbues upon him. "Nothing? What's the fleece do? Rohza?"

Ansebe speaks, "Rohza, would you access your archives and let us know what this is?"

"On it, boss... how unusual. It's an artefact of immense power, but this is only a shred of the original. How could it have been torn? It cannot be torn!" Sub-Rohza moves closer to examine the fleece, a beam of light exudes from out of her orb-like form. "In-depth analysis of structure. Interesting."

"What is it?" Ansebe looks to Rohza.

"The Golden Fleece—albeit a small part of it." Zara raises an eyebrow, wondering why they are unaware of the legend. Fez's patience runs out.

"What does it do, Rohza, what? I can't feel it working. It doesn't work!"

"The fleece is home to a microscopic life-form known as the Nan-arcons."

"Great, so I've got a fleece full of little thingies. How do I command them?"

"Not so. My analysis shows that these life-forms can both cure and fix biologicals from all ills but cross them and they can also create destruction. They cannot be commanded, they simply act when they feel the need to."

"Frak dat! I've been given a first-aid kit!"

Zara stands with her hands-on hips, curious, looking down at the other item. "It is left for you," Ansebe says.

"Is that my name in hieroglyphics?"

"Yes, it would appear your name is now an officially recognized one, both by the Eyt and the exalted ones."

"It is? How so?"

"Zara in our dialect is pronounced Zar. Your full name is Zar-Pyan. Pyan meaning pure or good. This is now your universal name throughout the local clusters. As you have been anointed an official title, I suspect the relic bequeathed to you to be most significant."

Ansebe's voice goes in one ear and out the other, for Zara is entranced, mystified at the artefact laying on the beach, she asks, "What on earth is it? Looks like a clock spring."

Ansebe kneels to inspect the item, his eyes widen, "By the stars! It appears you have been gifted with an Urumi or to be more precise the Lost Urumi of the Seventh Star Immortal."

Fez cracks up with a bellyful of laughter, "Hah, the Seventh Star Immortal, can't be. Go on, pick it up, pick it up—see what happens."

Zara kneels to take a closer look at the artefact. It is an exquisite weapon, one of fine art, its alluring white handle inlaid with gems and ornamental carvings of elephants are spellbinding to look at. Further up, attached to the hilt are two flexible sword blades coiled up like a spring, on each blade a myriad of interlaced engravings of eagles, elephants and foliate patterns which when looked at appear to elicit a strange fixation in the observer. Underneath lays the Urumi's satchel interwoven with fine silk brocade embroidery designs of elephants and birds. Ansebe places a hand on her shoulder, "Do not be afraid, it is a gift from beyond. It should be readily accepted." Zara breathes in deep and exhales, taking hold of the Urumi's ivory-white handle. All feels fine at first, but something tugs inside, her pupils dilate wide open. Then it hits. She goes catatonic, feels the odd sensation of falling through her eyes into another place, another time.

Chapter Fourteen
Many Lives

The ancient lands of Bharat, the jungle another time long past. It is a time between the ages. Three elephants ridden by royalty trek through mysterious thick forests and rugged trails, in pursuit of an unruly tiger. Mounted on top of the elephants in full battle armour, seated on glorious saddles laden with gold and silk, sits the warrior princess Rani, accompanied by two princes of a long-lost dynasty. Princess Rani looks resplendent in her royal garb of armour and jewellery. The princes flank Rani at each side, her brothers in arms. Their elephants' sunlit armour entwined with layers of silk brocade shines brightly. On the elephants' heads sit exquisite shaffron-defences, complete with flaps for ears and holes for the eyes; stained in warrior paints of red, yellow and green—giving an inexplicable appearance to the elephants' faces, whereby people would stand transfixed in awe at the sight of their approach.

The taller of the two sits with regal composure on the most stunning of elephants, adorned in silver battle armour. The prince himself appears god-like, with blue coloured skin, over which lays an armour of gold and silver inlaid with jewels, which glisten against the jungle background, giving a rainbow-like vision of splendour. Upon his head sits a silver headdress cast from the most precious of metals. A work of art adorned with six ears majestically engraved with scripture, made from a long-lost art of metal forging. This is Prince Achuta, the Imperishable One.

The other prince does not sit with composure befitting of royalty, in fact he has little self-possession at all, a truly uninhibited being of irrepressible nature. One that suffers from an unruly mix of personalities; rumours throughout the palace say that he has qualities akin to that of the snake and the agility of a monkey. Some say that he was left at the palace gates by the Gods. Such gossip is not helped by the fact that this prince always wears a resplendent silver face plate, although none know why this is so. Alas, whenever Princess Rani asks why he wears the mask, he always gives the same reply, 'So that even Serpents may shine my Princess, and this one shines brightly.' Henceforth, Rani would always affectionately call him 'Serpent That Shines.' He is Prince Fanishwar, King of the Serpents.

Prince Achuta raises his hand, that the elephants all stop on the trail. He dismounts his elephant and thanks it, "Praise be to you Ganesha, your holiness." The elephant Ganesha gives an almost human like nod, then pats the prince on the shoulder with its trunk. Achuta kneels to study the pawprints on the path.

"These tracks are fresh. Tiger is close, be on the lookout."

Princess Rani expresses her wishes, "Remember, we are only wanting to scare the tiger away. Krishna is all things. This we should respect."

"We only scare it away?" Prince Fanishwar says, "I do not like it so! No, I do not like it one bit!"

Princess Rani giggles, "Oh Fanishwar you are awful," she wags a finger. "We are not going to harm the tiger. Not even one bit!"

"This way," says Prince Achuta, upon which Ganesha lowers her huge body to allow him to mount.

On seeing this Princess Rani smiles, "Prince Achuta, Ganesha always shows you such love and loyalty, do tell us the story again of how you both met."

"As you wish Princess, as you wish. We try… the story starts long ago when I was far younger and found much fascination with our empire. One day, the royal procession was travelling north, to pay homage to a religious festival in one of the provinces. The journey was long and arduous, when from the corner of my eye I noticed a weary elephant, its four legs bound in manacles. Something heartwrenching called out to my very soul, thus I commanded my guards to stop. I approached the elephant, for it was in pain! Its legs mutilated by crude manacles, which made my very legs itch so. They were of a cruel nature with spikes and chains to prevent the animal from running amok. Although when love and the right relationship is present, the animal will be at one with its master.

99

"I then summoned the owner and asked how long the elephant had been chained so, to which the owner replied, 'From its earliest years, Prince Achuta.' This grieved me. So, I approached the elephant and gazed into her eyes for some time. I then gently unbound the manacles from her legs and proceeded to clean the inflicted wounds with water and herbs. On doing so, tears, so many tears ran from the elephant's eyes. There we both stood, I caressed the elephant as everyone watched their prince and the animal crying tears. From that day, I named the elephant Ganesha, for her human qualities. She has never left my side since."

Princess Rani clasps her hands with glee, "I love the story, but what punishment befell the owner?"

"None a punishment fitting can Prince Achuta ever dream. So, I left such considerations to Prince Fanishwar."

"Oh my goodness," she gasps, "Fanishwar, what did you do?"

"I did not like it, I did not like it one bit! Nevertheless, I knew the punishment straight away. The royal guard wanted to execute him, and I decreed no! Shan't do that. The royal guard wanted to beat him, and I said no! Shan't do that. The royal guard then wanted to cut his hands off so that he may never lay a hand on an elephant again, and I said no! Shan't do that."

Princess Rani asks, "What did you do so?"

"It was simple. I ordered that he be manacled like the elephant and his bloodline be shackled for four generations, one generation for each leg of Ganesha which had been so crudely bound."

Princess Rani teases, "Oh, Fanishwar, you are terrible so. Such a terrible one, your title and reputation is befitting, Serpent That Shines."

Prince Achuta shakes his head, "I could not allow such a cruel punishment to play on my mind—"

"We all know of your secret royal decree to pardon him after only four seasons brother," Fanishwar smirks, "it is said how he ran for joy when the manacles were removed, only to drop dead from exertion, his heart having gave out. I suggest you use your pardons more sparingly, brother—"

Rani cuts in, trying not to giggle, "I think that would be a good idea." Their sounds of laughter fill the air, but as they stop laughing the jungle falls eerily silent. Achuta raises a hand, for all to be still. Out of the shadows a whistling schhaff is all that is heard. Then an arrow is seen piercing Prince Achuta through his chest as he falls to the ground. Ganesha, his loyal companion, lets out an almost human scream, then stands over her master to protect him, gently touching his face with her trunk.

"Assassins!" Prince Fanishwar shouts, dismounting his elephant to give chase. A hail of arrows flies towards the Prince, quick off the mark he stops in his tracks, evades and turns, catching the arrows out of the air. A near impossible feat. He holds the arrows in his fist, screaming, "With these arrows your hearts shall bleed!" And with that said he charges off into the heart of the darkness. At first all that is heard is the whipping of branches, the clatter of feet, the slicing of weapons, and finally the piercing thud of arrows. Screams echo throughout the jungle as the King of Serpents attacks like a poisonous cobra possessed, striking down one assailant after the other. His true nature unleashed in a blood-curdling outburst.

Princess Rani runs to Prince Achuta, to hold him. Save him. Alas, the loss of blood is too much. The Prince lies dying. She cries, "You cannot die! You are the Imperishable One. I will not let you, I will not!" Rani caresses the prince.

He looks her in the eye, "It is my time Rani, it is so."

Tears run down Rani's face. With innate purity in her heart, she pleads to the Gods, "Krishna, please save my brother."

He squeezes her hand, "Rani, please, do not mourn for me, I am to depart this world with Krishna in mind." Just then Prince Achuta's breathing becomes shallow, he recites scripture, "The soul can never be cut into pieces by any weapon, nor burned by fire, nor moistened by water… nor withered by wind." He breathes out. He is gone.

Princess Rani bursts into tears, unable to catch her breath. As her crying subsides, she hears approaching footsteps. More killers. She stands fast to be confronted by seven in total, she draws a sharp intake of breath. Before her stand the seven fallen Arhats. The deadliest of assassins in all the land. With tear-stained eyes she stands before them, a shiver runs down her spine at the sight of their cold masks of metal—like demons the fallen ones take a ghostly step forward, unsympathetic, blades and axes to hand ready to be off with her head and the head of the fallen

Prince Achuta. But the power of grief releases a divine act of retribution. What occurs next appears incredible, too impossible to the human eye. As the deadly assassins prepare for the kill, Princess Rani unleashes an ancient steel whip from her side-satchel, an Urumi. A deadly weapon made of flexible steel, a rolled up sabre made from the sharpest of metal which when drawn works like a whip. Princess Rani unleashes Shiva's dance of destruction. As the blades uncoil only one figure eight movement is seen by her assailants. The follow-up, a circular whirlwind movement slices through all seven assassins in one cut. Her attackers fall. Hardly no time has passed at all. As they lay defeated, a vengeful Princess Rani cries, "Sabre or axe can only kill one person! Urumi unleashes the will of the Gods!"

Just then, Prince Fanishwar returns running, axes held high, shouting, "I have killed many assassins, shan't, can't ever beat the Serpent That Shines!" He stops silent in his tracks, looks at the carnage, then sees the lifeless body of Prince Achuta. He drops both his axes in shock, falling to his knees. Princess Rani looks at him, shakes her head. Heartbroken, she kowtows to the Gods, praying that they return a life.

THE RETURN. The jungle dissipates to show the sea and sand. The return through time blurs her senses, but as they focus, she begins to regain consciousness. Her pupils un-dilate, the sound of a voice booms in the wind, it is Ansebe. "Zara… she's coming out of the trance." Dazed she looks to the others, then to her hand, throwing down the Urumi, "That weapon… it's death's right hand!" Zara stands unresponsive, still in a trance. Ansebe claps his hands to awaken her fully, at which point she looks at him, "It was so real. It was me in another life, my name was Rani and you… you were Prince Achuta." She turns to Fez, "You're Prince Fanishwar… the Serpent That Shines."

On hearing this a madcap response from Fez, "I've lived so many lives, almost succeeded in some of them. Except for the Elb element. No one can ever plan for that, unless… one has more lifetimes, that's it! But it would take one hundred—no maybe with a thousand lifetimes. Yes, a thousand lifetimes! If we can't get them with a thousand, then we'll never be able to defeat them, they'll be with us forever."

"Are you okay, Fez?"

"I'm sorry—did you think I was talking to you?"

Zara shrugs, looks to Ansebe who circles a finger to the side of his head, pulling a funny face. She lets out a snigger, trying to keep the urge to laugh bottled up, which just leads to a louder snorting giggle—her shoulders shudder as she tries to keep quiet.

"I heard that! What's so funny?" Fez asks. Upon hearing this Zara bursts into uncontrollable laughter. Not to be outdone, Fez joins in the laughter.

"You see the funny side?" Zara asks.

"I just laugh at laughter," Fez replies, laughing, "sometimes I'll let out one little ha-har at the absurdity of it all, and then I find the ha-har funny. One day I spent ages laughing at my own laughter—and then it hit me! Red Wing, Minnesota the World's Largest Boot. Too big for the statue of liberty to wear, now if I could get that into space! Way better than an electric car, don't cha think?"

"Do not even think about it…" Ansebe says, trying not to laugh.

After a brief respite Ansebe holds up a finger, he speaks, "Considering recent events, it would not be wrong to suspect Kyubi-K has left us breadcrumbs. A trail so that we may find that which is hidden, even from the Elb."

"Can't the Elb read minds? Being omnipotent?" Zara asks, curious.

"No," Ansebe's ears twitch as he explains, "while we can achieve telepathy with our mind-link, the tech also provides protection. They can no more read our minds than humans can read the mind of a dog. Nevertheless, they may appear in the heavens to watch us if they so wish. As they did earlier."

"What's our course of action?"

"We continue to investigate the underground pyramid and if necessary shut down its energy core, that we may be able to defer the Elb's interest in the Terrans. On route, Rohza will attempt to retrieve the memories of your past life experience."

"Fine by me, let's do this."

"Fine by me too," says Fez, "but I'm doing the special stuff, leaving a trail of mayhem, explosions. Stuff like that!"

"Then we leave for Alaska. We leave now."

Chapter Fifteen
The Booger Man

Meanwhile an orbiting spy satellite processes data, electronic lenses focus on the ground hundreds of miles below. It detects an anomaly, transmits the data to a secure compartmented information facility (SCIF) located in the Nevada desert. Within the facility alarms sound, grabbing an operative's attention. On one of the large monitors an icon flashes amber, but when it turns red, an operator dives forward from his seat. He validates the data and cross validates, then calls out to an associate, "Bob, I think we have... data indicates an anomaly of the biological kind. Think this one needs a response team." Bob slides his chair over, then jumps up to verify the data, "What the..." his mouth drops. "We definitely need to call this one in."

The operative replies, "Ahh... I believe we can track this object." He uploads various commands to the satellite—multiple images download in the ultra-violet, infra-red, microwave and thermal spectrums. They confirm analysis of the images, and on doing so an urgent message is sent to Project Moon Dust: UFO detainment and retrieval task force.

Within the Offices of Project Moon Dust, a task team reviews the footage, along with images, high-definition pictures of the biological entity. Its exact location pinpointed to within several feet. An operative takes the printouts to the office of Director Bullock and places the photos on his desk, "Sir, we have an anomaly. Satellite images are clear, it's a biological entity, a living space-vehicle."

Bullock looks at the image, after a few seconds of silence he punches the air.

"Yowzah! Well done son, can we track it?"

"Sir, we have more checks to do, to make sure this isn't an anomaly."

"An anomaly? Tell me son, don't you think it's mighty strange the incidents we've had recently. A saucer impounded in Nevada. A retrieval team taken out. Now under quarantine, I might add, and then the very next day a biological entity shows up."

"Sir?"

"It's called interconnectedness son, and it ain't no goddamn coincidence. We need to assemble a team now!"

"Yes, sir."

"Make sure this team has NBC gear on the ready, just in case. Our enemy was prepared last time, used technology that we were unprepared for. This time we'll be ready, understood?"

"Yes sir, NBC suits."

"Well, don't just stand there, get on it. We need that team on the go."

"One thing, sir. With our men in quarantine we just don't have the numbers."

"How long to get more men?"

"It's complicated sir, the problem is the vetting… profiling new recruits, process takes several months."

"Goddammit!"

"We can boost the team sir, by calling in the suits."

Bullock sighs, shakes his head. "Make the call."

The clandestine administrations move fast, within hours Bullock is sitting in a security boardroom, a strategic meeting chaired by the ambitious black-suited Agent Orange. He begins his presentation. "Gentlemen, may I take this opportunity to thank you for calling in our department, following your ill-fated desert incident. We also suffered a less than successful encounter. As you can see…" He clicks a remote control, plays video footage of Fez-Pyan escaping from their arrest, leaving a trail of bodies in his wake. "We are left to wonder. How can we control beings of this calibre? That is the question, and until recently we had no answer… until now." Agent Orange smiles, clasps his hands together, "What if you had an ace-card up your sleeve, but until now you were prevented, circumvented by various departments from ever playing your hand. Well, we have an ace-card that tops all aces, and gentlemen, it is ready for deployment." He passes photographs around the table, showing what appears to be a humanoid figure walking on the Moon.

Bullock and other high-ranking military representatives study the images. Bullock waves a photo in his hand.

"What is this? The booger man? Mr Orange, you have my curiosity, please elucidate."

Agent Orange continues, "Gentlemen, we have an enigma. The following videos are freely available on social media. The think-tank guys felt we should hide this one in plain sight—the game is disinformation—the footage, however, is most definitely real." The presentation begins with mobile phone footage taken from the window, on board an internal USA flight. It goes on to show a giant-sized humanoid entity as it simply walks, levitating amidst the clouds. Its appearance has a spectral quality, almost surreal. Several of the onlookers appear visibly unsettled, but not Bullock.

"Well, bless patsy, this is one of ours… outstanding," he says.

"We've named them periodicals, or elementals for want of a better word. The cloud walker is not one of ours. The next one however most definitely is." He skips to another video, "Moving on, you will see footage from one of our lunar incursions." The clip shows the surface of the moon, nothing to see at first. Then a large charcoal coloured being comes in view, an elemental being filmed by two astronauts.

The onlookers are at a loss for words, one whispers, "What the hell…"

"No gentlemen, your eyes do not deceive you, what you see is real. Our scientists believe that our ally comes from a family of elemental beings. Gentlemen, I introduce to you one of our greatest discoveries, one of the periodicals, code-name Actinide. Or Actinide-15 to be more precise, on account of its atomic properties." The mood becomes solemn as all present witness a slim humanoid figure wandering with the astronauts on the lunar surface. Actinide walks unimpeded, without any life support apparatus. No suit. No oxygen. Nothing. One of the generals quite awestruck, whispers, "The man in the Moon."

A half-smile from Agent Orange on hearing the comment, "Gentlemen, we present body camera footage of our asset in action."

A third video plays, to the sound of Holst's orchestral suite, The Planets. "Mars, the Bringer of War," says Agent Orange. A miffed look from one of the generals at seeing Actinide wearing headphones. Agent Orange gestures to the general, "It's unusual, one has to say. Our asset likes to listen to a wide range of music, an odd quirk but amusing."

The footage shows the elemental being in action. A covert mission on the border of Syria, to rescue a team of special operatives, captured from a botched desert mission. A body camera reveals his capabilities; confronted with a steel door he touches the lock, releasing a bright plasma which cuts through the steel door in seconds. "One of our weapons abilities, as you can see, Actinide-15 can create a thermite reaction at will." Actinide's actions are filmed by the task force's body cameras, recording every detail of his abilities. As the door is opened, the guerrillas release an onslaught of fire power, but Actinide-15 raises his arm to shield his eyes, effortlessly deflecting recurrent rounds of ammo. A brief respite occurs as the enemy fumbles to reload. It's Actinide's turn. He marches forward with relentless tenacity, leaving a trail of destruction in his wake. As the accompanying soldiers drop back, their body-cams record the bloody screams of the enemy, at which point the video transmission ceases.

Orange paces around the table, "Four special services operatives were rescued on this incursion, the enemy—all of them were killed." All present gaze at each other, then look to Orange, who gives a self-satisfied nod. A deluge of dialogue follows as all present discuss how they may best use the new asset. In the melee of cross-talk, Director Bullock shouts out, "Will yawl cease this hugger-mugger, talk is cheap! Now, Agent Orange, just where is this phenomenon of yours?"

"Look behind you gentlemen, if you please." All present slowly turn their gaze to the rear of the conference room, at the silhouetted figure that is Actinide. The being sits silently in the shade, his aura is that of a foreboding presence. Director Bullock stands up, walks to Actinide. Even though the being stays seated, his height at rest beats all those present. Bullock gestures to the behemoth, "Stand to attention, son. Let's get a look at you."

Actinide-15 slowly stands. A dumbfounded expression from Bullock, as he looks up at the being's ominous height. "You must be all of nine foot tall and then some." Bullock goes to pat the giant on the arm, which elicits a confused response from the elemental, who looks to Agent Orange.

Communicating using a form of sign language, they sign to each other. "Don't worry. These are friends, have more games for you to play."

The elemental signs back, touching thumb to chin, then forehead, "Parents, you will help Actinide find them? Find where he is from—if Actinide helps you help Actinide?"

Orange nods, "We help you, but remember the Sun, it must rise and set many, many times… remember patience."

The titanic figure gazes at the floor, his stone-like complexion darkens, its leaden eyes turn jet-black, then without warning he stomps on a nearby chair, which combusts into tiny fragments to gasps from those present.

Agent Orange calms his asset, "In your room, I've got you more music to listen to." Actinide goes to leave, but Orange adds, "No manners? Then no music!" Like a petulant child the elemental walks around the room, shaking hands with the wary officials, then stomps off to his quarters.

"What the hell was all that about?" a high-ranking general asks.

Bullock adds, "Indeed son, do you have control of your asset? Please indulge us?"

"Gentlemen," Orange exhales a sharp breath, "we believe our asset is of… let's say what you'd call a low mental age, but he does follow orders. As far as we understand, the elemental believes it is playing a game."

"What happens when it figures out this is not a game?" an official asks.

Orange replies, "That may be some time, gentlemen. Our team believe it could be years. We just don't know, have no idea so to say as to the exact aging process of the elemental—some of the shrinks believe the being may have a condition, a brain injury of sorts. It won't be figuring out anything smart, anytime soon."

"Okay, so what?" Bullock says. "We can still deploy the asset, we'll cross other eventualities later. What I am interested in, as I am sure yawl are, is this Actinide's capabilities and limitations."

Agent Orange answers, "Director, we believe the abilities of Actinide-15 may be limitless."

A smirk from Bullock, "Well gentlemen, assemble the team. We have a spacecraft of the biological kind to find."

Chapter Sixteen
Deviations from Flight Plans

Night falls as Por-Pyan glides through the sky, towards Alaska; her outer shell glows green and blue. With the plan agreed upon, Sub-Rohza guides the leviathan's navigational senses, so that the tetra avoids the flight paths of civilian air traffic. Within Por-Pyan the team relax and make comfortable for the journey ahead. Inside, the belly of the creature is self-illuminated along with several transparent pores, which act as portholes. As Zara sits a gelatine reaction from Por-Pyan's innards takes place. The gel creeps up, grows around her body, "What… whoa!" she stands startled, upon which the mould releases.

"What's this?"

"Don't be alarmed, please sit," says Rohza, "it is the gel mould. It is protection."

"I guess it makes for a seriously comfortable sofa," Zara says, snuggling into the gel.

"It's a substance that protects the life-forms a tetraporphyrin carries."

"This protects? How? From what?"

"Phasic shift, changes in inertia and the electromagnetic pulse field."

"Electromagnetic pulse?" Zara raises an eyebrow.

"Tetraporphyrin can create a magnetic shield."

"Cool. So what speed are we going? Doesn't feel like we're going that fast."

"Our speed is capped so that we are not easily identified by your government's tracking systems," says Ansebe.

"Why doesn't Por-Pyan simply phase to our destination?" Zara asks.

"Energy signals, child—a small phase is hardly noticeable; however, longer phase shifts can be tracked, beckoning those who wish us harm."

"Oh, I see—"

"Never mind that!" Fez says. "We need to talk about your regression, are you linking with Rohza now?"

Ansebe's ears twitch, he raises a hand, "Brother, be patient. Rohza needs to assist with navigation, so that we travel on the safest path."

Fez shakes his head, "We can't afford to fail, we're at the last-chance saloon." On seeing his mood, Gnash-Byte jumps up, slobbering its techno-antennae all over his master. "You know what it's all about don't cha, Gnash." The family Pyan relax. For the first time they enjoy some peace, the peace you get after relaxing on a long flight, having realized it is one of the safest forms of travel.

What could go wrong…?

Slowly at first then like a tidal wave out of nowhere, a freak weather system blows in from the east. The type of weather that's so rare, it's experienced only once or twice in a pilot's lifetime. An American Airlines Boeing is caught in the maelstrom. Its pilots are in state of dismay, as the perfect storm causes errors in navigation, resulting in a severe deviation from their flight plan. Excesses in turbulence are the least of the pilots' concerns. They are lost. Battling the winds, they fight to gain control of the aircraft. A helpless fight. All on board prepare to meet their makers. The passengers, long past their initial fright, are praying, preparing for the worst outcome—total destruction, when suddenly the storm dissipates, full visibility returns, and navigation systems restore. The pilots breathe a sigh of relief.

"That was a close one, buddy."

"You're not wrong captain, not wrong at all."

The captain squints his eyes, out there in the distance a small bright dot of blue light, getting bigger, brighter. He shouts. "We have a UFO… move to the right, move to the right!"

At the same time, on board Por-Pyan…

"Boss, we have incoming. Por-Pyan initiate pulse-field— move to the right!" The combined velocity of Por-Pyan and the Boeing meet head on. The pulse-field pushes them apart, but results in the shoulder of the leviathan colliding with the nose of the airliner. A loud crack heard as a skimming recoil shakes everyone. Inside the tetra, the gel combined with the pulse-field creates a protective cocoon. All are unharmed. The Boeing is less fortunate, the jet's nose having suffered a large dent, resulting in extensive damage. It is the pulse-field that has caused a critical system loss, as one after another the airliner's electronics go down. The airliner begins to drop out of the sky, then starts to nose-dive and as it does the passengers scream in darkness.

"What the hell was that?" Zara yells.

Rohza answers, "We've suffered a mid-air collision, unfortunately our accident has taken out the airliner's electronics. This unit suggests that I am phased into the jet, that I should be able to take control and land the aircraft safely."

A fast decision made, Ansebe instructs.

"Rohza, I will guide Por-Pyan to the aircraft, get you near as possible. On my command we will phase intangible. You will have seconds to board the aircraft." He places two fingers to his temple and a hand on Por-Pyan. "We are used to traversing the stars. I fear getting next to the airliner may be somewhat trickier." Two become one as Ansebe merges with Por-Pyan's senses. The tetra dives at incredible speed, and within seconds it soars over the aircraft, for Por-Pyan to open her pouch. Sub-Rohza waits at the opening, she beams a searchlight, illuminating the precise whereabouts of the Boeing. The sound of the wind buffers away any chance of being heard. Ansebe mind-links.

"< Rohza, get ready, on my say… keep it steady—starburst! >"

Sub-Rohza exits from the leviathan and vanishes above the hull of the Boeing, only to rematerialize inside the cabin, travel class section. Some passengers gasp, believing they've seen an angel. One passenger sits frozen. His hands dig into his seat, then on seeing the glowing ball of plasma, his mouth drops. "Holy mother of Mary!" he says, rubbing his eyes. "What is going on?" Rohza continues at a fast pace, her last seconds of intangibility used to shift into the cockpit. Inside, the pilots gaze on in disbelief. They look to each other for verification and concur a silent yes. The ball of plasma inches in front of them. It is real.

Sub-Rohza speaks, "Your airliner has suffered a direct EMP. This unit will now branch off into quantum fractals, hack your controls and land your aircraft for you. Please do not interfere."

One pilot panics, moves from his seat. Sub-Rohza warns him, "If your actions are not good for everybody on board, then they are good for nobody. Stay still! If you wish to live." The pilot leans back into his seat. She begins. Her form expands to a large orb of light surrounding the entire cockpit, then collapses to a small pinpoint of light. Then from that point a light bursts, discharging never-ending fractals of plasma; filaments of pure light reach into every corner of the airliner as she merges with the Boeing. A strange harmonic resonance hums in the air, then a miracle. The airliner reboots. As it does it levels out, and the lighting returns to a loud cheer from all the passengers. Sub-Rohza begins a controlled descent, searching for the nearest runway. As they descend, astonished passengers peer out of their windows, their mouths open on seeing the tetra flanking the right-side wing of the jet.

A teenager looks out to the wing at the luminous object. He can see figures inside and quickly holds his phone to the window to record what he sees.

A short while later a small-town airport is approached. Sub-Rohza brings the Boeing down for a text-book landing, the plane brakes coming to a standstill on the runway, upon which the evacuation slides inflate. The crew assist the passengers to disembark swiftly, while within the cockpit Rohza's filaments diminish as she transforms back to normal. When done, once again she floats as a ball of plasma inches within reach of the pilots, her static field disturbing their hairstyles. She moves in for a closer look; stupefied the pilots gawp back, oblivious of their hair standing on ends. On seeing their hair in such a state, she sways to one side then to the other, her algorithms triggering such odd sensations. "Well gentlemen, I am sorry you have had a bad hair day! Ha! Ha! Ha! Oh… humour, it is new to me. Oh, I see—you see with your eyes but still doubt. This unit advises that your senses are correct. Yes, there are entities of an interplanetary nature, be happy in this knowledge." With that said Sub-Rohza departs the cabin, smashing through the cockpit window with the power of a canon-ball shooting high above. She stops abruptly, levitating; when from out of nowhere Por-Pyan appears, swooping down to pick her up.

From all the people below, only one person notices the unidentified object high above, it is the teenager filming from the window earlier. Awestruck, he holds his phone up to video the action. He is not left disappointed. At that very moment, Por-Pyan shifts into a phase, an acceleration mode which leaves a trail of silhouetted movements in its wake. Smartphone in hand, luck favours the prepared teen as he catches a few seconds of footage. He plays the video, an energy signature trailing off into the horizon. "Wow! This is going on line, for real."

Por-Pyan skims the sky, on route to Alaska. The family Pyan discuss the Boeing incident. Zara's face lights up with a smile as she voices her excitement.

"That was shit-hot! Some freakin' weird science stuff going on there, Rohza."

Rohza gives a modest reply, "Oh, it was nothing dear, it really wasn't."

"Really? You just saved all those people. You're amazing." Zara nudges Ansebe, prompting him to give some praise. He catches on.

"Yes… excellent, Rohza. Well done!" Rohza burns brightly on hearing Ansebe's praise.

Just then, Fez yells, "What's up with Gnash?" gaining everyone's attention.

They all turn to see the xylographitet skittering around the floor in a most unusual manner, having found something inside the underbelly of Por-Pyan. Gnash-Byte's techno tentacles wag vigorously, then it stops and sits looking to the others, gruffling, yipping and grunting. "Whirr… grrr… yip-guhok!"

"What is it Gnash?" Fez asks, "What is it? You found something…" From the belly of Por-Pyan a glow illuminates something moving, several feet in length and width. Ansebe looks on shocked, "Oh no… not now." While Fez with a devil-may-care attitude simply laughs aloud, placing a hand on Zara's shoulder, "Wait for it—the song, any second now." As if right on cue Por-Pyan emits a resonant frequency which echoes like a symphony. A beautiful sound, heavenly. Zara looks to Fez, then to Ansebe.

"What's up guys, what's going on?"

"Por-Pyan is going to give birth to a new one," answers Ansebe.

"Por-Pyan's in labour, going to give birth?"

"Yes... this is most inconvenient," he replies shaking his head.

Zara kneels to take a closer look, placing her hand to floor. "I can feel the calf moving." Then something odd felt. All is not right. "I've sensed this feeling before... she's not straining. Rohza, can baby tetra become breeched?"

"Yes, they can, but it is highly improbable." The quantum wonder investigates further, she shines a ray of light, scanning Por-Pyan's underbelly. "Oh! My oh my this isn't right. It appears the new one is breeched. Its rear fins are tucked under its belly. They should be pointing down the birth-canal. How could you have known this, Zara?"

"I spent my gap-year on a farm in New Zealand, helping with the lambing process. For some reason, I don't know why, I could always sense when there was going to be a breeched birth."

"Then it should be you who delivers the calf. We need to realign the tetra's fins, unfold them. Here, let me show you the problem and how to correct it." Sub-Rohza projects some holograms, a visual step-by-step process. Zara leans forward, nods at the instructions.

"Okay, looks straightforward enough."

"It is. Please, see on top of the oblong, grown are surgical gloves for you."

"Let's do this," she dons the gloves, takes a deep breath. "I'm ready." She begins, pressing an arm into the birth-canal. "Can't feel the fins. Ah hah, here we are... got to pull." Zara strains, huffs, a tense time felt by all as she struggles to deliver the birth.

Outside the interstellar leviathan looks up at the seven stars of the big dipper. A shooting star scatters a trail of white dust— a beautiful sight.

Its eyes glisten with light, close as it ever will get to cry.

A mother worries for a newborn yet to see the universe, glistening green and purple against silvery shades of moonlight.

Then, inside the tetra, "Got them aligned, it's coming, I can feel... here we are." The newborn baby tetra glistens and as it is pulled it into the light it cries. Zara holds it snugly in her arms and all is quiet. A warm smile beams from her face, her brothers gaze over her shoulders with intent curiosity.

"We have a new one," Ansebe says.

"I think we'll call you New... New-Pyan," Zara says, holding the newborn in her arms.

"No, we really do have a new one!" Ansebe adds, shocked, "I think we may have the resurgence of a very old family of tetra. Unless I am mistaken, we have a newborn superpositioning tetra. The rarest of the male of the species. Rohza, can you confirm?"

"On it, checking records. Features, resonance, harmonics— data match. You're correct, boss."

Ansebe gesticulates to Zara, a frenzied rush with his hands.

"Quick! You are the first contact, you must bond with the newborn, place a hand on its forehead." Zara lays a hand on the tetra and as if in acknowledgement New-Pyan's golf ball-sized eyes come from inside its head to the forefront, sparkling like sunlit eyes. A magical bond occurs. One that will last a lifetime, never to be severed. A surge of bio-electrical toxins imprint onto Zara's skin, creating purple blotches all over, which dissipate as New-Pyan processes their complex chemical bond. Ansebe smiles, congratulates Zara.

"Well done, it is so, we have a new family member. One that will serve you for a lifetime. As soon as we can we should tie its superpositioning abilities to Terra, to the present time. It is a relatively simple surgery—"

"Don't even think about it," Zara says, glancing with a furrowed look in his direction.

Fez smiles at the newborn held in her arms, "My, what big eyes you've got!"

To everyone's delight New-Pyan laughs in tetra on seeing Fez, a bubbly cackling tone fills the air. Zara's face beams with delight, as she rocks the newborn in her arms. Just then, something in the air changes, a feeling all is not right. High strangeness follows. New-Pyan glows transparent and discharges a surge of bio-electrical life-force, taking the wind out of Zara. The jolt of energy forces her back, letting go of the newborn she winces, but the baby tetra levitates. All appears fine for a few seconds, but New-Pyan turns a ghostly shade, barely visible. Then a dark whirling occurs in his innards and from nowhere six particles of plasma come into view. Sub-Rohza reacts, raising an array of holographic shields, she commands, "Elb, we have an Elb infiltration. Everyone behind me now!" They all scramble, dash to get behind her, where they stand wary, mystified. Next, New-Pyan's strange chemistry is manipulated. His shell transforms for the briefest of seconds, to turn intangible, and at that very moment all six Elb particles burst free, enlarging in size. A millisecond later they triangulate to specific orbits, circling the baby tetra, weaving holograms which behave like living organisms, mapping space-time—a superposition in time selected. Rohza booms loudly, "Starburst? They're going to starburst. Oh no! Not a starburst. It's a time-jump!"

Again, a dark void appears inside New-Pyan and in the blink of an eye all six Elb return into the tetra, reducing in mass as they descend into the void, into a singularity. At the very same instance New-Pyan collapses into himself, through the void and into nothingness. Leaving nothing except for a fine waft of purple mist. A few seconds of silence end with a cry from Por-Pyan, a long wailing tone of despair. A tear rolls down Zara's face, her bond with the tetra severed. It is a severance that tugs on her heartstrings as the break in the chemical bond feels like a broken heart. Fez paces forward, unhinged he punches hand to palm, "Whoa! I did not see that coming. Man… frak dat!"

Ansebe sighs, takes command of the situation, "Rohza, take us to Alaska, to a hard-to-find place—we need time to recover, to plan our next move."

Chapter Seventeen
Alaska

Meanwhile, operating from a mobile SCIF, Project Moon Dust UFO detainment and retrieval track Por-Pyan with an array of advanced technologies at their disposal. Director Bullock and Agent Orange work together as team-partners for the mission, but it is Bullock who barks orders, clapping his hands loudly.

"Gentlemen, fast track the data—give me a status report." An operative, one of two drone operators, responds, "Director Bullock, on screen data indicates a successful shadowing of the biological entity. Aurora stealth mode appears to be imperceptible, we are ghosts so long as we maintain a safe distance." A video wall shows camera angles from the triangular drones, when the second vehicle comes into shot as it flies past the first. At first nothing is seen, then thermal processing technology combines with software to reveal the drone's three-cornered corona emissions via on screen graphics. Bullock speaks.

"Son, are you sure our visitors can't see our drones?"

"So long as we maintain critical distance, sir. Our visitors haven't given us the slip yet, this is the closest we've got to monitoring a biological."

"Keep on their tail, son. Listen up team, I do not, I repeat I do not, want us to lose track of the biological. I want this entity bagged and tagged, this could be the biggest find since Roswell. Let's make history, people." Something alerts one of the drone operators, he calls out.

"Whoa! Sir, the bio has landed, several occupants have disembarked."

Director Bullock squints at the screen, "What're they doing?"

"Sir, I do believe they are making camp."

"How so?"

"A fire sir, they just lit a camp fire."

"They're in Alaska, son. What d'you think they're going to do?"

"Director," Agent Orange cuts in, "we need to deploy now, give me free reign of my asset!" Bullock looks to the floor, assessing his next move.

"Okay Agent Orange, but I'm coming with yawl."

"If you can keep up, sir."

"Son, you're speaking to former Green Beret. You'll be the one who needs to do the keep-upping."

In the meanwhile, in a remote wooded area in Alaska, the family Pyan have made camp in a clearing. Zara has just made a camp fire, she breaks the silence.

"That should keep us going for a while, how come you're not using your quantum dice for a fire Ansebe... Ansebe?" As if distracted, he does not answer straight away.

"Sorry, I have a strange feeling that we have been followed. I don't know how I know this. I just do."

"Is that going to be a problem?"

"I suspect so, which is why I wanted a real fire burning that we may draw our pursuers out from the shadows. Force them to reveal their hand."

"Not good," Zara shakes her head, disagreeing with such tactics.

"Yes, not good as you say. Alas, we must try. We try."

"Not good? Like getting stung by a moofy-bushwa?" Fez says, playfully shaking his hands. Ansebe walks to his brother and places a hand on his shoulder.

"Which is why I must ask of your service, brother. I ask of you to make a solemn vow. To do something which may be very dangerous."

"How dangerous?"

"A life-threatening danger, one that you may not return from."

"You mean I could die?"

"Yes brother... you could die."

A look of realization dawns on Fez, he protests, "No, shan't do it, can't do it, won't do it, I won't do it—what is it you want me to do?"

119

"Brother, you are far more adept than me at the fighting arts, a true battle-hardened adversary." Fez jumps up, punching a fist in the air, as if winning a game.

"At last, you admit it. Who's the best—say it!"

"You are, brother."

"I can't hear you," he cups a hand to his ear.

"You are."

"Yes! I knew I was, I just knew it. I am the law of one in its true essence." He jumps into a martial art routine. "I…" he spins, into the poison finger style salutation, "am…" a flurry of fast kicks low and high, "the greatest!" With a handspring he launches into a high backflip, over a large rock, as he lands he drops down and with an axe-like motion of his hand splits the rock in two. He looks proudly at the broken rock, then to his brother, and back to the rock.

"With hands hard as diamond, how can I know defeat? What is it you want me to do?"

"When we are attacked, I need you to hold our aggressors at bay. In order that the rest of us may escape, that we may break into the underground pyramid."

"We can do that, can't we Gnash," he kneels to pat his pet.

"You have taught the xylographitet warfare?" Ansebe asks.

"Gnash can use his mecho-maws to bite, crush and shear but there are a few more tricks I have taught him. Plus, I have this artefact, this ass-bone which should prove handy," he waves the jaw-bone in the air.

"I have faith that you can do this, brother."

Just then Ansebe turns his gaze to the mountains and placing a finger to his temple he closes his eyes and becomes one with the shamanic mind. On opening them he raises an eyebrow.

"Rohza I suspect there may be an alternative route. I need you to find us entry to the underground site."

"The pyramid is based at the foot of yonder mountain range, deep underground. I can carry out a reconnaissance of the area, to uncover a route of entry. I shall need to create several dark drones to assist me."

"So be it. Use an oblong to do so. Do it now."

Sub-Rohza goes inside Por-Pyan, to one of the oblongs and projects a laser onto it, branding a glyph onto its surface. A code that only the oblong understands. The matt-black surface turns gloss, then matt again. Then from the oblong eight miniature orbs float out from its dark dimensions; dusky-red and inky at first, but then quickly solidify, emitting a short-lived shard of light as they boot into action. Without a second wasted, all eight dark drones trail behind Rohza as she skyrockets away in search of the underground base.

Ansebe watches them disappear into the horizon when his brother speaks, "I'm off to sit with Gnash. To meditate, that we may both draw energy from Gaia for the forthcoming battle." Ansebe nods to his brother, then looks to Zara, sensing her emotions.

"Come Zara, let us talk, I sense you have something on your mind." She sits with him, and with a heavenwards glance begins.

"You're right, time to deal with it. Ansebe, I need, no… I want answers!"

"To what?"

"My life! I feel like I've always been waiting on answers, to questions I didn't know—but now I know, and I'm sure… I know that you're keeping something from me. I'm your sister. If I truly am the third one revealed, there are big questions gnawing away at me."

"Which are?"

"My mother passed giving birth to me. So where does that leave us? None of this makes any sense, that's question number-one."

"The future or the past cloud our judgement, you need to stay in the present."

"Hell no! No philosophy—just answer, goddammit!"

Ansebe mind-links with Rohza, but speaks aloud, "Rohza, please keep an eye on Zara's temperament. We may need to sedate her."

"What the hell?"

"It is for the good of the mission, until you get a hold of your new-found abilities."

"What are my new abilities? That's question number two."

"If you do not heed my advice, you may never know."

"Well, perhaps knowing might help? So tell me!" He looks away, so Zara yells, "TELL ME!" Ansebe's ears wince, he snaps,

"You want to know this, want to know that. Just like your mother."

121

An empty silence from Zara, her lip shakes, she places her hand over it. Ansebe, with all his intellect and patience, has said that which cannot be unsaid.

"You… you knew my mother?" she asks, as her eyes begin to well up.

"It is complex, the answers are not allowed to be given."

Tears roll down Zara's face, "Ansebe please… please, I need to know." He leans forward and with the tip of his finger gently lifts her chin, so that their eyes meet.

"Dry your eyes, child. I shall tell you the story of your mother and how you came to be."

Zara bites her lip and lets out a smile as Ansebe holds her hands.

"When you cried, I knew you had to be told, and on this you give a pretty smile—keep smiling child. Your story shall be told, I only hope you are ready.",

"I'm ready," Zara says, scrunching up her shoulders.

"We begin. Your mother and her mother, and many before, are but an extensive line of lineage holders of the Gaia sect of the family Pyan. You wonder how myself and Fez were born of the same mother? Well, we are all borne from your mother's egg, this is true, but at separate times. I knew your mother—our mother, because I worked with her on many missions on behalf of the Eyt—"

"What was she like, my mother?"

"Zaidee was a thing of beauty, very funny and wise, but also one of the most formidable of the Gaia Juhj-iz. At first, she was just like you Zara, not so different."

"She was like me? In what way?"

"In looks she resembled you, but in character she was very much the same."

"How did my mother really pass?"

"You mother passed giving birth to you. This is true. Alas, she was the victim of an assassination, by who we do not know. All that is known is that Kyubi-K phased into the hospital and desperately tried to save her; alas, he could only save you Zara. He kept your mother alive long enough to see you, hold you… and then she passed."

"Did she die in pain?"

"She did not, Kyubi-K removed her pain. Zaidee died happy, holding you in her arms."

"If you knew all of this, why have you acted so indifferently?"

"I have not, child—my memories were blocked for this mission. It was not until the gift of the shamanic mind was given to me by the Ternion that my memories returned."

"What else do you know?"

"We were all created with advanced genetics from the Eyt Ree-Juhns, to serve Terra as Juhj-iz in times of need. Think of us more like the heroes from your classical mythology. We help your planet, help humanity in times of need. The head of the family is known as the litigator—I am the current litigator."

"What's the shamanic mind?"

"It is a glimpse at the nature of omniscience."

"Are you able to tell how this mission ends for us?"

"It is only a glimpse. A mere particle of the all-knowing, although I am of the thought it may be as much a curse as a gift."

"How so?"

"I now know things—instinctively. For instance, just now it came to me that the Elb are but a small part in a large jigsaw, and the shard of the Golden Fleece that my brother wears is an important piece to the puzzle."

"So, what are my new abilities?"

"Every daughter inherits the mother's psychic skills, abilities and training, including those of every mother's ancestor, the ability to jump into past lives—to regress. The Urumi triggers this ability, but you must hold it, meld with it and control your fear."

"Wait a minute, are you saying I can regress into my mother's life?"

"Yes, but you should not go there. Not yet… not yet."

"If I can do this now, why not? Why advise against it?"

"I advise against it. Your mind experiences time in one direction like a flowing river, the watercourses one way. When we crosswire our senses we become aware that there are whirlpools, and other ways to reverse a little, or all the way back to the source. For instance, on a hot humid summer day the water of the river evaporates, forming clouds, which travel high in the atmosphere, in higher dimensions you might say. Then, on arriving at the source, forces of nature come together and at that moment the sky issues forth rain. The water arrives back at the source, back in time so to say." Zara waves a hand over her head.

"Whoa, you lost me."

Ansebe smiles, he poses a question. "What do you see?"

Zara raises one eyebrow.

"You… I see you." At that moment Ansebe uses his chameleon abilities, his skin melds with the background. His nanofiber uniform mirrors his skin. He turns invisible.

"What do you see now?"

"Nothing, but I know you are there. Your genetics and advanced technology allow you to do this."

"Wrong, you do not see nothing. Your mind has painted the scene that you now see. It is a created thing." Ansebe returns to visibility.

"Your point is?"

"Time, it is a created thing."

"'Man fears time, but time fears the pyramids.' Old Arab proverb," Zara says. "I've always thought it to be about time fearing the Gods. In the back of my mind, buried in my subconscious it feels as if I've always foreseen this mission—seen through time itself."

"Our thoughts can affect future and past time. Our subconscious is our lineage and ours are the stories of legend. The original ancestors of the family Pyan were from ancient Bharat, which is why the Urumi took you there. It regressed you into the mind and memories of the first and one of the most famous of the Juhj-iz, the Princess Rani. She is now a part of you, which you can call upon at any time; for instance, you have already inherited her martial prowess."

"I have?"

"You need only to draw the Urumi. And although you do not realize it, you can wield it with deadly accuracy." Zara smirks, and with a look of mischief places a hand on the Urumi, stands and draws the weapon, her pupils dilate—she moves as if possessed. Overcome with a flurry of uncanny skills, she unleashes the ancient martial way—she spins, twists, jumps and spirals as the deadly two-pronged flexible blades whip, whir and crackle. Overwhelmed, Zara turns to Ansebe,

"That… that was awesome, I feel like a ton-a-dynamite."

Ansebe claps.

"Bravo, a splendid demonstration. Tell me, do you feel the memories, emotions, and life of Princess Rani?"

"I do, it's overpowering. Wait… too many memories, need to sit down, take it all in." Ansebe places a hand on Zara's shoulder.

"Now you understand! You cannot regress into your mother's memories, your mind is only capable of experiencing past lives one at a time, in accord with the flow of time. Our mother was the last of the Gaia sect of Juhj-iz before you, you must unravel these lives in the correct order. Rani's first, and then the others."

"I understand."

"Let there be no doubts—your brother Fez tried to absorb all the lifetimes of his predecessors in one go, and it almost destroyed his sanity."

"Whoa… all of us have this ability?"

"Yes child, we do."

"You're chewing my kookie-dough."

"I am not chewing on anything."

"It's a saying."

"Ahh, I see. Now that I have chewed your dough, are you ready?"

"Yes, I believe I am," says Zara smiling, having found answers about her mother.

"Then we have progressed. We try."

"We try? No, Ansebe. We will."

Chapter Eighteen
The Quantum Wonder

In the intervening time, Sub-Rohza leads the dark drones to approach the mountain from high up so as to remain out of sight. Her arcane-tech surveys the ground below, spying the industrial complex housing the entrance to the subterranean mystery. Of the eight drones Rohza performs complex programming, she uploads personalities, consciousness and a general sense of survival into the fabric of their being. Once done their nano-bacterials make changes, they morph into interesting little-thingamajigs, each one with its own individual shell and oddball charm. They cajole, sput and clatter in their own language of bauds, bits and chirps. A whacky sight to behold, as the drones float, hobble and boat around the sky.

"Oh dear, this simply won't do. Some fine-tuning is needed, of course, that's it! The Fy gamer laws!" Rohza exclaims to herself, accessing complex algorithms, tuning the drones with distinct traits and behaviours. Once done, she names each one.

"Now, we can't have you all as nameless drones, that simply won't do. You are sentient little things, so naming you would be a fitting act.

"You my little blue one, the Sky-Fy you shall be.

"The next one to be named is you. How bright white you glow. Sun-Fy it is.

"And you, a reflection, like the reflection of a lake. You shall be known as Water-Fy.

"This one stays very still, like a rock. Mountain-Fy. That's you.

"And what of you? How vibrant and powerful your program design is—of course, a tweak of your algorithms. The Leader-Fy it is.

"This one is feisty. Running a tad hot, I see. Fire-Fy you shall be.

"And last, but not least is this one. My oh my, your program is neither here nor there. How odd. The Mid-Spring-Fy you are christened. Now reboot and be born anew."

The Fy spin around in a circle, and one by one speak in their own unique language that only a Sub-Rohza may understand. Then Rohza tattoos a unique glyph onto their shells and once done she instructs, "Now, I need to gain some height, for I need to be in two places at the same time. Listen carefully, I have activated the spectre protocol. You my little ones, are to anchor me to Earth's resonance. Oh, I do hope this works." Rohza ascends high into the atmosphere, to attempt the spectre protocol, a theoretical course of action, dangerous, but required nonetheless. She rewires her quantum state on this plane of existence, a combination decided, her systems start to disturb the surrounding physical space.

At first, she oscillates intensely, running both hot and cold, forcing the effect of entanglement to occur. Spinning into a wraithlike state, part of her skips off the line in space-time, transmuting into a quantum impression—two presences of divergent frequencies—and with that she drops abruptly with incredulous speed, leaving a shard of light in the sky. All the Fy descend with her, entrained to her form with spectacular precision, until near the ground seconds from impact, Rohza stops dead, upon which the Fy shoot off in separate directions pulling at holographic strings, affecting her elastic suspension in space-time. At that very instance, from the underbelly of her corporeal form, an intangible presence separates and disappears deep into the ground.

Several minutes pass when, without warning, from out of the ground an eruption, a displacement of the strings that bind, glue and mesh with what is real. Sub-Rohza's intangible presence slingshots high into the sky, her supernatural aura looking to merge with its natural presence. Quantum particles align, and in that moment the positive and negative reunite, she is one again. A moment later, "My oh my, that was intense." The Fy approach her, from eight directions, to give a stabilising effect to her resonance. They hum a reverberation in tune with Gaia's electromagnetic frequency, and in no time at all Rohza recovers, making her way back to camp.

Ansebe's ears twitch, sensing Rohza's return he looks skyward, likewise Zara looks up. "Rohza! You're back, what did you find?"

"The base is deep underground, Zara. It is a labyrinth not of humanity's making, a crypt most strange, of extra-terrestrial construction, no doubt."

"Its makers?" Ansebe asks.

"I suspect them to be of intra-dimensional origin. Something odd in the design. A pyramid, untouched by weather, but its condition remains pristine, with no signs of age."

"Time fears the pyramids," Ansebe says to himself, raising a finger. "Our point of entry—is it easily accessible?"

"I've found a cave system, boss. It isn't easy to access, but it's the best route to gain entry undetected."

Ansebe looks to his brother, who is sitting in deep meditation, gathering his resolve for the forthcoming skirmish, he walks to him, "Brother, we are going to leave shortly, the eight drones shall stay to assist you. I don't know for sure, but something tells me that you need to keep those watching at bay." Something in the sky catches his attention, "We have company! I see them above, cloaked but visible to my eyes nonetheless."

Fez opens his eyes, "Your animalistic senses are to be coveted, brother," he gives a skywards glance, "I see nothing, what do you see?"

"Two flying triangles spying on us, possibly unmanned. Wait… my bhedai-ears!" Ansebe's large wrap around ears open wide, "I hear twin rotor blades in the distance, getting louder. Our pursuers approach." The distinct sound of a Chinook heavy-lift helicopter increases, its rotor blades echo with thunderous intensity as it closes in. Ansebe shouts, "That which is on board may be our undoing, and so I must bid you well in battle, brother."

The brothers share a moment, everything is said in their eyes, their gestures. Ansebe turns to depart, briskly walking to Por-Pyan. He shouts, "We leave."

Chapter Nineteen
Everyone Knows
What to Do in a Fight

Fez-Pyan closes his eyes, sits in the lotus posture, waiting for the action to begin. Despite the overbearing sound of the Chinook approaching overhead he stays calm, ready, and decidedly upbeat. All eight drones levitate around him, in a protective formation. Rohza mind-links.

"< Fez, do you remember the simulation games you used to play on the unification reserves? >"

"< I do, the eight-directional law of one. >"

"< I have overlaid the game into the Fy and in you the remote interface. >"

"< Amusing, you named the little critters—all of 'em— this'll be a blast. >"

The Chinook hovers nearby, Fez waits making poison finger salutations with his hands, gathering up his internal energy. Within Por-Pyan the others wait. "We need to go," Zara says. "They're not here to play," her eyes widen, she shouts, "Ansebe!"

"We wait!" Ansebe replies, holding his hand up waiting for the Chinook to land.

On board the heavy-lift helicopter Agent Orange snarls, "Got you right where I want you Mr Pyan, time for the big payback!" He turns to Actinide-15, signals to him, "Actinide, you're up," he pats the giant on the shoulder, "break them, but leave them breathing." Actinide jumps out of the Chinook, at least a sixty-foot drop. The giant lands crouching carefully holding in his hand a large box, a boom-box. The Elementian slowly stands, placing the boom-box down, its large speakers facing his opponent.

"Look at the size of you," exclaims Fez in awe, "this is going to be… unorthodox." Fez waits, but nothing happens, "What's the matter, vikit-wasp stung your tongue?"

No answer is forthcoming, the giant that is Actinide just stands waiting. At that moment inside Por-Pyan, Ansebe signals his hand down, "Now!" A translucent shimmer is all that is seen as the tetraporphyrin phases and in an instant, they are gone.

"My Bio-ship, follow that ship," screams Director Bullock from the Chinook, but to his dismay Agent Orange cuts across, blocking his path.

"We know where they're going," he says, pressing a gun into Bullock's stomach. "We stay here until we're done." The Chinook descends to land behind Actinide-15, who stands still, waiting, ignoring the noise of the blades buffing against the wind. As the blades begin to slow, Orange operates a remote control—the boom box—its speakers play classical music from Holst's orchestral suite, The Planets. "Mars, the Bringer of War," he says gloating, "your ass is mine, Mr Pyan." On hearing the opening notes, Fez's metallic face turns a shade of red. He looks at Actinide, something familiar about the being, if only he had studied the Eyt's library of strange races.

Just then, Rohza intrudes inside his thoughts, "< My data banks have identified the being as an Elementian. Oh no! Music… they fight to music. >"

Fez smiles, a memory from his youth—the Bitter Sage's tales of the Elementians, "I know," he says, drawing the jaw-bone from his belt, "they always fight to music." Titan and gladiator square off. Fez walks a circle, gauging the best line of attack, with the Fy surrounding him in shield mode. Alas, hubris is his biggest weakness, and in a moment of insane over-confidence he waves a hand, motioning the Fy to stand down. Actinide's body tenses, Fez's silver nano-faceplate shines silver-bright in response. It is the percussive sound of the strings in the symphony that trigger combat. Without warning they charge at each other and in the moment, Fez recalls the Bitter Sage's words:

When an unstoppable energy meets an invulnerable force, Annihilation is King. Therefore, whatever is fluid, soft, and yielding is never easily ruled.

Just before they collide Fez drops, sliding feet first between Actinide's legs to strike the giant in the crotch area with the ass-bone, wielding it like an axe. The ground shakes, but the Elementian remains impervious to injury; the resulting force wrenches the weapon from Fez's grasp. Disarmed, he stands quickly and lunges forward to attack from behind, then in the briefest of moments the Elementian lets loose a harsh back-kick fortified with a thermite reaction. "Oh… life-flash, wait I'm not ready…" Fez says, as the kick burns a cauterised foot print deep into his chest. It is a life-eating wound, one he collapses from as his body gives out on him; his breath fades and as it does distant thunder clouds crack, filling the sky with flashes of light.

"Yes!" Agent Orange shouts, punching the air, celebrating his asset's victory but prepared they are not for the xylographitet. A terrifying growling noise comes from the heart of the beast, its arcane metalloid body boils with rage. Its master, who was so vibrant and full of life, lies on the ground silent and still; it reacts like a mad dog enraged, so much so that it switches to Mach-mode, something that should not be possible for such a small one. It attacks with an animalistic ferocity, and in the confusion mecho-maws find their mark, biting down hard on Actinide's hand. The Elementian desperately tries to shake off the living-metalloid but is unable to do so. Actinide is in pain.

In the melee the Fy swoop in to protect Fez's body, but something odd glistens from his shoulder shawl—photonic particles seep from the shard of the Golden Fleece. The Nan-arcons awake.

Meanwhile, Actinide tries smashing his arm to the ground, in a desperate action to shake off the metal beast, but all xylographitets feed on kinetic-energy and such movements only serve to drive its mecho-maws down harder. In a frantic bid to free his arm, the Elementian issues a thermite-burn, his arm shines bright hot. This only empowers Gnash-Byte, who uses the heat as an energy source. Harder still its mecho-maws crunch. Actinide lets out a grimace of agony, desperate he tries something else. Coldness. This time he transitions to a superconducting state, drawing the heat from the very air. The xylographitet struggles to adapt to the sudden drop in temperature. Seizing the opportunity, Actinide pulls open the beasts mecho-maws and slams it to the ground. Gnash suddenly skitters away out of sight. The Elementian opens and closes his hand, testing if it still works, when behind him is a sudden crash. A fragmented bang follows. The music stops playing. A hum of electrical feedback fizzles silent.

Actinide turns to investigate, sees the ground scattered with wreckage, and by the remnants of smashed parts stands Fez with ass-bone in hand. "That's better. That racket was beginning to annoy me," he touches his wound. "Hey, you back-kicked me. I didn't think Elementians fight dirty."

"No, no, no," Agent Orange shouts, holding his forehead, "my asset needs music." On hearing this, Fez lets out a maniacal smirk and faces the Elementian, who no longer seems concerned with battle, "So, you won't fight without music?" Actinide sits down, his attention intriguingly diverted. Fez's chromium features trace a raised eyebrow upon seeing the Elementian overcome with fascination, having just plucked a handful of daisies out of the tundra.

With a bellyful of laughter Fez keels over, hands on knees for support, shaking his head, "My Daemon! I did not see that coming, no I did not." On standing, he rubs his chest, inspecting his wound. A gawp of surprise. The wound has completely healed, and his uniform returned. "Now there's a witch-wizardry thing of wonder. It appears this fleece prevails over my state of being mortal."

On realising his newfound ability to cheat death, Fez snarls a look of vengeance in the direction of the Agent Orange. Pointing to the helicopter he signals to his faithful xylographitet, "Gnash, go chomp the blades, the blades." The beast jets off. Orange and his team desperately try to defend their ground, aiming at the xylographitet. Rapid machine gun trails chase the metallic techno-tet, but to no effect as its electromagnetic armour deflects bullets with ease. With right-angled turns Gnash-Byte evades, advances and in no time at all the beast attacks, tentacles trail in the wind as it makes for the twin rotary blades—a gnawing noise at first, then a splitting screech as mecho-maws find their mark.

At this point Bullock slips away, out of sight. A look of disbelief from Orange turns to despair at seeing the Chinook grounded, its rotary blades warped, twisted out of shape. He screams, takes further aim at the metalloid wonder, a trail of bullets shot ricochet off the beast. "Call in backup," Orange yells into his communicator, but Gnash-Byte pounces forward like a wolf possessed, forcing him to back up against the Chinook. The xylographitet slowly advances to meet him face-to-face. Orange turns his head to look away as it bares its titanium teeth and lets out a terrible psychoacoustic noise, causing a terrible nauseous feeling in Agent Orange, one that steals his very breath.

"No Gnash—down!" Fez says, with a grin on seeing his loyal companion discover another weapon from its arsenal. Gnash returns to his master, with techno-tentacles wagging as it receives a pat, "Well done Gnash, you learned another trick." Fez-Pyan turns to face his assailants, his demeanour changes. The frown etched into his forehead dissolves with a smile of mischief, his eyes narrow and as they do intricate engravings morph under his polished skin, reflecting his emotions. His penchant for mischief comes to the fore. Like a cat playing with a mouse. He walks to the Chinook, and opening both arms outwards, turns his palms up, upon which the Fy levitate, controlled by the very motions of his hands.

"Mr Orange, fancy meeting you here, of all places, never took you for the off-the-grid mountain-man type. Think you know people."

Orange shakes his head, his lip quivers as he whispers to his team. "He's coming, be careful he's real fast, fire on my command," but his nemesis stands still. "Why's he waiting? Why?"

"In my youth, I used to play a game called the eight-directional law of one, it really is a fascinating game." Fez holds one hand outward thumb and index finger forming a circle, "You move artillery through sets of movements. Hard to master. Players who reached the one-hundred-and-eighth level were said to have achieved the art of war. It really is quite an intoxicating game. Allow me to demonstrate." His hand movements change, a display of an open palm. The Fire-Fy is first up, its glyphs burn bright red. The embossed impression on its shell smoulders yellow, like an incense stick, but leaving a pungent smell of sulphur in the air. One by one his opponents prepare to aim, but Fez moves his hand, whereupon the Fire-Fy rockets through the air, crashing into an agent, stealing his consciousness in the blink of an eye.

A double-take, a look of shock from Orange, "Shit," he wails, stamping his feet, "shoot, smoke that thing!" A millisecond passes, another wave of Fez's hands; this time all the Fy move at phenomenal speed. Bullets fly in all directions. In unison, the Fy follow their conductor as he makes movements with his hands, intricate patterns of attack which the Fy mirror. A complex dance of destruction ensues, and with pinpoint accuracy the Fy find their prey like heat-guided missiles. One, two, six, then eight soldiers all taken out. The remaining members of the team beat a hasty retreat. Agent Orange attempts to flee also, but Fez claps his hands shut, "Not you!" he shouts, directing the deadly orbs to block his path.

"Aargh… dammit Pyan, you piece of crap!"

"Mr Orange, lonely was I until seeing you. Is that anyway to speak to an old acquaintance?"

"What are you going to do to me?"

"I don't know."

"What?" Orange says with a confused look of fear.

Fez casually takes a cigar from his belt, holds it for Gnash-Byte to cut the end off. He lights it, inhaling the fumes, he coughs while talking, "Did I ever tell you the story of how I got into these? About me, a dictator and a bedtime discussion we had on a hot summer's night in Cuba. It's a long story, some other time perhaps. Now, where were we?"

"Stay away from me."

"Ahh yes—what to do with Mr Orange? I thought I knew what to do, but that's the problem. Thought I knew. On the other hand, I just learned that everyone knows what to do in a fight—until they get hurt."

"Actinide," Orange pleads to the Elementian, "over here, help me."

"He won't help you. They communicate on another level. I know you thought you were communicating with it, but to the Elementian it was just playing a game. No more interesting to its intellect than noughts-n-crosses would be to yours."

"Keep away. Don't come near me."

"Don't worry. I'm going to help you to become enlightened. Hell yeah, I'll even let you join my special club."

Agent Orange begins to laugh, a nervous cackle of despair.

"What… what club?"

The instant Orange answers is all that is needed to trigger Fez's hairpin reactions. With breathtaking speed, he lets loose a straight-cross, punching his adversary clean in the eye. Then he answers, "The club of the bright-shiners!" Agent Orange does a slow-motion pirouette, his spaghettified legs wrapping around each other as he spirals to the ground, unconscious. "So, you can be graceful, but only in defeat? Didn't think you had it in you, Mr Orange." With that said, he leaves in the direction of the Alaskan mountain range. It is a trek and then some, but as luck would have it, he can move over large distances faster than any human.

Chapter Twenty
Mountains and
What They Contain

It is sometime earlier, Ansebe, Zara and Sub-Rohza have arrived on the mountain side nearby the entrance to a hidden cave. The wind whistles as they disembark the tetraporphyrin, stepping onto a rock-strewn ledge leading to the mouth of the cave. Ansebe hugs the leviathan and whispers, "Por-Pyan my loyal steed, it is not safe for you here. Rohza has laid within you a calling, that we may find each other again, but for now go hide in water nearby." A phase to the left, then to the right and Por-Pyan is gone.

Ansebe places one of the oblongs on Zara's back, which instantly melds, weaving straps to her body. He flips the other one onto his back. Sub-Rohza zips behind them and projects holographic lasers onto each oblong, branding complex geometric patterns, which burn bright then dissipate. It is an instructional code. The oblongs return to jet black, but from them a transmogrification of sorts; they weave around their hosts a wafer-thin layer, an armour of unusual complexity.

Rohza mind-links with Zara, "< Uploading to your mind an interface, a symbiotic relationship with your oblong. >"

"< It feels… odd. >"

"< The sensation will soon dissipate. Now, my earlier reconnaissance located this cave system; it leads to the underground pyramid. Follow my lead and instructions always. Warning. Route may contain obstacles, placed here and there by the original creators of the crypt. >"

"Hold on, rewind," Zara quits her mind-link to voice her concern, "are you saying this route may be booby-trapped?"

"< More akin to a complex obstacle course, which may contain curators of an artificial nature. >"

"Just how dangerous is this route?"

"Let us find out," Ansebe says, placing a reassuring hand on Zara's shoulder.

They enter the cave; the further in they go, all outside light dissipates. It gets too dark to see when Sub-Rohza transforms into a beacon of light, shining the way into the abyss. As if in symbiosis with Zara's sight, from her suit a translucent glow reflects off the cave hues of gold and blue light. The oblong, a living organism, creates light in the darkness. As she scales further into the cave, more artificial light juts from out of the gloves woven onto her hands. Overwhelmed, she looks at her gloves and says, "Let there be light—light is good." Further still they descend into the system, following Rohza's lead.

"Here it is," Rohza beams a hologram to the ground, then disappears into a cenote, a dark pit. It is one of unnatural creation.

Ansebe speaks, "Zara, follow my lead. Trust me, just drop. It is a leap of faith." He faces her, steps near to the edge and falls over backwards into the pit, but as he does from the oblong bursts free several cloak-like blades. All of them as flat as paper, and yet more tensile than steel, they open out against the walls of the pit with a springy flex, bringing about a controlled descent. On seeing this Zara smiles and takes the plunge. As she descends, she cannot help but admire the wonder the oblong has released. Descending at a controlled pace, sparks fly off the blades as they push out, brushing against the cenote, all the while making minute adjustments to keep her balanced. Then darkness, the cenote is no more. She speeds up, plunging even faster, into a large cavern. This time the oblongs reveal the amazing things they are when from them more blades sprout out in all directions, a myriad arrangement of fluorescent white blades, all catching the air. They ride the wind gently downwards. Below them Rohza lights up even brighter, revealing beneath them a large subterranean river meandering through the cavern. Ansebe is first to land, and as he does, multiple blades caress the ground under him, lowering him softly to the ground. Zara follows, leaving a slight breeze in her wake. Then as quick as they sprouted, all the blades moult and fall off, having fulfilled their task. Rohza mind-links.

"< This river system goes deeper still underground, we need to scuba-dive to the next cave system. >"

"Do you guys have any idea how dangerous cave diving is?"

"< Zara, use the mind-link. The oblong is weaving a scuba-suit for you. Don't try to fight it. >"

A black film grows around her face. The same with Ansebe. Except with Zara a moment of panic, her eyes widen as the strange coating covers her mouth, enclosing it.

"< There's no oxygen, can't breathe… >"

"< A few more seconds. Please remain calm. >" A few more seconds feels like minutes. Then the oblong kicks in, weaving two airways up either side of Zara's neck into a mouth piece. An inhale of relief, of bewilderment.

"< This is air? What am I breathing? >"

"< It's a bacterial gas, don't worry, it'll keep you alive. It has no after affects. >"

"< No, only the current effects, feels like I'm breathing methane— >"

Ansebe cuts in, "< Now that we are breathing comfortably again, we dive. >"

Ansebe and Rohza jump into the waters. Zara follows but underwater has trouble swimming, something out of the ordinary impedes her; from the side of the oblong's new growth, two massive wings appear, moulding around her body. The divers take on the appearance of stingrays. The best solution to underwater scuba-diving is found in nature, as the giant streamline wings propel them forward with one smooth motion, overtaking Rohza. The quantum wonder admires her program.

"< My oh my—my design works. >"

"< Wow… I'm a human stingray! >" Zara says, thrilled at her underwater manoeuvrability.

"< Fluid dynamics. The wings create pressure fields, pushing you through the water. >"

"< It's magic. >"

They twist and turn like fishes in water. Then a strange feeling overwhelms Zara. Her third eye brings on a bout of clairsentience, an ability inherited from her ancestor princess Rani. Sensing the past, an aura, some strange connection with the river. A vivid memory of an amber stone she once had as a child, but not knowing nor being aware of this psychic ability, she dismisses the vision from her mind. Rohza does not.

"< Is everything all right, Zara? I picked up a disturbance in your thoughts. >"

"< It's nothing. Just a memory of an old amber stone given to me. >"

"< Let me know if it proves troublesome. >"

From behind Rohza lights the way, combined with the fluorescence of the aqua suits they illuminate the dark depths, revealing a world never frequented by visitors in many a millennium. Strange unearthly markings, glyphs, pictures all decorate the walls of the river. Rohza's lasers probe every inch for information, but what extra-terrestrial entities placed them there she does not know. The river begins to flow faster, the current starts to tug and pull; it is not a problem for their aqua-wings until out of the blue at incredible speed a bright rod of light shoots through the water, corkscrew in shape it spirals past them. In its wake, it leaves a change in their vision and as their contrast settles, an array of solid light comes into focus; multiple holograms akin to sheets of glass in orderly rows appear as they move forward. Zara's heartbeat raises in tempo—she mind-links.

"< Something's wrong. This is a trap! >"

Sub-Rohza investigates the holographic layers, sending out lasers to analyse the light, trying compute its effect. As they swim through the phenomenon, the unusual sensation of slowing down takes place.

Another rod shoots past, leaving more layers, windows of solid light, slower still they go, then a strange sensation takes place as their thoughts seem to echo in time.

"< Oh dear! Quantum anomaly—time is being manipulated. >" Rohza burns bright, trying to find a solution. Two more rods shoot by, this time releasing frames of light, followed by three, five, then eight, all leaving the water filled with the weird phenomenon of solid light. It encloses, encapsulates, binding them within a green transparent hue. As the layers of light gleam brighter, the emerald waters solidify, trapping everyone like insects entombed in amber. And as they try to move, the dense river of light cracks, creaking like a frozen lake about to break— only with every movement it congeals together even harder.

"< Help… can't move, >" Zara says via the mind-link, her mind full of fear.

"< Hold on team, I'm analysing the situation. >

"< What were rods doing here, Rohza? >" Ansebe asks.

"< I can't move guys, can't get any air… aargh. >" Zara exclaims, getting agitated. Unable to move, a claustrophobic feeling takes over.

Ansebe tries to calm her.

"< Zara look at me! >"

From the corner of her eye she gazes at Ansebe's forehead, which mimics the mesmerising qualities of a cuttlefish, with hypnotic rainbow patterns.

"< Breathe with me, shallow breaths, let your lungs find the space. >"

"< I think I've got it. >" Zara finds the room to breathe.

Just then, Rohza lights up, and reports.

"< Solution! I have the answer. This trap is designed to ensnare biologicals. If I was on my own, I would have been fine. >"

"< How much time do we have? >" A feeling of dread sets in Zara's stomach.

"< Theoretically, this construct could last for an eternity. It appears we are now separated from the normal time continuum. Time is passing for us in the here and now, but to an observer in the world outside, time for us is at a standstill. >"

"< Nice to know—how long before the air runs out? >"

"< Not long, but I believe I can trick this technology into dissolving. >"

"< How? What do I need to do? >"

"< Nothing, Zara. I, on the other hand, need to reboot the both of you— >"

"< Best do it quickly, do not tell us when! >" Ansebe says.

"< Authorization, boss? >"

"< Authority level zeta granted. You may reboot us. >"

"< Whoa! Reboot us? What the hell is a reboot? >"

"< Oh, I just need to shut the both of you down. >"

"< Shut down? So now a reboot is a shut down? >"

"< It's a temporary termination, of a sort—are you both ready? >"

140

"< Wait! You don't mean death, do you? >" Amplified by the mind-link, Zara hears her own heart pounding, on realising Rohza's plan.

"< Don't worry Zara, you only need to die for a bit. I won't be that bad. >"

"< Hang on, how do you know—ick. >"

Without warning Rohza shuts down their minds, and shortly thereafter their vital signs begin to waiver as their life-force begins to leave them. Seconds lead to minutes but the amber trap stays solid as ice. Although a Sub-Rohza is incapable of panic, this one is unique, a one of a kind. From her sub-conscious an emotion, one of anxiety, the fear of losing loved ones. The fear of grief. Rohza does not realise it, but she was created to achieve the ultimate self-realisation. To be human-like—she tries to understand this feeling—such emotional complexity to which a question is pondered.

"Why do beings experience sorrow, grief, heartbreak? No, I won't have it!"

Rohza burns brightly, calculating their odds of survival as the amber light de-solidifies. "At this rate five more minutes shall be too long! That simply won't do."

More complex computations performed, then a result.

"Ansebe's quantum dice! Able to influence odds at the quantum level."

Decided, she beams a holographic string, lasers send instructions to the dice inside Ansebe's belt. No response. Again, she tries, this time fine-tuning the frequency, upon which a slight movement from the quantum dice is seen.

"Almost there! Quantum non-locality—shut up and calculate Rohza!"

Suddenly, the dice glow, sparkle with the manipulation of probability, and as they do the entire forest of light dissolves in an instant. Freedom, but at a cost. The built-up water pressure from the river—the raw power of nature—releases, firing them forward at break-neck speed. Rohza desperately tries to reach Zara; unable to do so, she goes back to basics, sending an electrical surge to re-start her heart. No good—she overlays a hologram onto Zara's mind, a slow reboot process, but it will have to do.

"Strange, she's limp, no response. Need to crosswire her senses, create an adrenaline release. There, that should do it."

The torrent does not subside. With no time to monitor her recovery, Rohza moves onto Ansebe, brings him back instantly, his genetic makeup able to make a quick recovery. On awakening, he realises all is not well. Washing around in the torrent he fights to gain balance; regaining his consciousness, he mind-links.

"< Rohza, status report! >"

"< The backed-up water released a torrent when the trap dissolved. Get to Zara, waterfall approaching. >"

A fast brushing noise rumbles near as Ansebe races towards Zara. Nearer to the edge he sees a faint gleam of light from her suit, but the waterfall snatches her from his grasp. As her wilting body rolls down the falling waters, Ansebe streamlines, stingray wings wrap around him like a cloak, allowing him to ride down the waterfall faster. But she is just out of reach, and so with outstretched fingers he concentrates, and as he does the oblong weaves from his gloves a thin-line akin to the feelers of a grapevine. The outgrowth descends downward, spiralling, twisting, and reaching out for Zara. A vine catches her foot by the ankle and wraps around tightly. Ansebe sighs a breath of relief and tugs, at which point the vine contracts, pulling her within reach. Not much time left, but time enough to tap some instructions onto her suit, which the oblong processes instantly. He mind-links.

"< Rohza, sub pilot Zara's new weave. >"

"< Accessed boss, ready? >"

"< Yes, lets open up. >"

The stingray wings wrapped around them open, only far larger this time, spreading out as wings as they soar from out of the waterfall. As they transit the emptiness, Ansebe gazes downwards with a look of disbelief. Immense is the cavern, the size of an underground city. His far-reaching eyes able to view from on high, he spies the pyramid then something catches the corner of his eye, amazing light sources from biologicals, floating plantae and algae providing enough luminosity to see. Insects, bats, and birds not originating from Terra reside in this place, an Eden with its own ecosystem hidden deep inside the earth. Ansebe sees in the distance construction work and temporary buildings. He spies the best place to land, a small forest on the banks of a large lake leading away from the falls. They swoop in to land, and as they do their woven suits interweave camouflage, a stealth mode blending them with the fauna in the background. Upon landing Ansebe rushes to Zara; tearing off her breathing apparatus, he holds her upright in his arms. He lets out a woeful sigh, looks to Rohza.

"Save her!" Rohza moves to face her.

"Hold her head back boss, this is a one-time shot." Ansebe leans so her head rocks back on his forearm; distraught at the sight of her limp body, he shakes his head.

"Whatever procedure you adopt… make it work."

"I'm sure this will work." From Rohza a dash of gold-dust falls onto Zara's lips.

"What is this?" Ansebe glances at the gleaming golden particles then at Sub-Rohza.

"I took the opportunity of taking some of the Nan-arcons from Fez's fleece. Only a few, I thought they might prove useful… look!" The Nan-arcons awake, something to fix. To make well again. They dissolve on her lips, and a few wondrous seconds later Zara bolts upright, gasping for air—only to complete out the rest of what she was saying prior to blacking out, "…you can bring me back to life?"

"She lives!" Ansebe says, his brow softened with a look of relief.

"My hearts about explode out of my chest," Zara says, trying to catch her breath.

"Try to calm. Your mind has triggered a substantial release of adrenaline," Rohza beams a light into Zara's forehead, returning everything back to normal. As Zara regains her composure, she looks around awestruck.

"The pyramid… we made it?"

"Yes Zara, we made it. I present the legendary crypt of the Gods. I have wondered all of my life if it even existed."

More on Zara, Ansebe and Rohza later.

Meanwhile top-side, Fez-Pyan has found the special access route to the unacknowledged subterranean complex. He spies from a distance a carved-out area, a small runway, a helipad, and prefabricated buildings housing the entrance into the mountain. "Well Gnash old buddy, we're supposed to be creating a diversion. It's diverting-time." He directs the eight Fy in first. A wave of his hands and they creep up to the entrance, changing an invisible hue, mirroring whatever surface they transit. At the entrance they roll around the tunnel wall in a loop-the-loop motion, traversing the ceiling unnoticed by the guards below. "They're in, let's roll Gnash, time for action." He sets out on a casual stroll to the entrance, lighting up a Havana, which he smokes in an arrogant manner. Such is the confidence bestowed by the mystical fleece that he wears.

At several hundred metres distance, security cameras record his every action. Inside the base alarms signal; a security operative in the communications facility squints, trying to make out an image on his monitor. He zooms a camera in for a closer look. The system scans for facial recognition but finds nothing. He tries again, a full close-up this time and still nothing. "What the hell?" the operative sounds the alarm, "get a look as this dude."

His co-workers turn, some roll their chairs over to watch the large screen. "That's… different," one says, gawping at the display. The close-up of the silver nano-face plate, glittering shoulder shawl and unusual woven uniform are one thing, but it is the gravity-defying xylographitet that leaves them dumbfounded. Its unusual shape. Its bulldog-like face. The cannonball-sized entity and its techno-tentacles leaves them in no doubt; time to sound the alarm. Seconds later General Stephenson, the head honcho, marches in, a stout military man who does not suffer fools gladly. He looks at the screen, a muscle in his jaw twitches.

"Status report!"

"Sir… look."

General Stephenson takes control of the situation.

"It's definitely not one of ours. Open all doors, lead them into the containment area—let's see what we're dealing with."

"Yes, sir. Setting the containment protocols up for beta-cell seven." The operatives issue commands to their terminals. Unbeknown to them however, the Water-Fy entered with the General in cloaked-mode and like a fly on the wall, it monitors the communications facility undetected. Out of sight, unseen.

Outside Fez stops in his tracks and placing his fingers to his temple, he synchs his vision with the Water-Fy. "What do we

144

have here? We have an eye-ball on the enemy! Time they saw my harem-skarem side." He marches forward, doing what he does best. No fear, no bravery, he just gambles on happenstance being in his favour. Even though he is not completely sure what is about to go down, he intuitively calls the shots. "When we get inside, they'll try to figure out what they're dealing with, so they will detain us, for interrogation." The xylographitet growls excitedly. "I know you want to get at 'em but not unless I say so. No matter what they try to do to me, do nothing unless I say."

They approach further and come to a standstill at the entrance to the military complex; from within a team of armed soldiers appear, and quickly forming a firing line, they take aim. A voice echoes in the wind, from a megaphone. A sergeant shouts out:

"Intruder, kneel down! Get your hands on your head!" Fez spits the half-smoked Havana out and kneels, with Gnash-Byte sitting by his side. The soldiers release a sniffer dog who goes over to Fez first, then to Gnash, wagging its tail. It does not sit, indicating there are no explosives, and returns to its handler, who shouts, "All clear!"

One soldier sprints over to Fez and secures his hands behind his back, binding them with cable-ties. "Prisoner secured," he shouts.

"Any weapons?" shouts a sergeant.

"Animal bone tucked in his belt. No firearms." Not sure what to do with Gnash, he retreats to back to safe distance. The soldiers surround their captives, marching them to a small hanger. An eerie rumbling noise echoes, the hanger is a tube-station; in the distance headlights hail the arrival of an armoured carriage, brakes squeal as it comes to a standstill. Two doors slide open. The soldiers point their guns in Fez's back and manhandle him on board, also kicking Gnash, who growls with indignation, only to scuttle into the carriage following its master.

With the doors shut, the train begins to descend at a steep angle; as they speed downwards Fez counts, trying to estimate how far they travel underground. After a while he gives up. "Screw it. We're going deep underground—real deep." He looks up at a camera in the train, and as he does his nano-faceplate engraves dragon-tattoos over his face; then as if showing off, he wipes them away, leaving a shiny chromium gleam and addresses the camera. "Pretty cool, huh? Check this out!" With an unsmiling twinge of insanity, he changes the colours of his nano-faceplate while reciting an eerie threat said in poetry and rhyme direct to the camera…

"Black as the soil. I bring trouble and toil,

"See me a radiant red. Wish you were dead,

"Back to a silver-white. I give all men a fright,

"See me turn purple. Poisonous am I,

"A change to off yellow-white. I strike like a thief in the night,

"Brilliant white, prepare to face my might,

"Green as the spring. I change like thunder, that's my thing,

"Blue as twilight, none survive my bite."

In the communications facility a solemn mood takes over on hearing the psychotic verse. The silence breaks with a threat. "We need to smoke this badass," growls General Stephenson, "give me a status report, let's find out what we're dealing with here."

At that moment Fez talks to the camera, "Gentlemen, may I suggest you search your data files for the Serpent That Shines. I do hope my alter egos haven't been kept hidden from history."

Just then more action from on top, "General, two Chinooks have landed up-top, patching through the intercom now, someone has the code to the hotline." General Stephenson picks up a handset.

"General Stephenson speaking, who is this?"

"General Stephenson, this is Director Bullock. I'm taking control of your base."

"The hell you are!"

"You'd better find out which side you're on son, and quick."

"Whose side are you on Director?"

"The right side son, the side you'd better step over to."

"I can't do that, Director Bullock."

"Now listen here son, the man up top has invested all the power in me, understand? Now check your goddamned security protocols, or you'll be buried up to your neck in a pile of shit in the Nevada desert."

"Check the protocols!" Stephenson shouts to his men.

"Son, the release codes have been issued. As we speak my team's biometrics have been added to your security mainframe. Tell your men to stand down. We're accessing the base."

Stephenson paces a circle, hands on hips. "What's the head count on the controlled access system?"

"Sir, forty extra men granted high security access just now," the operator rears back from Stephenson, "Bullock is on… a higher level than you, sir. He's effectively in charge of the base."

General Stephenson shakes his head, he speaks into a handset, "Welcome to project Tetragrammaton. We'll meet you down below."

Chapter Twenty-One
Project Tetragrammaton

In the meantime, the train transporting our two unannounced trespassers enters an underground station, the clunking noise of tracks changing is all that is heard inside the carriage as it is re-routed into a holding hangar. As it comes to a standstill, its armoured doors slide open, and over a megaphone an order issued:

"Leave the train!"

More soldiers meet Fez and his loyal companion, "This way," one shouts, "step into the circle!" Fez glances down, at a large circle scribed into the ground, and walks into the centre with Gnash skittering in behind him, at which point he addresses the soldiers.

"Did you know the philosopher Gurdjieff wrote about his encounters with the Yezidis—how he once saw a Yezidi boy distraught, struggling to break out of a circle drawn in the ground by other boys. Try as he might the boy just couldn't step outside of the circle. The other boys teased and taunted him until Gurdjieff erased part of the circle, whereby the boy was able to escape. Perhaps the philosopher wants us to think carefully about the Yezidis—perhaps you should think carefully about me." Out of the floor a circular glass wall made of toughened glass shoots up, stopping at a circular lip in the ceiling, trapping them like a ship in a bottle. "A prison—how quaint, never been in a prison before. When do I get my medication?" No one answers, but Fez spies a security camera in the ceiling and stares into its lens. "You think that I think you can't hear me, but I know that you don't know I can."

"What's he on about?" one of the operators asks in the control room.

"Something about us hearing him."

"He's bluffing," the operator replies to his co-worker, "mic is off, he can't hear us." The operator checks his controls, glancing at the captive in the glass prison on his display screen.

"Now I know you can hear me," Fez says, still glaring at the security camera.

"Mute the speakers, this freak is messing with us."

"Indeed!" With that said Fez presents his cuffed hands to Gnash, who shears the cable-ties. He shows both his hands to the camera then sits, leaning against the glass. The xylographitet moves to his side, he looks into the beast's eyes and whispers, "Soon Gnash—not long now."

In the intervening time Bullock and his men enter the base and proceed to a conference room, where General Stephenson and his men join them.

"Don't worry General Stephenson, I've had time to acquaint myself with this project. Now yawl know I'm doing work for the big man, so tell me all about the extra-terrestrial in the holding cell."

"The extra-terrestrial, if indeed that's what he is," Stephenson says, pointing a remote at a large plasma-screen, "take a look." Fez's impromptu threat said in rhyme plays out.

"Remarkable," Bullock says, "its face, the colour tones, like something out of a movie."

With that said, Mr Orange steps forward with Actinide-15 in tow, "Gentlemen, we need to incapacitate the prisoner, by whatever means necessary. We're not dealing with a movie villain here, we're talking a phenomenon, a force of one that may well destroy us."

"Don't worry men, the big guy is one of ours," Bullock says, trying to calm the men from the sight of the Elementian, but it is Agent Orange appearing like a madman, looking a sorry state with one eye now completely swollen shut, that steals their attention.

He begins to rant aggressively, "We have the enemy in a Darpa confinement and interrogation unit. We need to take him out now, or he'll be up to something in no time… no time at all!"

"That won't be necessary, Agent Orange." Bullock orders his men, "Disarm this man, escort him and his companion to a holding cell. Until he comes to his senses."

"You can't do this. You've got to take the enemy out of the game."

"Out of the game, son? I'm just starting to play the goddamn game. Information extraction. This alien fella is going to tell us everything we want to know, and I do mean everything." Bullock waves his hand, "Get him out of my sight."

Agent Orange struggles to break free, and as he is dragged away he calls out, "You're making a big mistake! He'll beat you, you'll see, he'll beat every last one of you."

Bullock replies, "Son, you don't know what I know about this base, the potential resources we have," he looks to his men, "time we spoke to this alien fella."

Director Bullock and team march into the hangar where Fez and Gnash-Byte are being held captive. An interrogator follows, proficient in a specialist skill-set; the modus operandi of the Darpa confinement and interrogation unit—the innocuous-looking glass holding cell, that Fez finds himself in. Bullock approaches the cell, "Stand up, son." Fez stands to face his captor; a few inches of glass separate them. Bullock looks his captive up and down, and nods to the interrogator, who turns the two-way speakers on.

"Now, like it or not you're going to tell us everything we need to know."

"I am? Is that how this works?"

"That's how it works son."

"I don't think so. There are nine levels to this game, and we're only on level one. You're hoping to compete in a game you can't master, against a level-nine player. One who uses all the cheat-codes." Fez's eyes narrow, an unsettling maniacal expression takes over, one that sends the fear of God into the men the other side of the glass.

"Why the need to cheat, son?" Bullock says, wiping sweat from his brow.

"The short answer, because it is fun. The long answer—is there a long answer? Let's make up one! Why does the cat play with the mouse? It can easily kill it, but still it plays. A cheat of sorts. Maybe it's more interested in playing with the game than playing the game. Seeing what diversions the game might offer, rather than test its skills."

"That's all very well son, but we have you at a disadvantage."

"It is so, or so it would appear."

"Son, the glass cylinder you find yourself in is appropriately named the pokey, piece of equipment from the days of project MKUltra. The CIA's endeavour to master mind control by any means possible." Bullock faces closer to the graphene cylinder, "You're in a world of hurt son, my world." On a whim Fez head-butts the glass, causing Bullock to panic, to jump back agitated. "Well, speaking of cheat codes, son," he turns to the interrogator, "water-mode, fill it!" From the ceiling a rim opens, and the glass cell rapidly fills with water, moving quickly Fez jumps up to steal a breath of air. He floats in the water, time passes by.

"Director, monitoring the biological's vitals… no rise in audible heartbeat." Several minutes later Fez sinks to the bottom of the cylinder and relaxes into the lotus posture, while Gnash continues to swim around, looking like a metallic octopus.

Ten minutes pass, "No rise in heartbeat, director." The fifteen-minute mark, "Heart beat picking up." Twenty minutes, "Director, he's about done."

"Flush it!" On Bullock's order drainage plugs open in the floor, the water flushes away as fast as it had arrived. He steps forward and taps the glass.

"Are you ready to speak, son? Heart almost given up the ghost?"

Fez rolls over onto his hands and knees, and gasping for air, he holds a finger up, "Ask… ask your men to monitor my heartbeat again!"

"Director, his heartbeat has stopped!"

With his fist closed, Fez opens his fingers one at a time, all the while looking at Bullock he counts to five.

"And now it beats," he says, laughing, pulsing his fist open and closed.

"My God, he's right. His heart's beating again," a miffed look from the interrogator.

"Take away the air! Let's see this smart-ass deal with that," snarls Bullock. The oxygen extracts from the cylinder. Alas, Fez cannot endure the vacuum nor the reduced air-pressure. He keels over. Bullock shouts, "Oxygen, now!" The cell re-oxygenates and as it does Fez takes a sharp intake of air.

"Okay, you've got me, I'll... I'll talk."

"A sense of survival after all, see we're not so different, son."

"I guess we're not... I'll tell you everything you need to know, our theory of quantum gravity, bacterial-mechanics, the works," he holds his hands together pleading, "but only after I have heard Adamski can I do this."

"Where do we find this Adamski, son?"

"You'll find him on your... internet?" Bullock signals his men to get on it.

"Director... we have an Adamski on file, we're looking at one George Adamski, a medium to Nordic aliens. Ah, he's deceased, sir." Bullock taps the glass again.

"Adamski is deceased, son. Was you supposed to meet with him, pass him info?"

Fez gives a puzzled look, he waves his hand.

"No, the song by Adamski—I believe it's called Killer."

"You trying to play me, son?"

"No, song acts as a code, unlocks my mind. As soon as I hear it, I will be able to tell you what you need to know."

"Sir, we have the track downloaded, do you want us to play it?"

"Go ahead, let's see what he's got."

The eerie opening beats of the tune begin to play, as it does Fez taps his feet and slaps his thigh. He shouts over the music. "The artist who composed this score named it Killer, as it sounded like a murder movie soundtrack—by the same token I've often thought the same but wondered how it would play out. Shall we dance?"

At that moment Fez sends the Water-Fy in the control room into action. From earlier, it spied the control panel and, most important of all, the large red-button named POKEY EMERGENCY RELEASE. Fez claps his hands, sending the Fy racing towards the release button. A direct hit. The glass cylinder descends back into the floor. "Speaking of cheat codes!" Fez leaps over the glass rim, landing with the finesse of a circus acrobat. Gnash follows behind, and within a few seconds they have Director Bullock backing up.

"Now steady son, we can work something out," he pleads, holding out his hands.

"I'm not your son!" A thwack to Bullock's neck, followed up with a two-star poison finger touch, leaves his would-be captor paralysed. Unable to move, Bullock can only watch as Fez drops, spinning around to strike his metal fingers against his shin—a dreadful snapping noise is heard. Bullock instantly faints, dropping to the floor, and as he does alarms sound throughout the complex, accompanied by the echo of fast-moving footsteps. At this moment Fez places a finger to his head, and mind-links with Ansebe.

"< You're up brother, I'll maintain confusion—disable the Tetragrammaton. >"

"< We try, but we may have to leave by the front door. >"

"< I'll see if they'll play. >"

The Serpent That Shines launches into action, cutting off the escape of the team sent to interrogate him. He strikes and kicks, breaking bones, taking the operatives out in a few seconds. In the melee Bullock's paralysis wears off enough for him to speak over handsfree. "Transferring command of this base to Agent Orange, release code zero-one-six," he manages a few more words, "you were right… he is dangerous," before losing consciousness. Next, into the hanger a crack-team armed with stun-batons charge to meet Fez head on, led by General Stephenson.

"No guns I see. Aww fellas, that can only mean one thing, you want me alive." He waves his hand for Gnash to sit, to stay out of the way. The soldiers advance cautiously, closing in to surround their man. Many against one. Unfavourable odds for a man, but Fez-Pyan is no normal man. He looks around, a head count, forty against one. "It's been an unusual day, fellas. I've tasted immortality—and I got given this bone," he draws the ass-bone from his belt, waving it in the air, "I'm ready to put it to the test. It's half the jaw bone from an ass."

The soldiers glance at each other, smirking. "Get a load of this guy, he's really going to fight us with a bone."

Stephenson shouts, "Let's do this clean-n-quick." The soldiers attack, charge, scrap and bustle. A riotous melee ensues. Taser-batons swing in a disorderly array, but the ferocious assault meets with empty space as Fez turns, side-steps, and ducks. A barrage of batons swipe at his head.

"Too chaotic," he says, back-dropping out of harm's way only to retaliate with whirlwind kicks, breaking legs and knees. "He nutmegs a 5-hole," shouts Fez, as he slides between the legs of one the soldiers in the free-for-all out of harm's way.

The soldiers shout, "He's gone."

"Where's he at?"

"I'm in the red-zone," Fez says, standing behind them, catching his breath, "kick-off time!" Out of the crowd the tallest, toughest soldier charges to meet him head-on, but Fez craftily circles to his side, hooking the jaw-bone behind his neck. He turns fast, "So that happens?" Fez stands taken aback at the bone's power, seeing his opponent propelled into the front-line with such a force, that many are injured. Seeing this, several soldiers drop their batons and flee, but Fez blocks their escape and incapacitates them one by one.

"Let's go down fighting," barks the general, leading the rest of his detail in to attack.

This time Fez tucks the bone in his belt and uses the poison finger hand. He spins and turns, throwing his fingers out like darts, more go down in his wake. A brief pause ensues as two soldiers flank him on either side; they attack simultaneously, cutting their batons downwards, but he circles behind one attacker and pushes him to meet the other's baton head-on. He quips, "Where fast waters meet opposing currents, there is an abyss."

"Aargh…" screams the other soldier, having taken out one of their own. He charges in, but Fez ducks, bumps his shoulder into the soldier's ribcage, a loud crunch is heard as the soldier collapses.

"Still waters hide deep roots," Fez says, waving a finger. He turns, a head count, six standing, including the general. "And now gentlemen, it's your honour to witness that which I have learned from legends," and with that said he releases the full untainted force of the poison finger hand. His fingers transform into metallic digits of dread, moving with eerie speed he turns, slashes, strikes, cuts and chops, mowing all six men down in less than ten seconds. "As the waters build up to a torrent, there is endless change in which I easily absorb attack. How could I know defeat?"

As he stands over the fallen, one of the injured lets out an anguished yell, "How… how can you fight like that?"

On hearing this Fez kneels to face the soldier, "I'll tell you my secret—evil is sweet, so I keep it hidden under my tongue, saving it for a rainy day. Remember that's the secret—save it for a rainy day." Just then the Killer soundtrack ends, and as it does Fez stands, walks away talking to himself, "Interesting, fighting to music. Now I see what the Elementians get out of it."

Fez departs the hangar with Gnash-Byte to enter the crypt of the Gods. As he does he claps his hands, and on hearing this all the Fy come out of hiding to meet him. The clap echoes, and as the sound reverberates, his eyes widen, taking in the view. "Monumental," he says, gazing around the large cavern. In front of him a city long abandoned, lit up with light extruding from biological plantae and algae. And running through the centre a pathway, a giant's causeway leading to the pyramid. On top of the giant structure is the light source, a golden hue of heavenly light created by the Tetragrammaton.

He stops to gaze at large glyphs on a massive stone tablet, underneath it scribbled in chalk an interpretation left by a cryptologist. "What's this? The Tablet of Stars… an army guards the pathway to the stars." Fez looks at the path and shrugs, "What army?" Just then Gnash-Byte growls. "What is it, Gnash?" The xylographitet skitters to the edge of the path, sniffing, as if sensing danger. Fez kneels on one leg, touches one of the hexagonal shaped stones and waits. "Nothing, whatever was here appears to be long gone." With a half-shrug he stands and gingerly places a foot onto the path, then another. He mind-links.

"< Brother, I'm on my way. >"

"< Excellent, guard the pyramid steps, we are near the summit. If we are unable to disable the Tetragrammaton, half the universe will come looking for this place! >"

Chapter Twenty-Two
The Army of the Gods

Something inside pushes them on, it is destiny that beckons Ansebe, Zara and Sub-Rohza as they ascend the final steps of the pyramid, arriving at the apex. "We've reached the Ben-Ben," Ansebe says, stepping onto a narrow ledge. "Behold the Tetragrammaton." As if in response an intensified harmonic hum emits from the golden capstone, discharging a colourful corona high into the air. Ansebe places a hand on Zara's shoulder, "I don't know how I know this, but you can decode the Tetragrammaton."

"I can?" Zara says, at a loss for words.

We shall return to the pyramid shortly. Meanwhile, on the outskirts of the underground city, Agent Orange has been released from his cell and stands in the communications facility. A sergeant addresses him.

"Sir, Director Bullock has relinquished command of the base, you are now in charge of the facility—"

"He gave you all an ass-whipping, didn't he? Bullock injured?"

"Well…"

"How bad?"

"He's severely hurt, sir."

"Shame. Tell me, what artillery do we have at our disposal?"

"We can't use any munitions in the city sir, the pyramid goes crazy at any kinetic activity. Ground starts vibrating, as if it senses our armaments."

"If it can't be used, then it's freakin' useless!" Orange closes his eyes, a slow exhale, "Tell me, is there anything we can actually use against the alien?"

"Well sir, there is one thing, but it's not tested," the operator looks to a member of the science team.

"Talk!" Orange says.

"Well, sir," the scientist replies, "we have, theoretically speaking, an army at our disposal."

"Go on."

"Several months ago, after years of work our cryptologists finally deciphered a message on the large stone tablet. Not messages per se, but a warning left by the Gods—"

"What kind of warning?"

"The kind of warning scribed in two-foot-high glyphs, the one which says...

"'Malevolent is the end,

"'Which waits any mortal,

"'Who treads the pathway to the stars.'"

"What does it do, this pathway?"

"It activates an army, a swarm. Interred inside the path's inner recesses are catacombs in which the children of the path sleep. A defence mechanism to cleanse the city of mortals who dare to enter. Or so it is written."

"Where is this army now?"

"The army waits patiently, watching... the path senses, knows if it is being walked on. When awakened, they kill those who walk the path without the Gods' permission. We lost a lot of men to that path. Eventually, we found a way to switch it to a deactivated state by our broadcasting an infra-sound frequency, inaudible to us—"

"Activate the army."

"This is highly irregular."

"Turn the infra-sound off," Orange says softly, then shouts, "Do it!"

"We might be opening a Pandora's box. Something we can't close." Orange aims a gun at the scientist, who complies, switching off the amplifiers.

"Interface power released—it's working!" They all gawp at a monitor screen, at an array of weird phenomena on the pathway as the giant causeway shines faintly, revealing a honeycomb mass of transparent hexagonal cells.

"Here we go... look, there's movement," Orange says, obsessively viewing the live-feed.

In the intervening time, Fez-Pyan and Gnash, having walked half-way along the path, stop on hearing movement. They take a closer look at one of the hexagonal cells, when it begins to rise out of the ground. A few inches at first.

"What's this?" Fez examines the protruding cell, as it elevates sluggishly from out of the ground. "Gnash, stay away... could be dangerous." He turns, on seeing movement from the corner of his eye. "Oh krill, not good. Not good at all!" From everywhere cells rising out from the ground, some faster than others. "What the harem-skarem's inside of these things?" then a sixth sense or even a touch of fear, "Gnash, we need to move... fast!" In each cell a skeleton, each one encased in a transparent hide. Some small, others tall, some with four arms, others with four legs, but all armed with weapons forged by the Gods. The glistening of silver swords, axes, daggers and shields shines all around them. Fez mind-links, as he sprints forward, avoiding the ever-rising obstacles.

"< Rohza, need an analysis. What are these things? >"

"< Skeletal-biologicals, synthetic, part bacteria. No, it can't be, there's too many. Get out of there Fez, get out now! >"

He waits not, switches to breakneck speed, and as he does some of the cells that have risen begin to dissolve, revealing that which lies inside. On seeing this he runs faster, but even more cells rise, a sea of hexagonal columns blocking his way. Some a few feet out of the ground, others several metres. His training kicks in, he uses the columns as stepping stones while Gnash and the eight Fy shift up a gear, levitating over the obstacles.

"< A little help here, Rohza. >"

"< They're a part-sentient race, created by the Gods of the crypt. >"

"< How do I deal with 'em? >"

"< Use the bone, and the xylographitet. >"

"< Oh yeh, my ass-bone. Almost forgot. If I get out of this one, I'll start believing in the above-beyond! >"

We leave Fez for the moment, and return to the top of the pyramid, where Zara tries to work out Ansebe's prediction.

"I'm not sure how to do this, decode something I have no knowledge of?"

"Try the Urumi," Ansebe says. Zara reaches into her side-satchel, holds the ivory handle, "Nothing, it's not working."

"My computations show a key is required," Rohza analyses the golden capstone, "I'll try entanglement," she tries a quantum-merge, but the Tetragrammaton defends itself with a field of pure energy. "Oh my, data received, processing… Zara, you're the key!"

"So now I'm a key?"

"Yes, that burst of energy was a transmission, a message. Hidden inside you are psychometric abilities which trigger the claircognizant mind—the ability to acquire psychic knowledge without knowing how or why."

"How am I supposed to know about all of this?"

"How do you know that you do not?" Ansebe says, to which Zara nods her head.

"Okay," she exhales, closes her eyes and dissolves her mind to a state of emptiness. Inside her head, an instinct, a compulsion triggers her next action.

"I'm ready…"

Zara slowly reaches forward, touches the Tetragrammaton with her index and middle finger, nothing at first, then an odd sensation, a feeling of divine power and knowledge. "It's beautiful," a surge of information overwhelms her senses—she turns her palms face up, as she does they turn transparent to reveal the constellations, "I am that which is not, born from the imperishable stars." With that said her skin transforms a dark blue, filled with a star-blue sky, photons of rainbow-light encircle her body; she stops dead, lifeless, in a suspended state of animation. Just then she finds herself above, looking down at the pyramid, at herself, the entire universe all stopped dead in single frozen moment of time. And then it is all gone, she awakes in another place, another time-line. Ancient Egypt. The Pyramids of Giza.

From the heavens, a diamond-shaped vessel descends, it stops aside the great pyramid. From out of the interstellar craft levitates the princess Nut—Goddess of the Stars and Sky. Fully clad in a magnificent space-suit, star-wings unwrap around her body opening wide, her dark-blue skin fills with diamonds of light, iridescent like the stars. As she soars the sky, her long locks of jet-black hair sway unaided as if alive, her body appears almost invisible against the star-lit sky except for the shimmer of golden wrist, ankle and neck bracelets. Gliding effortlessly toward the pyramid, landing on a small ledge, her star-wings close behind her—in front of her the Tetragrammaton. She holds her hands together, to form a triangle with thumbs and index fingers and on doing so the golden capstone hums, energy crackles all around it. Keeping the shape, she places her hands on the stone. A strong magnetic force repels her hands back, revealing a golden eyelid. It slowly opens to reveal a human-eye, a gloss-black pupil sits inside an opaline-blue iris. It blinks once, then once again—the Eye of Horus awakes.

The Goddess Nut opens her arms out sideways, palms up. She speaks, "Oh Horus, I know not why you ask this of me, this is the last but one of your conduits, alas there is one Eye I cannot find. I fear we shall spend an eternity looking for it, my love."

The Eye, a sentient state of consciousness inside Nut's mind, blinks one last time, "Is it so?" the Eye blinks again, releasing a tear onto the pyramid, and in turn tears stream from Nut's eyes,

"So be it, my love." And with that said the Goddess Nut pushes against the Eye of Horus, and in an instant, it implodes, upon which the golden capstone disappears to where no one truly knows.

The next instant she is back in the crypt of the Gods at the exact moment when everything stopped dead in time. The present moment reignites, and she is Zara once more. "I was a Goddess!" she says, then faints only to fall backwards, losing her footing, but Ansebe catches her by the arm, pulling her back to the safety of the ledge. Holding her in his arms, he calls out to Rohza to help bring her around.

More on this part of the story later, for now the action kicks up a notch.

The scene goes on to find Fez-Pyan running for his life, "A little help here, Gnash," he stops to catch a breath. "We ain't going out like this." No sooner than he avoids one skeletal-biological, more rise to block his path. "We got no choice Gnash, war-mode pal." And with that said, Fez holds his arm out and as he does the xylographitet swoops down to clasp onto his hand, morphing into a gladiator's mace. One that bites. The eerie army prepares to attack, but he lashes out with bone and techno-mace as if possessed by the very devil itself. Biologicals go flying high into the air when hit by the bone, and once caught by the mace, its mecho-maws chomp arms, crack swords and snap spears. And still they come. He barely manages to fight his way to the foot of the pyramid, but the worst is yet to come. The sentient army evolves, learning from mistakes, their fighting strategy improves. With no mouths to shout, the children of the path vibrate their bodies like speakers. They make a terrifying shrill, it is their battle cry.

"Zykut-u!" As the echoes subside, the army clanks its weapons together.

"Zykut-u!" Again, they shout. The echoes reverberate everywhere. "Zykut-u!" Three times in all, a terrifying sound. Its meaning... death.

A brief respite of silence follows, the calm before the storm. Suddenly, fast footsteps, the army of darkness forms into battalions, pressing forward in attack formation, swords, spears and axes all pointing forward with pinpoint accuracy.

"Oh krill, the impossible odds scenario," Fez says, wondering how or if at all he will make it out of this one. "Gnash old pal, prepare to meet your maker..." The xylographitet lets out a sharp explosive growl and grinds its mecho-maws ready for action. Just at that moment, between them and the army appear several white spots of light, revolving in a pattern like the symbol of the atom. Then a bright sparkler enlarges from the centre, to such a size that the army retreats several paces. As the bright star fades, it leaves in its wake two silhouetted figures. With a squint of his eyes, Fez's vision returns to see the shimmering outline of a golden crown headdress. Its gold-leaf feathers shine with a soft wavering light, and as the being turns, a golden pendant necklace shines underneath its robe. "It can't be!" Fez's eyes widen with amazement, "It... it's an Ascetic."

The Ascetic announces his entrance, "The time has come for a guiding light to take control of the situation, and Æther the Golden Ascetic is that light. Of this let there be no uncertainty— foreseen is my arrival—arrival is foreseen!"

"They sent the Golden Ascetic," Fez says, his eyes noticing the other figure, "New-Pyan? It is you."

"Go, get behind me now," commands Æther, who then marches to confront the army, holding his infamous quasi-cudgel in hand, a mythical short-staff of legend. "This staff is named the eight-ways-emergence, passed down to me by my teacher, and his teacher before him," and with that said he displays his skill, a straight-thrust sends a wave of kinetic energy through the staff, releasing an ear-splitting crack. "The Harij-ans call this cudgel

161

the golden-ratio, for its ability to even odds in battle," he walks back several paces. "Allow me to demonstrate."

He holds his arm high and with all his might pile-drives the quasi-cudgel into the ground, setting it into stone. All is quiet at first, until the ground begins to rumble, and a strange mechanised energy transforms the staff into a large pillar, several times higher than it was. Æther advances several steps forward, stops, and snaps his fingers together, upon which two walls of lasers fire out from the pillar, creating walls of light. With a powerful movement Æther brings his arms together, and as they meet the lasers begin to form a narrow corridor, instantly carbonizing any skeletal-biological that meets with their touch. "The odds have somewhat improved." Æther reaches out to touch the laser wall, and as he does it fades, only to return when he moves away.

"In sync!" he says, standing ready. "Creatures of the darkness, bring me your wrath." The hordes of death charge, their skeletal-bones shine an intimidating glow under the ultraviolet light created by the laser walls. Still some try to cross the beams to flank the Golden Ascetic but are instantly incinerated or badly injured. They slow their pace of attack as they funnel down the corridor, realising only a few can approach to fight at once. "Ah hah—you've got the idea."

A four-armed beast sways to and fro, holding in its arms sword, mace, axe and club. It swipes with the axe first in a downward arc, but Æther side-steps the motion, slapping the axe blade to one side with a phenomenal force that the living thing teeters off balance. A moment is all the Golden Ascetic needs as he pushes the monster into the lasers. A second beast attacks, this one taller with two-arms, wielding shield and mace. It swings the mace violently in a sideways arc, but the Golden Ascetic sees through time itself, a second or two in advance before things occur—might as well be an eternity as he avoids the ball and chain, swooping down to uproot the beast. He upends it into the lasers. "Two down!" he says, as two more attack, both flank him and in unison they swipe mace and axe wildly, he waits a second—steps forward—mace and axe surf empty air at first, only to complete their arc, meeting both their wielders head on. "Four down!" Æther says, only to meet three more attacking in unison. With mystical speed he flanks the first creature, pushing it into the lasers, "Once," he says, turning to catch a kick, throwing the second beast with a circular motion into the searing walls of light. "Twice!" he exclaims. This time the third one armed with shield and sword attacks with a forward thrust, but the Golden Ascetic sidesteps, catching the blade between fingers and thumb. The beast appears perplexed and pushes even harder—the blade bends—then in the blink of an eye he grabs the beast's wrist, turning it up as his fingers release the blade, upon which the flexed sword springs back, hitting the beast head-on. "Thrice!" he shouts, as the creature falls. Æther stands holding the beast's sword, "How quickly the odds change," he says, testing the sabre with a cut, parry and thrust. "A tad off-weight, but it will do." And with that he attacks. "Time is tight, I can afford no clemency!" Ten, twenty, forty of the beasts fall at his hand, and still they come. The melee ensues, and in a short time the numbers rise, one hundred of the beasts slain by the Golden Ascetic.

"How?" Fez asks himself, watching awestruck, admiring the god-like being in action. "How does he do it?" Yet still they come, clambering over the uneven causeway the darkling hordes advance, eager to get a shot at the lone fighter.

More on how the battle wages later.

In the meantime, atop the pyramid, Ansebe holds Zara in his arms. He pulls out one of his quantum dice, wafting it under her nose. Dispensing an icy white vapour... her eyes flicker.

"Are you okay, sister?"

"Fine, I think."

"You know what to do?"

Zara stands, takes a deep breath, "Let's see," she paces the ledge aside the Tetragrammaton. "Here goes," again she holds her hands together, to form a triangle with her thumbs and index fingers, gently placing her hands on the stone. The capstone repels back her hands, she places her hand over mouth on watching the surface morph into a golden-eyelid. It opens. On seeing Zara, the pupil inside its large opaline-iris dilates wide open. "I give you the Eye of Horus," she says, overwhelmed as a tear rolls down her face. As if in synchronicity, a large tear wells up in the Eye of Horus. From the Eye, an intense look of sorrow. It talks inside Zara's mind, "No, it's not enough," she cries. The Eye blinks, "You want me to keep going, to have faith?" It blinks once again, "Persevere with compassion and love? This is the key to the ultimate-salvation?" The Eye blinks once more, "I… I don't understand," she sighs, as the Eye closes one last time, "I'll try." Zara gently touches the Eye, and in a space between time the last conduit of Horus folds inwards, disappearing to a place beyond the realms of imagination.

"Well done, sister," Ansebe says.

"You usually call me child."

"The child is no more."

"It's not enough," she sighs. "The Eye told me, our journey so far has been for nothing."

"Nothing, you say?" Ansebe stops, closes his eyes and searches his thoughts, "Not for nothing! I see possibility, everything to fight for. The shamanic mind tells me so."

Just then, something appears next to them, they turn. "It's New-Pyan!" yells Zara, happy on seeing the baby tetraporphyrin levitating beside her. "You've grown." Then from inside the tetra a glow, which expands into a bright sphere and vanishes along with everyone on top of the pyramid. A second later they all reappear near the foot of the pyramid. In front of them they see Fez sitting with Gnash and the Fy, but it is the battle that wages in front of them that steals their gaze.

"Good boy Newp, you've brought them down," Fez says, patting the tetra. "Hi, guys."

"Is… is that the Golden Ascetic?" Ansebe asks.

"The one and only."

"We should help him," Zara says, stepping forward, "he's on his own out there."

"Wait and watch," Fez says, holding her back, "history's being made, why spoil the story I'm planning to write."

"What story, you nut-job?"

"I think I'll call it… Golden Ascetic Defeats the Army of Giants."

"Most of them are little, not an ogre in sight."

"Hmm… semantics. You should've been here earlier."

As the battle ensues, Æther notices the family Pyan behind him. "Time to end this," he says, walking through the corridor and once free of the lasers, he snaps his fingers. In an instant the laser walls close, leaving behind in their wake a sea of fallen creatures.

"The battle is over!" shouts Fez.

Æther walks up to the large pillar and claps his hands, upon which the eight-ways-emergence winds back down into a normal-sized short-staff, which he retrieves out of the ground. Fez applauds the Golden Ascetic, "Extraordinary… and to think I could have been your disciple."

"Alas, Serpent That Shines, your destiny was to train with the Bitter Sage," Æther says.

"I was forced to train with him."

"The Ones-and-the-Zeroes chose your path."

"And we all know how that worked out!"

"The Bitter Sage is my equal, had you returned to complete the final levels of your training, you would also have been—as you say—extraordinary."

"Those numbers are full of it," Fez says with a lopsided grin, only for Æther to thwack him on the head with his staff.

"Don't disrespect the Ones-and-the-Zeroes. The trouble I went to retrieve them. Now, kneel before me."

"Why? You're not my master!" Fez says touching his head, his indignation roused.

"And you don't want me to be?"

"What? Oh yeh… I mean yes great master." Fez kneels before the Golden Ascetic.

"Fez-Pyan the Serpent That Shines, I accept you as my next disciple."

"The greatest system ever devised. I thought I'd never get to learn it."

"There is one condition," Æther says. "Answer me this," he holds up a finger, "a pride of targabats go hunting. The hunt involves an innate combination of instinct and learning. Instinct drives their overall strategy, use of stealth and ferocity. What does the learning improve?"

"Their odds?"

"No."

"The hunt?"

"Not in the slightest, nature is a hard taskmaster."

"Their method of killing?"

"Last chance. As I want to mentor you, ask yourself—how you have all got this far?"

"Teamwork?" Fez replies, hoping the answer is right, at which point Æther prods him on the brow with his staff.

165

"Exactly! Single-mindedness has power, but multiple minds have unity of purpose and with that comes possibility."

"So, does this mean I'm a disciple of the Ultimate Salvation?"

"You are indeed, arrival is yours," the Golden Ascetic chuckles. On hearing this Zara raises an eyebrow, in response he turns to face her.

"Zara Hanson, how you've grown. You are wondering why Sifu Wang's school bears the same name."

"Yes, my master's school had the same name... I'm curious."

"Tis a story for another day," he walks up and touches a finger to her forehead. "Now you are also a disciple."

"What? She has to kneel as well," Fez says, in an indignant tone.

"No, she doesn't. It is I who should be kneeling to her. This is your first lesson, to gain from loss of ego—"

"I've always been afraid of dreams," a voice shouts, "of what may come to pass and all that fearfulness." All turn to see Agent Orange standing side by side with Actinide-15.

"You know, ever since I joined the black suits, the worst of the worst—unacknowledged emissaries tasked with keeping your kind from ever indulging the likes of the quintessential American family, I've often wondered, why all the hullaballoo?" Orange, paces up and down like a madman, balanced on his shoulder sits an RPG7 rocket-propelled grenade launcher. He continues, "Then I saw the light, I realised that the people—the lemmings—can't handle all of this," he turns, to show with his hand the city. "Hell no, they can't even handle a presidential election. If they knew one iota of the shit that I know, they would all be running for the hills—abductions, illegal experimentation, that's just the tip of the ice-berg."

"Sir, perhaps we can talk," Zara says, trying to appeal to Agent Orange's human side.

"Don't!" he screams, pointing the RPG7 at her. "Just don't," he nods at the pyramid, "it's stopped working, nothing to stop me from firing. Say... you shouldn't even be standing, lost two of my best men to you girlie."

"They were grade A losers, like you!" Zara says, realising he sanctioned the hit on her.

166

"No, they kept shit from getting out," shouts Orange, pacing back and forth. "My first day on the job, we had the curious case that we called the oyster files. Our think-tank worked out the truth behind so called alien-implants, and it scared the hell out of me... made me realise why we do what we do."

"That is nothing to do with us, it is the Maitra. We deliver harsh justice to any of them found wandering your skies," Ansebe says, trying to calm Agent Orange.

"You don't think I know that? Look, I realise you're the good guys, I get it."

"We are not Maitra, we are peaceful."

"Peaceful, huh?" Orange appears to calm down, "Hell... you're free to leave. Just go, get outta here." As they begin to leave, a grimace from Orange, "Wait—not you!" he shouts, aiming the grenade launcher at Fez, "you're coming with me. If anyone has a problem with this, Actinide is locked-n-loaded. See his headset, it's ready to play his favourite tune—and when he hears it, he'll kick ass at my command."

"It's okay, I'll go with him," Fez says, holding his arms high.

"That's more like it, now have a nice day the rest of you. It's nothing personal, it's just business, that's all."

"I shan't allow this deal," shouts the Golden Ascetic, marching in front of Fez, "this one's interaction may yet save your world."

"Well, then..." Orange aims the RPG7, but in a moment before the moment Æther throws the eight-ways-emergence like a javelin, it spins out a sharp tip piercing Orange's trigger arm. "Intoxication," Æther says, and with that Orange's arm drops limp, paralysed.

"God dammit, Actinide, attack! Kill... kill them all!" Actinide leans forward, ready to attack. Orange adds, gloating, "Look at the lucky man. Well Mr Fez-man, you know Actinide's undefeatable, 'bout time your luck ran short. Time to pay the piper." An insane chuckle leaves Orange's lips, which Fez mimics, preparing to meet the attack head on.

"I will handle this," Æther says, throwing a small device to the floor, which opens out in the shape of a star-fish, and projects a hologram many metres high. Inside the hologram appear two giant-sized Elementians. The giants relay a sign-language while tracing with their hands holo-geometric shapes and patterns. On

167

seeing this Actinide-15 stands mesmerised and takes off his headset. Æther adds, "I warn you this Terran, these two are the Elementian's parents, from a world most advanced. They can see their son, and shall star-jump into the hologram to arrive here shortly, of that I assure you—"

"Actinide, attack," shouts Orange, but his instructions are unheard. "Aargh!" he screams, holding his arm. Æther walks to Agent Orange and retrieves his staff.

"Your arm will recover. Heed my next words carefully. It was a star-jump malfunction that stranded the one you call Actinide on your Moon, wiping his memories in the process. The Elementian's parents have been searching for him, when they arrive, his mind shall be restored—and when that happens, you shouldn't be here." And with that, from out of the star-fish device a large expanding-sphere of light, inflating ever so high. The sphere evaporates to reveal Actinide's parents, far taller than their son and no longer a hologram—before them stand two majestic giants. The father places a hand on the son's head and goes on to restore his mind. With an upwards glance the Elementian's eyes burn white-hot, and as they do, so does his hand. Smoke billows from Actinide's head, but when it dissipates, it reveals his eyes, no longer fixated and dark but alive and moving. The father turns and gazes at Æther with a look of gratitude, both nod at each other in acknowledgement. It is at this point that Actinide's eyes dart to one side on seeing Agent Orange, after which he turns to face him, shaking his head ominously.

"No, not happening, can't be!" Orange cries out, then flees desperately, trying to escape over the uneven path of octagonal stepping stones. Fez goes to give chase, but with his staff Æther blocks his path.

"Let the Terran go! We can trace his movements, he may prove useful."

"Trace him?" Fez punches his fist to palm, "Nano-transmitters! The toxin was laced with nano-transmitters."

"Exactly!" Æther says, as he walks to New-Pyan, "You have been patient, little one. Now you can take us all to your mother."

A nearby lake, a bright sphere expands for a second or two then bursts, leaving in its wake our intrepid team. They barely have time to adjust when New-Pyan shrieks with delight, on seeing Por-Pyan breaking out from the water's depths—she swings around, levitating playfully, reunited with her offspring. They sing the song of the tetraporphyrin, beautiful harmonics resonate from the astonishing creatures.

"We are re-energized," the Golden Ascetic says, "a few minutes of tetra-song combines the six healing sounds into one," he holds his arms out wide, "each sound restores our vitality and enhances our perception." All feel the effect of the miracle-frequencies, then no sooner had the song started, it ends.

"Golden Ascetic, how'd you know about the Elementian?" Fez asks.

"On receiving Rohza's status reports, I ran a search and found the Elementians had contacted Tranquillity some time ago—to report the one missing—and left with us a star-fish holo-drive, should we ever locate him."

"What's Tranquillity?" Zara raises an eyebrow, curious at such a name.

"It is a place of peace," Æther opens a hand, slowly tensing it into a fist, "of unity," he smiles. "You'll see, when we arrive there, although we best not to use New-Pyan, he tends to wander some—"

"Where has this little one been?" Zara asks, hugging New-Pyan affectionately.

"I do not know, he was brought to Tranquillity by the Elb. On learning this, I returned to Tranquillity to investigate further, and on arrival I found seven Elb waiting for me, led by one that called itself the Elb of Paradoxes."

"What did they want, so close to Terra?" Ansebe asks.

"Worry not, they came in peace to return the tetra, then they departed. As they took their leave, the Elb of Paradoxes said to me, 'One day will sense make.'"

"Sense... make sense of what?" Ansebe's acupoints glow, he's ill at ease.

"Of this I do not know, it was at this time I decided to take a more direct interaction in your mission," he looks Ansebe in the eye, "that and receiving a writ that the trial of strength is to take place within nine solar-winds."

"Then we are out of time," Ansebe says, with a solemn expression.

"Not so, I felt no fear… according to the Ones-and-the-Zeroes, I should have been fearful. I was not. This troubled me so, I could not sleep nor meditate and then it hit me—I remembered something in the writings of Kyubi-K. Ansebe, can you recite the inner verses of Kyubi-K, more specifically the one that mentions the Elb?"

"I can," Ansebe closes his eyes and recites the verse in question,

"Two intra-dimensional entities met in Kyubi-K's dream, to sing of designs of that which is not. Unconcerned that the dream-holder would question or recall, for to recall the infinite using the finite was folly.

"Hitherto, the dreamer awoke.

"A quirk, a rift, a strange change.

"Dimensions separated, and yet, recall he did.

"So, the recording of the higher ones began.

"The writings of Kyubi-K speak not of such things.

"And hence knowledge of the mysterious Elb is never attained."

"Bravo!" Æther says, "on recalling those same words, I was left with a notion, one I could not clear from my mind. At first, I dismissed it as farfetched, but my thoughts kept returning to it. So, I said to myself—what if?"

"What if?" Ansebe replies, with a curious frown.

"Yes, what if divine revelation is hidden in this prophesy. What if Kyubi-K had somehow stumbled upon hidden knowledge about the Elb, such knowhow he was desperate to keep secret."

"Those verses are nothing more than philosophical poetry, Kyubi-K said this himself."

"Are they?" Æther stomps his staff, "Tell me, why would Rohza start processing hidden algorithms now, for this specific mission, one that involves the Elb?"

"This we have wondered, she has already hinted at a cypher."

"Rohza, has this mission affected your sentient-being in anyway at all?"

"Query. Yes, the Painted Symbol mission unlocked a sub-routine, hidden algorithms on my ghost-drive."

"Exactly!" Æther says pointing a finger skywards, "We shall talk more on this later, for now we leave for Tranquillity." And with that said they all board Por-Pyan, for the space leviathan to phase them away.

Chapter Twenty-Three
Tranquillity

The tetraporphyrin phases into orbit around the Moon, familiar with the journey, the space-leviathan swoops down towards a large dark, uninviting crater, disappearing out of sight. As the tetra descends into the subterranean darkness, a complex of interconnected geodesic domes comes into vision, appearing like faint glimmers of aquatic-spawn clinging to the side of the crater. Æther taps some glyphs on his arm, and on doing so one of the larger spheres changes its luminosity, shining bright with a chromium-iridescence filled with a rainbow hue.

"That one Por-Pyan, head for the brightest." The tetraporphyrin approaches; as it makes contact, nano-technology reshapes the dome's surface tension to absorb the leviathan, and once inside they dock safely. The belly of the tetra opens for all to disembark.

"Welcome to Tranquillity, haven for weary travellers from all corners of the Eyt Ree-Juhns, a place of peace," Æther says, showing the way.

"Where are the travellers?" Zara asks, looking at the empty spheres, holographic walkways, walls and corridors.

"We are on lock-down, that none may interrupt our plans."

"A wise choice," Ansebe says.

"Never mind that, is the safe-haven serving intoxication?" Fez asks, eager to drink.

"Of course, we have a variety of liquids from the farthest reaches of the Eyt Ree-Juhns."

"I'll see you all in there later," Fez says, "I'm taking a spatial-spa." He jumps into a smaller sphere, upon which Gnash and the Fy follow. Zara looks on taken aback, as they seem to turn invisible inside it.

Seeing this Æther chuckles, "Privacy mode." He beckons the others, "Take a spatial-spa if you please. We shall regroup after some much-needed rest."

Zara takes a tentative step onto one of the bubble-like orbs. She pushes her foot down, it sinks inside; she smiles and takes the plunge. As she submerges—thoughts, emotions, breath, energy and time seem to stop, a side-effect of the oxygen created by the sphere's molecular chemistry in synthesis with its harmonic eco-resonance. Zara closes her eyes, meditates for what seems like minutes—time passes—a holographic alarm awakes her from a deep slumber. The sphere talks to her.

"< Welcome, Zara Hanson. We are Tranquillity Sentience. We are self-aware, pleased to meet you. >"

"Oh, a talking sphere?"

"< Yes, we are Tranquillity Sentience, you are the Zara Hanson. >"

"I believe so," Zara says, slightly amused.

"< You will be pleased to know your health score is 98.756. We have taken the liberty of washing your bone-marrow. We also strengthened your sinews, irradiated your body tissue, and best of all, boosted your auto-immune system to near perfection. >"

"You have?" Zara opens and closes her hands, "Whoa… that feels exceptional."

"< You are exceptional. We have also taken the opportunity to weave you a new suit, like your old one but far more advanced, please see… >"

In front of her an orb appears, inside it an all-in-one black body suit, woven by Sentience. Like her old suit it has thin white strips running down each arm, except it is made from billions of nano-crystals as is the new-design Z on the chest, which sits under a hieroglyph, a white outline shaped like a flying saucer. She reaches into the orb and holds the garment up.

"I guess I should thank you."

"< It is our pleasure to serve the great Zara Hanson. >"

"Please, just call me Zara."

"< Zara, why don't you try the suit on? >"

"Sure, oh… how do I get into it? It's seamless."

"< Just place it over your shoulders. >" Zara discards her old suit.

"What the…" As the nano-crystals touch her skin, the suit morphs at the molecular level, wrapping around her body, even weaving a set of boots.

"Now that's neat. How'd I get out of it?"

"< The suit is a combination of xylo-oblong technology. After some practice, you will be able to control the tech by thought alone. >"

"I see… what does it do?"

"< Nothing yet, it is new, it is still learning, growing. It is like Sentience. When it has grown, it will make its presence known, it will communicate with you. >"

"You mean it will talk to me?"

"< It will, among other things. >"

"Then I'll call it Presence," looking at her suit, a smile spreads across her face.

"< Zara, your attendance has been requested by the Golden Ascetic in the safe-haven. Have a wonderful stay. >"

Tranquillity Sentience directs Zara to safe-haven, a recreational sphere which stimulates enjoyment, fine-tunes emotions, thoughts and intuition. She enters the sphere to be greeted by Æther and Fez.

"Zara, come and join us," Fez shouts, slightly woozy from drinking. "Here, have one of these," he grabs a tumbler, and pours from a bottle, "it's a green-mist, let's get intoxicated."

"You know me so well," she jokes, downing the drink in one. "Another."

"Wait for it, wait for it!" Fez says with an expectant smile.

"That's nasty…" she shuts her eyes, a sour-taste, "hits the spot, and then some!"

"Nice threads, look-ing good."

"Why thank you, a present from Sentience."

"Have you ever been intoxicated, Zara?" Æther asks, also slightly the worse for wear."

"You obviously haven't been with me in Camden on a Saturday night, give me another."

"Let's do this," shouts Fez, lining up fifteen shots of green-mist, five for each person. "Let's not forget Gnash," he adds, pouring directly from the bottle for Gnash-Byte to guzzle away, only to burst into a fit of hiccups, bouncing around with each one. "Technical glitch," Fez says, as he goes to pat the xylographitet, only to fall off his stool. Zara and Æther cannot help but burst into fits of laughter and shortly thereafter safe-haven is alive with their merrymaking and games.

In the meantime, Ansebe and Sub-Rohza wander in the jungle geodesic dome, a greenhouse with its own mini ecosystem. Ansebe walks, deep in thought.

"It is peaceful here Rohza, perhaps we can untwine that which is written in your code, the shamanic mind presses me—what secrets troubled Kyubi-K?"

"Boss, the first riddle was answered by Zara and the answer was DNA."

"It was, I do not know how we missed the answer," Ansebe says, shaking his head.

"The other oddity was when she made physical contact with Fez, a codec synthesized with the nano-tech you administered to allow her to pilot the Newara. These two aspects must have conspired with pre-existing specialities in her genetic code—creating the messages on her arm."

"Which said she is both a primer and a cypher, the one which unites the three. We already know that us three were united, but what does this have to do with Kyubi-K?"

"Boss, only those coded may gain access to Kyubi-K's burial chamber, to confer with his spirit-waves."

"What is she the primer for? What cypher does she hold? I wonder… Rohza, please bring up a hologram of the chamber." Sub-Rohza projects the main entry to the burial chamber. Ansebe walks around inspecting the layout, thumb and fingers against his head, concentrating.

"Zoom into the onyx-rock." The hologram zooms into a large rock with two engraved handprints. "The Lyrian caretakers gain access to the chamber by placing their paw-hands on here," he places his hands on the hologram, and as he does his jaw drops. "How could I have not noticed?" Hidden inside the large handprints an outline for a far smaller set of hands, human hands.

"Rohza, overlay a hologram of Zara's hands onto the handprints." Sub-Rohza overlays a hologram of Zara accessing the onyx-rock, her hands fitting snugly into the finely chiselled recesses.

"Worlds apart!" Ansebe's eyes widen, "We need to go to Kyubi-K's burial chamber, to Tik-Ingkeyk."

In the meantime, in the safe-haven Fez and Zara are playing a game of slaps with Æther, both frustrated at their attempts, both unable to beat his uncanny reflexes.

"Haven't had this much fun in ages," Zara says, resting her chin in both hands. "So tell me Æther, why the Ultimate Salvation school, why me?"

"You really wish to know?"

"Try me," a tad inebriated she slips from of her stool.

"Well," Æther catches her, "I suppose—"

"Try me!" Zara yells, and with a merry smile sits back on her stool.

"There is a tale, you really wish to hear it?"

"Yes, we want to hear it!"

"This I've got to hear," Fez says, downing another shot of green-mist. Æther tells the tale…

"It is the late nineteenth century, the last days of the Silk Road in China," he grabs his staff and stomps it to the ground. "It was a time of great change on Terra, but the old ways still flourished—the ways of the warrior!

"Now a merchant's caravan was making the perilous journey along the Silk Road accompanied by bodyguards, an infamous Chinese boxer and his band of brothers. Stopped in their tracks they did, on seeing from the west a strong wind picking up, a sandstorm brewing. Unseen by the travellers, high in the sky a flying saucer flew overhead—the Yún! In the distance it landed, then no sooner had it started, the sandstorm began to dissipate, as if it had never been. The sand cloud cleared to reveal a lone figure, a Grey. The Ascetic known as Oracle of the Four Winds. The one that never dies, whom for the sake of this account we shall call Lives-a-long-time.

"The story goes on to tell how Lives-a-long-time held up a hand for the caravan to stop, upon which the leader dismounted from his camel, and said to the Ascetic, 'What is it you want demon, you dare to stop Wang-Yin?' 'I do!' said Lives-a-long-time, at which Wang-Yin roared: 'Then prepare to taste my iron-palm heavy-as-the-world!'

"Lives-a-long-time wasn't worried by such threats and simply said, 'I come to offer you divine salvation, the heavenly immortal way of universal form.' Now, Wang-Yin was a young man, a famous boxer who did not suffer fools gladly, especially strangers of unusual appearance, and so he readied to fight. On seeing this Lives-a-long-time shouted: 'Stop! I am of the way that is all ways, bow to me as your teacher—this is the easy path.' 'The hard path it is,' shouted Wang-Yin, who stepped forward to attack. 'So be it,' replied Lives-a-long-time.

"And so, Wang-Yin, never bested before in all of China, went in to attack, as he said he would, and struck Lives-a-long-time on the shoulder with his iron-palm, but the Ascetic simply absorbed the strike and retaliated with the unknown-technique. The action seemed at first to Wang-Yin like a gentle tap, but as Wang-Yin went to follow through, he looked on in disbelief unable to move, paralysed. Lives-a-long-time then said, 'The intangible hand cannot be subdued, even by ghosts and spirits.' 'Who are you?' screamed Wang-Yin. 'My name is unimportant,' replied the Ascetic. 'What is it you want?' asked Wang-Yin. Now at that point Lives-a-long-time simply smiled and said, 'Your assistance.' Well Wang-Yin just stood there speechless. Lives-a-long-time then touched him a second time, and he could move! Overcome with emotion, Wang-Yin fell to his knees humbled.

"On seeing this Lives-a-long-time said, 'Over the years a dream-form shall teach you this art of mine called the Ultimate Salvation, which you'll master. One day, a relative shall ask you to teach his son, and you will. He will become the next generation master, but he shall only pass his skills onto a girl— this is my boon to you.' Wang-Yin then asked, 'What do I gain from this?' 'You become legendary,' said Lives-a-long-time.

"The Yún then came in to land beside them, whereupon Lives-a-long-time stepped into the saucer, but before departing, he said, 'When three bright shiners descend from the heavens, the second generation shall pass the system onto a young girl.'"

Zara and Fez gawp at the Golden Ascetic, both starry-eyed and speechless, a moment's silence sees them both reaching to neck another shot of green-mist in one. "Whoa, that's a mad story," Zara says, profoundly affected, "but why go to all that trouble?"

Æther leans over to hold her hands, "Lives-a-long-time was a seer of prophesies, the odd things he's done are many."

"That's quite a story," Fez says, drinking another shot in one.

"It is time for us to retire, come Zara, I shall escort you back," Æther says.

"You two go, I'm staying here for one more."

"We'll see you in the morrow then, Fez."

"Yeh, we'll see ya later goopy face," Zara says, giggling to herself.

"So, tell me all about the Ascetics," she says, clutching onto Æther's arm as they leave. "It all started with the first Ascetic…"

Fez stays to carry on drinking, his penchant for self-destruction masked by his merrymaking. Ahead of safe-haven barring his access to yet another bottle of green-mist, he quickly grabs all three remaining bottles. Gnash-Byte and the Fy all sit on the bar looking at him, he raises an eyebrow, and slurs, "What are you looking at…?" then has another drink. "Green-mist leaves no after-affects," he says talking to himself, "I'll just get where I want to be, and then that's it. No harm done."

On his way back, having just walked Zara to her quarters, Æther is met by Ansebe. "Golden Ascetic, we must leave now for Tik-Ingkeyk, time is of the essence."

"Too intoxicated, no travel till ready," Æther replies, waving his hand.

"Leave we must, it is most urgent."

"Universe is going nowhere," Æther stomps his staff, "Tik-Ingkeyk is not going anywhere, we'll find it later."

"But I have made a crucial discovery, one that we need to investigate urgently."

Æther stops in his tracks, looks at Ansebe as if reading his mind. He closes his eyes, trying to glimpse the future and answers with a solemn tone.

"If we leave now, we'll only get into trouble. Those who rush into battle are easily fatigued. How much worse would the already fatigued fare?"

"We are not going into battle."

"There's always a battle. We live in a universe inhospitable to life. It's a miracle we live at all."

"And yet here we stand, while precious time passes," replies Ansebe, keen to leave.

"It is said, make the host and the guest exchange places. Are you not doing this with your mind?" Æther touches a finger to his forehead, "Defeat the enemy from within by infiltrating the enemy's camp under the guise of friendship. In this way you can discover their weakness and then, when the enemy is least prepared, strike directly at the source of their strength."

"I defer to your experience, Golden Ascetic."

"Now you know how to go into battle, without first going into battle. This ends the lesson. We leave in the morrow."

In safe-haven, having downed the last of the three bottles of green-mist, Fez lurches to and fro, holding his arms out as if walking on a tightrope. "One foot in front of the other," he says to himself, carefully trying to retain his balance. After some time, he sobers up ever so slightly thanks to his advanced metabolism. On the way back he passes a sphere, when something inside seems to talk to him. It is the gallery of gold and silver, a domain which houses historical artefacts and advanced technologies. He kneels to take a closer look, a strange ticking noise coming from inside calls out to him. "Tat… tat… tat… tat… tat…" He places both hands on the sphere and bends forward to listen, whereupon he falls into it, followed by Gnash who lands on his lap. The Fy follow, several of which bounce off his head onto the floor. He shakes his head, and as he looks around, his mouth drops at the sight of the artefacts on display. Sentience queries his presence.

"< This is Tranquillity Sentience. You have not stated your access rights, on what authority are you here? >"

"Ahh… I have a xylographitet?" Fez says, knowing they are only assigned to high-ranking officials.

"< We see. You are an Ascetic or one of the Juhj-iz perhaps? >"

"I'm a disciple of the Golden Ascetic," he replies, chancing his luck.

"< Confirmed. Access allowed. >"

He gives a once over look around the gallery, "It's a freakin' arsenal!" The ticking noise draws his attention to the largest artefact and on seeing it a shimmer of light reflects off his face, coming from a giant Arthurian sword. He walks to it, stands under it mesmerised. A weapon made for Titans, its size end-to-end as long as he is tall. He reaches up to touch it.

"Sentience, what's this sword called?"

"< It is the Sword of Mars. >"

"Interesting," he turns to inspect a large looking-glass construct in the centre of the sphere. "What's this?"

179

"< A hyperspace quantum bridge. >"

"You mean a wormhole."

"< Not quite. It is only stable enough to transfer inanimate matter one-way. It can send but does not receive. >"

"I see, where's it looking now?"

"< A secret location, on earth. >"

Just then Fez has a crazy notion. "Can you view the planet Mars, with this contraption?" The looking glass shimmers, power surges through the device as glyphs dial new coordinates, and the surface of Mars appears through the glass device. "Mars!" Fez says with a quirky grin. "Tell me, can you find the NASA rover?"

"< Here it is, viewing it now. >"

"Is the bridge open?"

"< The path is open… what is it you are doing? >"

"Orders from high command!" With that said he takes the Sword of Mars in his hands. "Heavier than expected, like a dead weight," he says, swaying to and fro as he steps towards the looking glass with the giant sword. He holds the cross-shaped handle and supporting the blade with his other hand, throws it with a shot-put technique, aiming for the rover. "Shot!" shouts Fez, but the sword lands nowhere to be seen. On Mars, however, the giant sword hurtles through a shimmer of light, landing upright like a cross for a brief second, only to topple over onto the planet's rust-red surface.

"Where's it gone? It's nowhere to be seen," Fez says, upset at missing his target.

"< We are viewing a magnified telescopic view through the quantum bridge, the actual location of portal and what we are viewing differs by some distance. >"

"Frak!"

"< You were hoping to hit the rover? Why would high-command want you to do such a thing? >"

"To keep a certain team of black-suits busy. The look on their faces would have been priceless, a rover with a giant sword run through it. I guess we're going to have to settle with the possibility of NASA snapping an image of the sword sometime."

"< That was an act of attempted sabotage. >"

"I can't help it, I've got a rare genetic disorder that makes me contemptuous of consequences." With that said, Fez sits down, reeling from the effects of drinking so much green-mist. A few seconds later he falls to one side, sleeping in the gallery of gold and silver.

Chapter Twenty-Four
Transition

Having slept on matters, Æther calls an audience in the Sphere of Meditative Traditions—a place where the probabilities of events are forecast using the sixty-four divinations, whereby the proper course of action is decided. The Golden Ascetic stands at the end of a large hall, in full regalia, wearing a robe made from the finest weaves and silks the universe has to offer; his golden crown headdress with feathers of gold all preened back and out on display, looking like a bird of paradise. Ansebe, Zara and Sub-Rohza approach quietly. His back to them Æther waves a hand for them to sit. He stands blindfolded, inside a circle of eight divining holograms, and begins to chant the first incantation of the guiding light ceremony, "I, Æther the Golden Ascetic consort to Kae-Rai of the Eyt Ree—where is Fez?" He pulls off his blindfold, "Was a message not sent to his quarters?"

"You didn't?" Ansebe whispers, shaking his head.

"Did what?" Zara replies in a low voice, a part of her already knowing the answer.

"You didn't leave him on his own, with access to the green-mist supplies?"

"Oh… we did."

"The last time this happened, he stole a Maitra ship and intercepted Beagle 2, the British Mars Lander, as it was touching down on the surface of Mars."

"He did?"

"Yes, he did! Shot it with an electro-magnetic pulse, caused it to fail."

"Why?"

"His words, 'Because they were neglecting Venus.'"

"What?" Zara says, with a snorting giggle.

"He said it made sense at the time."

"Fez is clearly incorrigible," Zara says, biting her lip so as not to laugh.

Marching out of the hall Æther stops, shakes his head then speaks. "Sentience, where is Fez?"

"< Asleep in the gallery of gold and silver. >"

"What mischief has he been up to?"

"< He said he was carrying out orders from high command. >"

"Tell me no more, my imagination already runs wild."

The Golden Ascetic stomps away to confront Fez, "You three stay, we shall return shortly." And with that said he upswings his staff, "Escalation!" The word triggers a change in the wooden stave, upon which it clicks and whirs, transforming into the eight-ways-emergence.

The scene goes on to find Æther standing over Fez, who lies sound asleep, curled up, snoozing contently. He leans down to lay a hand on Fez's head, draws a deep breath and whispers, "Sssss," followed by, "shhhh." As he removes his hand, Fez bolts upright wide-awake. He looks around, as he does Gnash rouses as do the eight Fy.

"Where am I?" asks Fez, rubbing the back of his neck.

"The gallery of gold and silver, it has no name. More's the question, why are you here?"

"I'm not sure."

"The Sword of Mars?" Æther asks, turning to gaze where it once was.

"It… it talked to me. It needed to return."

"Where is it now?"

"On Mars… why would it be there?" Fez holds his head in hands, "Oh yeh… it's definitely on Mars," he shakes his head. "Threw it thru-a-looking glass—it told me to do it."

Æther chuckles, reaching over he tugs at Fez's shoulder shawl, "Maybe these little things were talking to you?"

"The Nan-arcons?"

"Let's see… Sentience, a holo-circle if you please." A holographic circle appears. "Place the Golden Fleece inside the circle." Fez lays his shawl down. "Sentience, please request an audience with the Nan-arcons."

"< Sentience running. >"

The presence that is Sentience coalesces into complex holograms, geometric shapes spin over the fleece. Attempts to communicate are simple at first, circle denotes a circle, square equals a square and so on, building up in complexity. After a brief pause, Sentience fast-tracks through a myriad of geometric symbols, light spectra, sound frequencies and harmonics, until…

"< Sentience has established contact. >"

The micro-life forms transmit a voice… "Who requests an audience with the Nan-arcons?"

"I am Æther the Golden Ascetic, consort to Kae-Rai of the Eyt Ree-Juhns."

"We are the Nan-arcons, created as a negative effect to the Elb. We come from beyond. Once we were one, one race, one form, one purpose. That which we were given refuge was torn into three shards, by deviant Arcons re-weaving your reality."

"Who are the Arcons?"

"Our creators."

"Why did you manipulate Fez into moving the Sword of Mars?"

"No manipulation, only the suggestion."

"Then why the suggestion?"

"We were unable to complete our course, to free you from the capricious whims of the Elb, from their intra-dimensional syphoning of life-potential."

"Why return the Sword to Mars?"

"Suggestion."

"Suggestion? Please elaborate."

"We use suggestion to steer events."

"Why were you steering such events?"

"For an audience—and future events which shall be of benefit to all."

"I see."

"No, Nan-arcons see all. We see the Elb bringing dark ages to your Eyt Ree-Juhns."

"Can you prevent these dark-ages?"

"Not directly, only influence events for positive outcome. This is why the Ternion bestowed our presence to your mission. We must now sleep, hide from view, five Elb are approaching. We shall return."

"< Sentience has lost contact. >"

"To the Hall of Meditative Traditions," shouts Æther, moving at uncanny speed.

"On it!" Fez yells. They both sprint to meet the others. As they make their entrance, Sentience sounds the alarm. Everyone stands ready for action.

"We have visitors," Æther says, stomping his staff three times, upon which Sentience produces a holographic view from outside the crater, high above the Moon.

"The Hand of Ice!" Ansebe shouts, on seeing the hologram of the supermassive crystalline structure. Its uncanny appearance made from five separate vessels all docked together, giving the appearance of a giant-hand carved from rock crystal.

"It is the full hand, all five of the Elb's Celestial Witnesses have assembled," Æther calls out, "Sentience, deploy shields!" Outside from one of the five glacial digits an orb materialises, it is the Elb of Tropical Convergence. The First Celestial Witness. Downwards the Elb descends, once inside the crater, it shines an incandescent light, burning through Tranquillity's shields. Holographic defences fail, with the Elb's tangibility neither here nor there nothing can stop it. The lone Elb advances past the shields as if they were no more an obstruction than sunlight.

"It approaches," Æther waves a hand, gesturing all to stay calm. Outside the Elb appears levitating like a translucent apparition, and with a ghostly breeze it appears inside the Hall. Its transparent surface reveals a panoramic window into a tropical forest world within, so vibrant that it glistens a green hue. As the lone Elb comes closer, the fragrance of the rainforest, exotic plants and flowers fills the air. A sweet scent at first, but then it turns a pungent aroma, one that alters the sense's grip on reality when breathed in. The Elb's toxic attack turns their minds into a weakened state so bizarre and unfamiliar that they are unable to stand. All except for the Golden Ascetic.

"Your kaleidoscopic tricks won't work on me, I am neither in the mind nor in the body."

The Elb announces itself inside Æther's thoughts.

"< We know. This one, the Elb of Tropical Convergence, first Celestial Witness requests a parley, do we have a truce? >

"We do, parley it is."

"< Then we have terms. >"

"You are here to deliver your ultimatum?"

"< We are. You know what follows, Golden Ascetic. The Terrans are facing oblivion, change is not in their nature. Do you still wish to defend them? >"

"That is our wish."

"< And so, a new trial of strength will take place. Do you have a litigator? >"

"Ansebe is still retained as counsel for the Terrans."

"We… we request a deferment," Ansebe says, struggling to speak as he fights off the effects of the Elb's toxins.

"< Denied, we have already served the notice of the nine solar winds. >"

"Then… so be it," Ansebe says, with a mystified look, the words he meant to say having just been altered by the Elb.

"< Where do you wish the trial of strength to take place? >"

"The centre of Milky-Way," Fez shouts, catching the Elb off guard. "Now frak-off toadstool face, back to whatever enchanted woods you came from." Now, this may seem a strange thing to say, but as far as Fez is concerned he is looking at a giant red-mushroom, peppered with white and yellow spots.

On hearing this the Elb of Tropical Convergence departs, leaving a chilling message, "< We have terms. The silver faced one has chosen, centre of this galaxy it is. >"

Æther turns to the others. Ansebe is the first to recover while Fez sits in a dreamland-state, the Elb's toxins still in control of his mind. Alas, Zara is the worst affected, down and out for the count. Æther takes control of the situation.

"Rohza, please see to Zara. Sentience, analyse this Elb's foul toxins, synthesise an anti-toxin, we need some protection against it." They go to work. Sub-Rohza beams a hologram into Zara, flushing the toxins out of her system—she wakes, rubbing her eyes. Next, Æther rubs his hands together, and placing a hand on Fez's head, he whispers, "Hawwww." As he removes his hands Fez jumps to his feet, on guard ready to fight. "Take your time, breathe. You've had quite a mind-bending experience, made you blurt out the most absurd location for the trial of strength."

"Wha… what location?" Fez says, with a slight stammer, still recovering from the toxins.

"The centre of the Milky-Way. The location is either the chance choice of folly or serendipity in action. We shall see."

"Perhaps it's fate," Zara says, supping tonic-water from a beaker, "I just had the weirdest dream, but it seemed so real."

"A dream?" Æther asks curiously, as he gives her more water, "Take your time."

"It was vivid, so real," she raises her eyebrows, "I was lost in it. It was like parts of me were scattered all over time itself. The past, future and present all in an endless causality loop, every moment co-creating slices of time."

Zara trembles, suffering a flash back, but Æther intervenes, "Breathe! In—out, that's it… now tell me what you saw."

"At first, I saw a black-hole swirling around, then something was taken from me and given to a giant-being made of stars. Then another place, feared by some and not by others, a black planet—it spoke to me…" Zara suddenly stops talking, unable to breathe, but Æther acts quickly, slapping her on the back.

"Just clearing out the cobwebs," he says. "That's it breathe— now tell me what you heard?"

"A sound, repeating over and over… Tek, Tek… Tek-n-kek."

"Are you sure it wasn't Tik-Ingkeyk?"

"That's it! It was saying Tik-Ingkeyk."

"We leave for Tik-Ingkeyk now, Golden Ascetic?" Ansebe says, in an I-told-you-so tone.

"Yes, we leave now. Sentience, prepare the Three Kingdoms!"

"The Three Kingdoms?" Zara asks.

"Wait and see," answers Ansebe, "I never thought they would be called upon in my lifetime; we're about to see something special."

Everyone makes their way to the large sphere, in which they docked on arrival. The sphere changes its luminosity, once again scintillations of swirling colours turn the orb transparent.

From the bottom of the crater's bedrock, something buried stirs, a rumbling noise akin to a moon-quake follows as it breaks free from its resting place. Then from out of the resulting cloud of moon-dust appear three colossal saucer-shaped craft, in eerie triangular symmetry. As they ascend they shift their angular formation and coming to a standstill, they rotate to dock with the large dome. The lead saucer and dome bond together, creating an airtight seal, whereupon Æther shepherds the tetra and the others through large cargo-doors. Once inside the giant craft, Æther plots a path via a holo-interface. "The Three Kingdoms has no bridge, it is operated from anywhere on the ship," he swipes a hologram in the direction of Sub-Rohza, "the operating-system, I need a good co-pilot."

"Oh… our course is via Rai?" Rohza asks, uploading the hologram.

"We go to the Alcazar of the Lords Temporal, if I have read Zara's dream correctly, then Lady Devanagari and Master Antariksha play a role in our mission. Of what it is I am unsure. Nonetheless, it's time to bring on board our heavy hitters." And so, they set on their way, from out of the crater the Three Kingdoms rise and with a flash of light they are gone.

Inside the vessel, "Here, come and take a look at this," Ansebe says, guiding Zara to a view screen, he waves a hand to reveal a glimpse of the space they travel in.

"Wow… what's this?"

"Hyperspace!" Ansebe says, his face lit up a rainbow glow from the view screen.

"It's nothing like anything I ever imagined it to be."

"It takes some getting used to, no matter how much we try."

Suddenly, the view changes, back to normal space-time as Rai comes into view.

"We have arrived, the Eight Moons of Rai," Æther says. In no time at all the Three Kingdoms arrives at the Alcazar of the Lords Temporal, stopping at the pathway to the fortress doors. Outside waits Lord Kae-Rai, along with the two giant automatons.

"Wait here," Æther says to the others as he disembarks the vessel to greet Kae-Rai. He kneels, "My Lord, you are well?"

"Please rise Golden Ascetic, we do not have time to waste on frivolous formalities."

"Yes, my Lord."

"You have the girl on board?"

"Yes, she is with us."

"What is she like?"

"This one is different."

"Does she know what she is?"

"Not yet my Lord," Æther lays a hand on his heart, "even I am unsure of what she is."

"Best let events take their natural course." Kae-Rai places a hand on Æther's shoulder, "The Eyt are indebted to you, but what of the two brothers?"

"We have two great Juhj-iz in the making, perhaps even an Ascetic shall one become."

"Is it so?" Kae-Rai asks, with a pleasant smile.

"It is so, my Lord."

"Then take leave with Lady Devanagari and Master Antariksha by your side," Kae-Rai says, gesticulating to the automatons. Before they leave he says, "It is foretold that she may teach us the way of the just, for the light of the universe is in her eye." Æther bows, and with that marches on board with the two giant-size automatons.

Inside the vessel the giant beings stand silent behind Æther, "We head for Tik-Ingkeyk, my Lady," he says, pulling up a hologram, "to the Black Planet." On seeing the two giants, Zara arches her eyebrows, their uncanny complexions on the face of what appear to be transparent membranes takes her aback—she looks at one, then to the other, unsure which one of the two is the most astounding.

"Take your breath away, don't they?" Ansebe says, at seeing Zara's astonished look. "There are no words to describe them."

The brothers Pyan both step forward to show their respects. Having met the automatons before, their awe is short-lived. In fact, Fez feels a strange compulsion as Lady Devanagari steps forward, offering the hand of friendship. Ansebe follows tradition, placing his hand on top of hers, but Fez has quite a different idea when she turns to him. He looks at Antariksha, who as usual is quite unconcerned with matters, and with a penchant for mischief kisses Lady Devanagari on her giant-size hand. As an empath she senses the thoughts behind the kiss, upon which her complexion changes from blue sky to red. On seeing this Fez looks up, his metallic features narrow around an eye—he winks—and in a flirtatious way.

"Are you sure you can't take human form?" he says, infatuated by Devanagari's feminine ways. "Still you can't speak," he turns to Master Antariksha walks up and kicks him. "Why won't you allow her to speak?" Alas, the one that is the stars finds his comment unworthy of reply. Not one to be ignored, Fez positions himself for an audience with the giant and holding hands around his mouth he shouts, "Hey, big guy! Have you ever heard the story of Echo?" He smirks as the giant turns his head. "Now, the Terrans tell the tale of a playful nymph who diverted the attention of the goddess Juno so that Jupiter may court other nymphs. When Juno learned of this, she transformed Jupiter's loyal plaything into nothing more than an Echo, unable to speak unless spoken to—and even then—only able to return as an Echo of that which was said." Master Antariksha kneels to face him, having gained his complete attention. The giant appears irked, unconcerned that automaton could smite him with but a thought, Fez steps closer.

"Fez-Pyan!" Æther shouts, "Kneel and apologise!"

Fez reluctantly kneels, albeit with a defiant stare at the giant. "Yes, Golden Ascetic," he says, kowtowing to the automaton.

Æther turns to Antariksha, "Please allow for this one, Master Antariksha. Ill fortune has made him a sufferer of the absence of reason." The giant gives a slow nod and stands.

Having noticed Zara, Lady Devanagari turns her attention away from Fez. Her faceless form appears fascinated as if never having seen a Terran female before. "Ahh yes, please meet Zara Hanson, my Lady," Æther says. Devanagari clasps her hands together joyously and kneels to face Zara, tilting her head to one side and then the other. Although Devanagari has no face as such, her colour takes on auroras of red, blue and yellow as she gazes on mesmerised.

"You can talk to her, Zara," Æther says.

"Does she ever talk?"

"No, not speech as we know it, but still she understands everything we say."

"Hello Devanagari, I'm Zara."

Devanagari nods enthusiastically, tilting down to look at Zara's hairstyle and with her giant fingertips she gently touches her hair then clasps her hands with delight as if a hairstyle was a fantastic cosmic arrangement. Her complexion changes to a beautiful cloudscape. An odd thought from Zara. Is she smiling? Again, Lady Devanagari nods.

"Whoa… you can sense my thoughts?"

"Not thoughts Zara, Devanagari is an empath—she senses your emotions," Æther says.

"I think she likes me." The automaton nods again.

"It appears you have a new friend, Zara," Æther chuckles.

"Best friends forever, by the looks of it," she says, with a quirky smile.

Just then, the ships holographic display hails their arrival at Tik-Ingkeyk, the Black Planet.

Chapter Twenty-Five
The Black Planet

"We have arrived. Alas, I cannot accompany you to the planet," Æther says, shaking his head.

"Of course, the Ascetic's Oath," Ansebe exclaims.

"All Ascetics, as you know, must abide by the Oath and honour the way of the Lyrian, for theirs is the way of the Eyt."

"The way of the Lyrian?" Zara asks, looking at Æther somewhat mystified.

"Lyrians abhor all forms of spirituality bar one, the traditional practice of Shangari. So, when they agreed to join the Eyt—on their own terms—an accord was struck, one which forbade my kind from ever placing a foot on Tik-Ingkeyk. Thus was borne the Ascetic's Oath."

"I see," she says, with a half shrug, holding her hands open, "but what are Lyrians?"

"Freakin' cat people," Fez replies. "They're sneaky, manipulative and cunning. I could never be like that."

"What? You're describing yourself." Zara rolls her eyes at his double-standards.

"Am I? Am I like that?"

"Yes," reply the others in unison.

"Iron my socks!" Fez replies, with a lopsided grin, extending his middle finger.

"What does that even mean?" Zara asks, throwing her hands up in the air, trying not to laugh.

Æther cuts in, "Time for banter later," his expression hardens as he faces the brothers. "Do you recall in your youth how Kyubi-K used to teach you the Lyrian art of stealth?"

"Naturally," says Fez.

"It was a good lesson taught, that one day you both may have dire need of such skills."

"The hell it was," an agitated frown from Fez, "his burial chamber is in the middle of the jungle of a thousand-and-one-eyes! We're good, but not bat-shit-crazy good."

"Then perhaps we should try the ways of old."

"How about the ways of the new? Take the Three Kingdoms down and have a shoot-em-up." Fez mimes firing a hammer-ray.

Æther's eyes blaze a shade of yellow, "You forget our history," he prods a finger to Fez's head. "This ship was once manned by an elite team of undefinable Juhj-iz, named the Unseen Nemesis of the Third Way."

"No one ever saw them, according to legend," Ansebe says, as the answer dawns on his face. "That's it, this ship must hold their secrets."

"Exactly!" Æther stomps his staff.

"What secrets?" Fez asks, none the wiser.

"All Juhj-iz of the Third Way had to pass a rigorous selection process. To prove themselves," Æther raises a finger, "they had to survive unseen for seventy-seven nights in the jungles of Tik-Ingkeyk!"

Ansebe nods his head, "But no one knows how it was done."

"Impossible!" Fez protests, "Their scent would have been picked up, or they would have been tracked," his eyes narrow on seeing Æther shake his head. "It's not just a legend, is it?"

"It is not," Æther says, with a chuckle.

"How'd they do it?" Fez gives a half-shrug of his shoulders.

"How indeed. Legends are popular history yet to be authenticated," Æther pulls up the ships holo-logs. "Ah hah, here it is," he swipes a hologram and with that a pallet arrives from storage. "They're a little musty." Inside the pallet are furs, from a bear-like animal from Tik-Ingkeyk. "I present the skin of the even-clawed-devil," he holds up one of the pelts, "otherwise known as the Grizzly Tahy-Gar. Now, the Third Way knew this was a holy creature revered by Lyrians, that the Shangari faith considers it a sin to glance at a Tahy-Gar—"

"And the slightest scent of a Tahy-Gar is enough to send most Lyrians in the opposite direction," Ansebe says, his third-eye point glowing. "It is a textbook strategy, we try."

Æther waves a finger, "Now we have faith in our plan. We go to the Northern Shangari Temple. Or nearby as we have no precise mapping."

"One thing," says Zara, looking at a view screen, "its atmosphere looks pretty much the same as Earth's, so why the Black Planet?"

"To the Lyrians Tik-Ingkeyk is a holy planet, as such all forms of tech are barred from the planet. Hence, the term Black Planet—entire planet is a technology black-spot."

"Then we ignore the law," Zara snaps her fingers, "and take some tech with us."

"I said the planet," Æther loads the ships hologram, "this map shows the satellite array around Tik-Ingkeyk, which enforces the black-spot."

"I knew it," Fez paces back and forth, "no freakin' danger, except for the kinetic orbital bombs. A satellite system of guided carbide-rods, projectiles with pinpoint targeting accuracy, more kaboom than a meteorite," he smashes his fist to palm. "Take some tech down to the planet—you'd never know what hit you!"

"Precisely," Æther says, "which is why you won't have any tech on you," he walks over to New-Pyan, "and this little one will take you to the surface."

Our team of would-be heroes make their preparations, leaving all their tech behind they suit up. Sub-Rohza guides an oblong to knit a nano-weave emergency space-suit on everyone making the journey, "Boss, I can't accompany you on this one— the nano-suits will activate in space, should New-Pyan port you off-target on your return. Be careful down there, you won't be able to mind-link."

"Do not worry," Ansebe closes his hand, "we are a team, we try."

"We try…" Zara says, drawing a sharp breath she looks to Fez. "We ready?"

"I was born ready," he says in a deep macho-aggressive voice. Zara bites her lip, knows she should not laugh at a time like this. And with that said they don the skins of the even-clawed-devil.

"Ugh, these pelts reek," Zara turns her face away.

"Be thankful," Ansebe says, "you do not wish a Lyrian to pick up your scent."

They stand aside New-Pyan, their hands on the tetra's back, and with a burst of light they find themselves standing in the jungle of a thousand-and-one-eyes. A giant-sized tropical forest, with trees reaching high into the sky. It is still night, there is no light except for that of the mysterious glowing critters flittering about from tree to tree. The song of insects fills the night with chirps and trills, but it is the eerie sounds of the larger creatures in the darkness that strikes fear into their hearts. They crouch down, waiting for their eyes to adjust.

"My spine's tingling at what things might be salivating, looking at us," Fez says.

"Shhh… you will awaken the jungle," Ansebe whispers.

"Frak! It's pitch-black, can't see my hands," Fez talks as quite as he can, trying to stifle his giggles. "We'll have to wait here till dawn."

"Be still, you forget my nature," Ansebe stands, able to see in the dark. His large wrap-around ears open wide, all six ears attune his ability to sense magnetic fields. He points, "this way is north." The others follow closely behind him, after a while beams of daylight begin to break through the forest canopy.

"What about Newp, he's going to be seen?" Zara asks.

"Tetra roam free on this planet, New-Pyan is the least of our problems," Ansebe says. "Once we locate the temple, you know what to do?"

"Place my hands on the onyx-rock, and we're in, but then what?"

"I have no idea, we'll have to see what we're faced with."

"That's the plan?" Zara asks, lifting an eyebrow.

"That is the plan." Just then Ansebe's ears twitch, he raises a finger to his mouth, "Be still, something approaches—into the trees!" Ansebe jumps high onto a branch, holding a hand out he pulls Zara up, "Into the treetops, climb for your lives…"

Fez, moves faster, higher than the others, his fingers able to claw into the trees like nails. He stops to help.

"Higher still," shouts Ansebe. They ascend higher.

"What are we getting away from?" shouts Zara.

"Stampede!" Ansebe's skin-tone alters colour, blending with the tree, "Here they come!" In the distance a rumbling noise, a herd of giant creatures hurtle through the jungle, trampling everything in their path. Their huge bone-tails clank and scythe a pathway in their wake.

"They're like a giant-sized herd of ostriches," shouts Zara, "but with hammerhead tails."

Their heads pass within touch. "The seasonal migration of the giant Tik-Onidae," Ansebe replies, "nature's mighty powers have smiled upon us."

"In what way?" Zara drops onto a lower branch to face him, as the feathered creatures fade into the distance.

"Their northern migration heads to lake Tikanaki, a stone's throw from the temple," Ansebe jumps down to another branch, "Lyrians avoid these migratory routes—we are twice blessed."

It is daylight as they descend from the giant tropical trees, onto the newly laid trail. "There is little point in stealth now. We make haste!" Ansebe darts off along the trail, the others dash after him. Further on, he suddenly dives to the ground behind a rocky outcrop. They lay in wait, as the echo of footsteps, wooden sandals against stone approach.

"Lyrian monks, at least three of them," Ansebe whispers.

Zara takes a peek, "Whoa, bigger than I expected." A monk stops, she ducks. Too late. Her heart pounds, hands tremble on hearing the giant cat-like being sniffing. The head monk picks up an odour, draws a deep breath. Whiskers span out, hairs stand up on the back of its neck.

It roars loudly, "Show yourselves. I said show yourselves!" The monk extracts its toe-claws, scraping them anxiously against the wooden-soles of his sandals.

"We've been made," Zara whispers.

"Frak-this!" Fez pulls the Grizzly Tahy-Gar's head over his, and raises on all fours, just enough to be seen. The head monk catches sight of what he believes to be an even-clawed-devil and averts his gaze. Just then Fez mimics the call of the Tahy-Gar. "Aieoooh!" On hearing this the monks scatter, running away, arguing amongst themselves as to who had seen the Tahy-Gar, the head monk feeling aggrieved that only he should pay penance for their holy indiscretion. As they disappear into the distance, Fez rolls onto his back, laughing, a rare moment where he finds peace from the voices in his head.

Zara bites her lip, trying not to giggle, "Sorry guys, didn't think they would see me."

"They didn't," Fez says, smiling, "but they sure did pick up on the scent of something, your pussycat maybe?"

Her eyes narrow, she nudges his shoulder, "You're an idiot. I haven't got a cat."

"Be silent!" Ansebe says, looking left to right, unable to decide which path to take. "Guys, those monks must've come from worship."

"How do you come to that view?" Ansebe eyes dart at Zara.

"Well, on the one hand, because they weren't bearing gifts, meaning they must have left them inside the temple."

"That is a guess at best."

"On the other hand, the stone path they came from starts further up. As it starts where there is no temple—"

"Then it must lead to it. Very good," Ansebe says, slightly irked at not noticing the path, but nonetheless impressed with Zara's logic. He leads on.

The expedition presses forward, following the path, "The Shangari Temple," Ansebe holds a hand above his eyes, he sees in the ultraviolet spectrum, "we make haste."

"You see it with those farsighted eyes of yours, brother?"

"Not only do I see it, I feel its influence on the planet's magnetic fields."

"Where's Newp?" Zara panics unable to see the baby tetra.

"He's near," Ansebe's ears twitch, "I can hear his harmonic hum, try looking up."

"There you are," she beckons the little one to ground level, "here Newp, stay close."

New-Pyan swoops down, affectionately nudging Zara's thigh, and moves up front to go with Ansebe. As they trek along the path, a strange whipping noise followed by a thud occurs, then an abrupt breeze blows at Zara's hair—she turns around.

"Where's Fez?"

"Zara, run!" Ansebe shouts.

Too late. From out of the ground a massive trapdoor of woven soil, roots and silk bursts open, and a giant-sized arachnid-insectoid snatches Zara, throwing her into its burrow, closing the trapdoor behind them. Landing inside its larder she finds Fez, crouched, staying very still. "Don't move," he whispers. In front a multitude of eyes stare at them, shimmering a bio-luminescent hue of green and purple like a grapevine in sunlight. It moves close, so close that they feel the breath from the beast's lungs on their faces. Then it turns, ignores them to finish off a half-eaten rat-like mammal. The giant-sized arachnid-insectoid chomps away, tearing the mammal to shreds with its spiked praying-mantis appendages.

"Ugh… what is that thing?" Zara's shoulders shudder.

"I don't know—but I do know food should always be eaten with your mouth closed."

"It's going to eat us—"

"Nah, it's got no jaws," says Fez shaking his head.

"Those things making a crunching noise, they're jaws—"

"You know how Æther explicitly told us not to take any tech with us."

"Tell me you did."

"Found some nano-tech in the ships munitions, some real cool-gizmos."

"What are we waiting for?"

"This!" Fez gives a sudden gut-wrenching movement and from his mouth he flips out a matchstick-sized nano-bullet into his hand. He whispers to the tech, "A858 arm, put an end to threat." And with that the match sized tech unfolds into a beautiful butterfly on his hand. He calls out to the giant insectoid, "Hey ugly-face," the monster turns, "have you ever seen a butterfly that eats crocodile tears?" With that Fez blows into his hand and the butterfly takes off, fluttering towards the beast. As it gets close it shines a radiant white, lighting up the darkness. "Wait for it!" The butterfly lands on one of the giant-insect's eyes, a second later a surge of energy as the oddity closes its wings, upon which it explodes, taking with it the head of the beast. And with no head the beast drops, lifeless. Zara cringes, and looks away, at which point Fez says, "I told you it's got no jaws."

As the dust settles, they look for a way out. "No digging out of here," and with that said Fez flips a second nano-bullet out of his mouth, into his hand. Again, he issues instructions, "A858 problem, trapped under ground—find solution." This time the bullet eerily unfolds into a dragonfly and takes off towards the ceiling. "Oh no…" Fez shouts, "brother, stand back," and grabbing Zara he makes a mad dash to the other end of the burrow. From the dragonfly, a burst of explosive light sears a hole through the massive trapdoor, it travels high, searing through the forest canopy. An ever so small pinpoint of white light, visible from space. It does not go unnoticed by an orbital satellite, which whirs, kicking into action. Inside the burrow light shines through the newly made tunnel.

"Boom! I give you light," Fez shows the way out, they scramble to the surface.

"What did you do?" yells Ansebe, his shamanic mind sensing danger.

"Saved us—"

"We need to get out of here… run!" Ansebe shouts. For high above in the atmosphere an earth-shattering projectile has been set in motion, set free from a kinetic orbital bombardment satellite it hurtles downwards. A carbide-rod plummets to the location where Fez had used his nano-tech.

Ansebe blazes a trail down the path, his uncanny senses pickup something, the way the air flows, the smell of fast running water and its echo pounding against the steep sides of a narrow gorge. "This way, we have little time." They veer off the path, coming to the edge of a cliff, below a fast-flowing river, "We need to jump…"

"You're crazy," Fez yells, "why would we do that?"

And then it hits. Where they once stood the ground meets with such a force of energy that the impact unleashes destruction. From the jungle a shock wave, a brief look shared by all three as they jump off the cliff, and from a mighty height they hit the waters, into a fast-moving tributary of Lake Tikanaki. The waters swirl, opposing currents try to draw them under as they tumble downstream. Zara struggles to keep afloat, the fall having left her dazed.

"My hand… take my hand," Ansebe reaches out and rescues her, able to swim in the heavy seas of Rai, his creators designed him to be one with water. Fez fares just as well, being able to slow his heartbeat and make each breath count, but the forces of nature are not so forgiving. Upstream the bombardment unleashes a landslide into one of the smaller lakes and when it hits the river, the large displacement of water gives rise to a wall of water. A mega-wave rumbling in the distance.

"Oh no!" Ansebe signals to his brother, who turns to face the torrent.

"Brother, we must use the tetra," Fez yells, with a look of dread in his eyes.

"Tetra has been scared away."

"We must do something—"

"Boat!" Ansebe shouts, desperately making his way to it. They tussle, grabbing the decking to clamber on board a fisherman's sailboat.

"This your best move?" Fez asks, but Ansebe ignores him, grabbing some rope.

"Here lash yourself to anything you find!" After a frantic struggle, they secure themselves just as the wall of water hits. The boat rises with the wave, but something tugs it to one side.

Fez's eyes widen, "Frak! The boat's anchored." Higher still they ride the wall of water, until the anchor rope snaps away a cleat, the loosed rope whips and whistles, unreeling from the capstan. Even higher they rise, as the taut anchor rope tugs the boat on a near vertical climb. "It's been a blast, brother," Eyes closed, Fez prays, "I believe in the above-beyond, believe in the Almighty. I repent… I repent…" As if his prayer was heard the anchor rope snaps, and high on the crest of the wave they surf. The skiff creaks and scrapes but stays in one piece, butting against the swell it defies the downward pull, riding the giant force until the waters release. The torrent quickly subsides, with giant breakers dispersing into the vast waters of Lake Tikanaki. Then with a sudden bump and a jolt, they open their eyes to find the skiff washed up onto a rocky outcrop, behind them the great lake wetlands teeming with thousands of giant Tik-Onidae. In front of them, the Shangari Temple.

"Whew! That was gnarly. I knew we'd be all right. I always knew," a maniacal laugh bursts free from Fez, one of relief.

"We have little time brother, we must leave," Ansebe helps Zara up. "How are you?"

"Shaken…" she clutches her chest, her eyes widen, "that was level thirteen insane."

"We must make haste."

"Where's Newp?" the tetra descends to Zara's side. "Newp," she hugs him, props her chin on his head.

"To the Shangari Temple," Ansebe says, leading the way and shortly thereafter they arrive nearby the entrance. In the meantime, a rummaging from under the deck of the fishing vessel. A Lyrian fisherman awakes, having slept through the entire upheaval. Whistling happily, he climbs on deck to retrieve his catch, but stands dumbfounded, scratching his head at the view of the giant lake. As his shock subsides he notices three sets of footprints trailing off in the sand, foreign footprints. The fisherman gasps, then quickly grabs a large conga drum, and begins drumming an alarm call. If you want to know what happens next, then keep reading, as the story goes on to tell of unforeseen revelations.

Chapter Twenty-Six
The Unveiling

After a fast-trek they approach the Northern Shangari Temple. "We wait until we know for sure we can approach," Ansebe tells the others, waving his hand, signalling them to keep low. Zara holds Newp down, keeping him by her side, out of sight. After some time lying in wait, Ansebe cuts the silence, "I hear nothing, sense nothing—we go now." They sprint towards the temple doors, Zara stops at the onyx-rock, placing her hands over the giant chiselled paw-prints, and into the smaller recessed hand-prints within. An exact match. As the huge temple doors begin to open, they waste no time entering. Once inside, they tread lightly, unsure of the exact layout of the temple when a sudden creaking noise echoes, and the giant doors begin to slowly shut behind them. Ansebe glances sideways, spying a second onyx-rock used to gain exit.

"Newp, quick!" Zara beckons the baby tetra inside before the doors shut. Once shut the onset of darkness quickly turns pitch black. Ansebe, able to see in the dark, places his hand upon New-Pyan, whereupon the tetra turns fluorescent, lighting up the way for the others. They walk down a passageway, and either side of them are giant statues of cat-people—fierce and ominous their shadows appear as if moving with them as they walk onwards. At the end of a long corridor they find a large cubed structure inscribed with hieroglyphs. Ansebe reads aloud, "The last resting place of Lord Kyubi-K." The brothers kneel, paying respects to their creator, whom for the best part of their life they knew as a father. Ansebe turns to Zara, showing her the onyx-stone adjacent the cube, "If you please, we have attained our goal." And with that said she places her hands on the stone, upon which one face of the cube turns a translucent shade of green, whereby a doorway appears. They enter warily, anxious at what they might find inside.

"We're in!" Fez says, he looks around taken aback, "It… it's empty?"

"Ahem… all this way for nothing," Zara says, with an upset croak in her voice.

"Is it so?" Ansebe's face glows a radiant blue, "Kyubi-K knew this was the last place anyone would suspect him to keep any tech—he could easily thwart the satellites."

"How so?" Zara arches an eyebrow.

"He made them."

"So?" her eyes widen. "We're inside an empty shell… it's hollow."

"Ah hah!" Ansebe smiles, "repeat that last word if you please."

"Hollow?"

"Now there's a word pleasing to my ears. This place is far from empty, it is in fact—a holo-lab." Ansebe walks up to a wall, touches it closing the doorway behind them. They wait when a hologram of paw appears, and with an outstretched motion it opens to expose its claws. Moving eerily in front of them, it scratches words into the wall. A message scored in blood-red in front of them. And then the paw is gone.

"That paw," Fez says, his face transformed with awe, "it was his."

"The prophesy!" Ansebe reads the words aloud, "The Ultimate Salvation is written within the Painted Symbol. Its spirit is reborn in the host when freely received."

"Argh!" Fez gives a half-shrug, stamps his foot, "What the frak does that mean?" Ansebe closes his eyes, he says out loud, "From the need to save races from their self-destruction was borne an equation… the Painted Symbol."

"For operating probes," Fez throws his arms in the air, "to search for intelligence."

"What if it applies to something else?" Ansebe holds up a finger, "Something tangential perhaps—a story hidden inside a story—by the ancients no less." He repeats the line, "From the need to save races—"

"Wait!" Zara recalls the text she sent at the café days earlier, accepting the mission, "I received the Painted Symbol freely," she slaps her forehead, "that's it!"

"Please explain."

"My mission was named the Painted Symbol. I sent a text… Painted Symbol Received… accepting the mission."

"Intriguing. What are you thinking?"

"The riddle says the Ultimate Salvation is written within. If the Painted Symbol is a complex equation, it can be written anywhere—its spirit or code reborn or triggered in a host when freely accepted."

"The cipher!" Ansebe's face lights up a golden hue, a look of awe.

"Snap! Exactly what I was thinking."

"The shamanic mind wonders—how best to hide something written within."

"This is a holo-lab you say?" Zara asks, smiling, her eyes flickering with an idea.

"Already on it…" Ansebe waves a hand, pulling up holo-tools from the lab. He turns and plucks a hair from Zara, gently placing it into a holo-scope. "Holo-lab extract molecular structure, inspect for encoded cipher in DNA." The advanced tech runs through a complex series of computations, a result found in which it displays a hologram of a cipher.

"What does it say?" Fez asks.

"I have no idea," Ansebe opens all the holo-files. "Lab, add cipher to all stored data. Use it to open any encoded files." The holo-lab finds a file named Zara. Ansebe draws his lower lip between his teeth, briefly closing his eyes. "Holo-lab, open file named Zara." From the cube a surge of activity as two holograms phase together to reveal the image of Kyubi-K. The brothers gasp as he walks among them, resplendently dressed in a long white silken tunic, his robust panthera body towers above them. A serene figure, with a near-black coat of fur upon which his lighter spots are barely visible. He opens his eyes, which instantly cast a magnificent golden glow—the Kyubi-K hologram speaks. "My handsome sons," he smiles, tugs at a whisker, "you have awakened my essence, which can only mean one thing." He turns, "Here she is." Zara steps back, gazing at the dark jaguarian giant. Kyubi-K kneels to face her, "You wonder what you are, child?" Zara looks into his cat's eyes and nods—he answers with a smile. "A chrysalis, one day to become something wondrous."

"What is it… this thing I'm to be?" she asks nervously.

"The Ultimate Salvation, a convergence—from the need to save races was borne an equation, ordained by the very Gods themselves that one day you should arrive as the Painted Symbol."

"I'm still human. I'm only human… why me?"

"Of course, you have questions. How this came to be? Sent to me as a dream by an Elb of good virtue the secrets were whispered two-fold. The first, how the Elb may be defeated, but moreover I was given sacred knowledge of the sixty-four codecs. The divine combination, which I have written into you. Creating the cipher and amending Rohza's code brought you here to me. That was the easy part. Alas, to protect these secrets from the Elb I had to partake of the ultimate forfeit, which is why an image you find me."

"What of the Golden Ascetic?" Ansebe asks, "He realised something, a revelation hidden in your writings."

"A back-up plan, a page I sent to him, asking him to read it daily in my memory."

"Hold on, I'm none the wiser. What am I?"

"There are Juhj-iz and Ascetics Zara Hanson," Kyubi-K faces her, "but the rarest of all are those painted with the sacred codecs, for those are the Symbols."

"It's in my DNA… I'm to become one of these Symbols?"

"We live in a time of marvels, to witness the arrival of a Symbol is a magical thing. Moreover, the arrival of the Gaia Symbol—able to tear asunder the hearts of the Gods with but one teardrop." With that said his holographic hand touches her forehead, after which she drops to her knees, overcome with emotion, for Kyubi-K's touch has a profound affect.

He turns to face the two brothers. "My astounding creations, my sons," his arms open wide, he hugs one then the other. "Time was revealed to me by the Big Teacher, the Elb of Virtue. And so, I must reveal to each of you what roles you play—and more importantly—what you are to do." He picks from the air a hologram, a small translucent bubble. "Time in consciousness is time in space, your future role is written within," he nudges the purple bubble in Fez's direction. The neuro-sphere passes straight through his head and out the other side, where it bursts into nothingness. Fez's shoulders judder as a shiver runs through his body on receiving the information, which hides within his subconscious.

Then, to Ansebe, Kyubi-K turns, "The information I have for you my son, is for your own ears," and with that said a transparent holo-cube encloses them. The others watch but cannot hear Kyubi-K talking. Ansebe's skin tones change colourful hues of green and gold, then something said by Kyubi-K drains the colour from his skin, turning it a ghostly white. Ansebe drops to his knees, and just as the cube dissipates he is heard saying, "I… I see." Kyubi-K helps Ansebe stand, "Be brave my sons, remember do not share this knowledge with each other, if you wish to find counsel seek it with the Golden Ascetic," he turns to Zara, "and you child, you have no idea how much you are loved. See that you return it. Now go, leave my essence be." Zara gives the giant Lyrian a hug, as do the two brothers. As they leave, on the way-out Fez touches his metallic face, feeling something on it, it is a tear from the one who rarely cries.

As they exit the Shangari Temple, they freeze at a standstill, from everywhere an army of Lyrians encircles them. It is the Lyrian Guard, an elite task force made up of the most powerful Lyrians. The guards move at a phenomenal speed, surrounding them in seconds, the panthera giants point the tips of their spears within inches from their throats. Their growls reverberate deep into the ground and backup into their spears; a paralyzing effect sets deep in the pit of Zara's stomach, she draws a sharp breath and tries to calm. They quickly separate their captives from the tetra should they try to use it to make their escape. Suddenly, the army moves to make a pathway for a tall foreboding figure. It is King Hagonite. The giant cat-being advances, wielding a chakram, a giant circular bladed weapon, its circumference as wide as Zara is tall. He walks around his captives, inspecting them, his grey and white spotted fur fails to give a true impression of his fierce nature. The king looks at Fez, gives the most subtle of nods and raises a finger ever so slightly—both respond with a wry smirk.

"Harrumph." The king voices his displeasure at seeing them in the pelts of the even-clawed-devil, "Why are you wearing these?" King Hagonite kneels to face Fez.

"Why are you not averting your eyes?" Fez says with a defiant look, countering the king's question. The king stands, gives an impromptu speech, "In my younger years, I used to keep a pack of boolabirri. On one outing into the jungle one of the pack met its death, the most playful one of them all. Her name was Mil-ee," the king closes his eyes takes a deep breath. "The dam and her siblings nursed her until she passed, but when she was gone they only looked at her the once, as Mil-ee did not seem to have been any more of their kind. What..." King Hagonite becomes upset, slaps himself on the face to snap out of it, "what they loved was their sibling, not the body which contained her, but that which animated and made the body what it was." The king holds his arms wide open, addresses his army, "This thing we call our essence is without outward form. As are the pelts these intruders wear, and as such we are not bound to avert our gaze."

The Lyrian guard roars, cheering loudly for their king.

"Well then," Fez says, "if there's no harm done, we'll be on our way."

"Not so quick..." King Hagonite raises his hand. All falls silent.

"You know, come to think of it, that story was a tad mediocre," Fez says, looking for a rise, "not very, what's the word... kingly." The king scowls at Fez, as does Ansebe, but Fez pushes on, "In being kingly isn't one supposed to be like heaven?" The king laughs incessantly and kneels to face Fez, "Serpent That Shines, you are forgetting that I too trained with the Bitter Sage—your ruse to anger me shall not succeed."

"Then you know I could call upon the Bitter challenge?" The king lifts his giant chakram, stomping it once on the ground and walks away from Fez. He stops in his tracks, "The king does not accept challenges..." then in one fell swoop King Hagonite spins around, throwing the giant chakram with all his might. Fez's eyes widen! His viper-reflex kicks in, and in the blink of an eye he back-drops to the floor. A heavy thud. The vibrating zing of metal. All the troops gasp at seeing the circular blade imbedded in the temple wall. Moreover, they wonder how the ringed blade missed its target.

The king's hair stands up on the back of his neck. He missed! He never misses. He tugs at his whiskers, both impressed and irritated. A frown turns to a look of amusement as he speaks, "The snake knows its bite is poisonous and with but one bite its adversary shall die, but that is all it has, so it waits for the most opportune moment to strike."

Fez replies, "True, but the cat also waits, strikes at opportune moments, but knows come hell or high water, it must not get bit. Not even once."

King Hagonite roars with laughter, "Brother Fez, you are still as quick with your wit as you are with your feet." He walks up to Fez, whispers in his ear, "Think of a wager or feat that I can grant clemency." The king turns to address his army.

"These interlopers have committed only one crime—holy pilgrimage—to see their father the great Kyubi-K."

The troops cheer, "Kyubi-K!"

Just then, the three Lyrian monks who fled from Fez earlier step forward, the head monk addresses the king.

"Sire, they have committed holy crimes."

"Speak!" King Hagonite roars, far from happy.

"They not only actively impersonated the even-clawed-devil, one of them mimicked its call. Sin above sins! You know the punishment, my King."

"Then their only saviour is the unforeseen wager."

"That's it!" Fez says.

Ansebe whispers to Fez, "What is?"

"Yes what?" Zara adds.

"Just watch this," Fez calls out, "King Hagonite, I have an unforeseen wager."

"And what is your wager?"

"That with this holy-pelt a miracle can be done."

"What is this miracle?"

"That I can make this pelt cover the land around this temple."

"That's a stretch," the king roars, laughing at his own words, "this I must see."

"And you grant us three leave once the miracle is done?"

The king smiles and raises his arm, "You have my word as king."

"Well then, we start but I warn you—this may take some time."

King Hagonite watches on amused, wondering how Fez is going to accomplish the feat. Fez looks back at the king, smiles and pulls a small knife from his boot. Seeing the knife Ansebe's skin turns a radiant shade of blue, "I know this!" he says to Zara with a reassuring nod. Fez begins by laying the Tahy-Gar hide to the ground and spreading it out he carefully cuts away a small strip from the edge and keeps on cutting. Time passes, it is slow, meticulous work.

"What's he doing?" Zara asks Ansebe.

"He's working a spiral pattern, cutting the hide from edge to centre."

"Why?"

"Watch. We try."

He works on relentlessly, as night falls he carries on through the night, cutting, unravelling the hide. Once again dawn breaks on Tik-Ingkeyk, at which time his Majesty has fallen asleep.

"I'm done," shouts Fez. The guards take him to the king.

"The wager is complete great King," Fez says, awaiting inspection of the task.

The king awakens from a half-slumber and stands, "Show me the fruits of your wager."

"This way, your Majesty."

"We agreed I would cover the land surrounding the temple with the hide."

"We did," the king gives a double-take, "but I see no hide."

"Then follow me." Fez shows the narrow strip of the unravelled hide surrounding the temple, "As you can see the hide covers the land surrounding the Shangari Temple, great King."

The king looks on astounded, a look of awe turns to laughter. King Hagonite places a hand on Fez's shoulder, "Free to leave you are, the unforeseen wager was true. You have won your freedom." The king commands his Lyrian guard, "Stand down, these people are free."

King Hagonite walks to Zara and Ansebe, "You are now my guests," he claps his hands, "bring these weary travellers refreshments." The king's servants quickly prepare a large table, laid out with a mouth-watering selection of fruits, delicacies and juices. "Please sit that we may drink and eat well." An advisor kow-tows aside the king, "Sire, it is unusual protocol for the King to eat alone, without his advisors." King Hagonite waves a dismissive hand.

"And this is a far from usual situation. Leave me."

"As you wish, my King." The advisors scuttle away.

"I apologise for the theatrics, my new-found friends," King Hagonite reaches over and resting his giant arms on Fez and Ansebe's shoulders, he looks at Zara. "Pray tell me the name of this girl."

"Meet our sister sire, Zara Hanson."

The king smiles, "A Terran, I presume?"

"Yes, my King, I am from Terra."

"I sense something good in you. It is pleasing to my eyes."

"Thank you, your Majesty," Zara replies, but Fez keeps nudging her leg whenever the king speaks—biting her lip, she tries not to laugh.

"Your mane is also pleasing to the king's eyes." Another nudge under the table. This time she returns the nudge with a sharp kick. A sudden jump of surprise from Fez leads to a choking-fit, his airway obstructed with food. The king leans over and casually slaps Fez's back with such a force that the obstruction is cleared in one go, allowing him to breathe.

"Your eyes are too big for your belly, Serpent That Shines," King Hagonite laughs.

Zara looks daggers at Fez. Their little set-to goes unnoticed by the king, who has become quite captivated with her. Some quick thinking from Zara, she asks the king for his help.

"Your Majesty would you be so kind as to assist us with leaving immediately for our ship—there are urgent matters that require my attention."

"As you wish Zara Hanson, tis my duty to ensure your safe return," the king claps. "Hail the royal tetraporphyrin—hail Mah-Hagonite!" A squadron of troops assemble, they begin pounding their swords against shields until a unique rhythmic percussion ensues.

"My tetramyrmidon, crew of the Mah-Hagonite," the king says, smiling proudly at his elite guard, trained to serve him from birth. The king opens both his arms wide, "Zara Hanson, see the great lake awaken—I give you Lake Tikanaki!" In the distance, the sky darkens over the lake, as if influenced by something stirring in the deep. As the tetramyrmidon drum faster, an electrical storm rages in the distance. Out of nowhere a squall of winds hit the shore, buffering against the temple walls. And then it rises, a colossal entity for which leviathan is an ill-fitting word.

"Oh… my… God!" Zara's words fall short of describing the moment, "It… it's ginormous." The huge entity draws closer. Its appearance is like a tetraporphyrin, except it has a hard shell as opposed to a tetra's translucent biology.

"The giant Tet-Tet," Ansebe says to Zara, "they have a symbiotic relationship with all forms of tetra." The giant Tet-Tet advances, gliding to a halt some way in the distance. Then from its underbelly a tetraporphyrin jets out, circles the temple to land aside King Hagonite. It opens its pouch. New-Pyan hides behind Zara, but the king sees this and kneels to face the scared tetra. He whispers, "Do not fear Areta little one, she is harmless." They board the tetra, and in no time at all Areta glides into the inner recesses of the giant Tet-Tet. Once inside, the titanic beast turns and shoots off into orbit, shortly thereafter they approach the Three Kingdoms. The gigantic Tet-Tet stops a safe distance from the Three Kingdoms, upon which Areta disembarks to dock with the lead saucer. On approach the cargo-bay opens to allow the tetra inside, where Æther and Sub-Rohza stand on guard, armed and waiting. As Areta lands, her pouch slowly opens, inside which the formidable figure that is King Hagonite is seen kneeling. The king calls out.

"Golden Ascetic, great grade-beyond-grades, I ask your pardon. I have held up your mission." Æther approaches King Hagonite, beckons him to stand. As he does Æther gazes up at the giant Lyrian.

"You are far bigger than me, friend. It is I who should ask your pardon."

"I defer to the great grade-beyond-grades, teacher of the divine martial-ways."

"Thank you for the honourable title, I am undeserving of it. Never been graded." The king and Æther laugh. On seeing Gnash-Byte rushing to greet the others Æther adds, "I hope my warriors have not caused too much trouble for you?"

"A king must always maintain balance when faced with trouble—" just then King Hagonite stops mid-sentence. His eyes widen on noticing the two giant automatons behind Æther.

"The… heavy-hitters," the king kow-tows before them. "Great deities, I never thought I would have the privilege." Lady Devanagari clasps her hands with delight, then leans down and with a finger guides the Lyrian King to stand by his elbow. Master Antariksha on the other hand remains indifferent to the king's reverence.

The king faces Æther, "Your mission is most serious Golden Ascetic."

"It is, and we must make-haste—"

"Then my army is your army," King Hagonite proudly roars.

"We are honoured Majesty, but the resources required at present are those of stealth."

"If you change your mind—"

"Then we shall be the first to call for your help."

"Then I bid you safe passage," the king turns to Zara and kneels. "You have been a pleasurable diversion Zara Hanson, and so I must depart—but before I do please accept this gift."

The king waves a finger, one of his loyal tetramyrmidon steps forward to present a necklace, adorned with seven sapphire blue pendant stones—a thing of exquisite beauty. The focal point is a large triangle-shaped locket, with the other six stones trailing either side, fashioned as circles, squares, and hexagons.

"This necklace is the spirit of Tik-Ingkeyk, magnificent and flawless—it is named the Seven-Photonics," he places the necklace around Zara's neck, "'tis a bringer of good-fortune, but moreover, no Lyrian shall dare harm you when wearing it."

"Why thank you, your Majesty," Zara blushes, smiling at the splendour of the gift.

"The Seven-Photonics grants the wearer safe passage throughout the Lyrian Empire. It is the royal seal. Its real power, on the other hand, allows its wearer the ability to call upon any of the Seven-Photonic-Titans in times of need."

"Thank you for the honour, great King."

"The honour is all mine."

"What are these Titans?"

"The less said about them the better. Just know they have a pact to honour the necklace. You shall find three of the seven on Terra," he looks Zara in the eye, "they shall make themselves known to you in time. Be frugal in asking for their help, it is wise not to become too familiar with them."

"Yes, your Majesty."

And with that said King Hagonite bids farewell to the others and boards Areta with his loyal tetramyrmidon. Areta spins around but before leaving places her forehead against New-Pyan, and then against Por-Pyan's head, whereupon sparks of bio-energy criss-cross to and fro. Æther nods, knowing what has occurred. Unbeknownst to the others, King Hagonite has instructed Areta to entangle herself with the tetra, so that they can call upon her in times of dire need. For Areta is one of the rarer tetraporphyrin. A shadow-tracker.

Chapter Twenty-Seven
The Foreboding Arrival

"Come, time is of the essence. While you were on the planet, we had a visit from the Elb," Æther swipes a hologram, images play of their visit. "The trial of strength is to take place soon… we must prepare." Æther walks over to a circle engraved into the deck and as he nears, it transforms into a five-pointed-star, and as it does an azure-coloured mist fills the air. He beckons the others to sit. "Each of you choose a point on the pentagram, we follow the ways of old, the ways of the undefinables—the ways of the Unseen!" They sit at each point, at the heavenly-point of the star Æther, at the two mid-points Zara and Rohza, and at the two earth-points Ansebe and Fez. Æther stomps his staff, upon which the floor begins to hum.

"This sacred geometrical-frequency prevents the Elb from listening in, this I have learned from that which was left by the undefinable ones." Æther's gives a warning, a glint of yellow appears in his eyes, "I say this once, never sit in the centre of this star," he turns his gaze on Ansebe as if looking into his very soul. "Tell me, has the trip to Tik-Ingkeyk proved useful?"

"It has Golden Ascetic, we discovered the essence of Kyubi-K," Ansebe's skin turns from a rusty red to a solemn-grey, "I have been told of possible future events… outcomes of which I cannot reveal, except to an Ascetic."

"I see," Æther nods, "we shall talk alone later," and turns to Fez. "Will you also have need of my counsel?"

"I know exactly what I'm going to be doing."

"Which is?"

"I have no idea. That's the idea!"

"Ahh," Æther smiles, "the ideal-scenario—a holo-memory?"

"Yup."

"It will trigger when it needs to," Æther chuckles, turns to Zara, his eyes burn a glint of yellow. "We are done."

"Whoa… don't you want to know more details?"

"Details?" Æther places his hands together, "didn't you know that I am aware? After all, I am a Mystic. Were you aware of this?"

"Yes, Golden Ascetic."

"So, tell me of the great mystery you have unearthed?"

"How'd you know?"

"It is written on your face—yes?"

"Yes," Zara lets out a wry smile.

"Go on."

"Well… in a nutshell," she takes in a deep breath, "there's a code, the Painted Symbol, used in probes for detecting the rise of intelligent life. Except there's another code used for creating genetic codecs, and that code hacks another code, one that has to be freely received by the one with the codec, and that's me, the Gaia Symbol." She breathes, and casts a self-approving smile at Æther, "Oh—wait! I can't be a Painted Symbol yet because I'm only a chrysalis, so no one really knows what I am. Were you aware of that?"

"Ahh… so the legends are true," Æther replies, to a baffled look from Zara.

"You knew of this?" She asks.

"You knew of this, Golden Ascetic?" Ansebe adds.

"There are old scriptures, that when intelligent life reaches the first great filter—annihilation by the atom—that one member of that race ascends, chosen by the very Gods themselves. That they may assist their race through that filter."

"No!" A stunned realisation from Zara, "I'm supposed to save the human-race from self-annihilation—"

Sub-Rohza cuts in, "Oh dear. We have visitors."

Alarms sound. Æther yells, "Prepare thy selves," and operates the ships holograms. "Retrieve your tech, the Elb are here." Above the Three Kingdoms the giant Hand of Ice emerges into the surrounding space-time. The huge crystalline structure expands its five shards in an open-hand configuration. Each of the icy shards slowly close together, encircling the three saucers like a hand getting ready to click its fingers, and then the mysterious Elb appear to rearrange the very fabric of reality itself. They do not travel through the vast expanse, instead space becomes a cocoon as they weave the strings of the universe into a silken-case, only to break it open, emerging at their destination. A form of travel so inexplicable that the Eyt have not developed the conceptual awareness to even measure the basic mechanics of such phenomena.

A second set of alarms sound, these ones signal a more serious warning as holo-view screens show outside—the super massive black-hole at the centre of the Milky Way. Zara stops to look at the view-screen, her face lit up from the image. "Oh my God," she takes a step forward, "Sagittarius A-star... it's nothing like I thought it would be." Just then the ship's star-drives moan a sickening hum as they try to balance the change in gravity back to normal. "Oh... feel heavy." Zara drops to her knees, then on to her hands as the Three Kingdoms' power output rises to compensate.

"Gravitational anomaly!" Ansebe shouts, still able to stand, "The engines can't keep this up." He takes over the holo-controls, trying to calibrate the ship's gravitational field—a useless endeavour—he tries desperately but to no avail. Just then his ears twitch, something is behind him.

It appears by their side as if it had been there all along, and as it does the gravitational anomaly is no more. The Elb of Tropical Convergence, the sphere that they are familiar with makes its presence known.

"< The problem of the singularity is no more. >"

"Oh my!" Sub-Rohza analyses the space-time configuration, "How unusual," she creates holograms showing the Hand of Ice, encircled in a giant ghost-like bubble, next to the supermassive black hole. "Analysis. It appears the Elb have created a negative-emergence—made-us-imaginary—we are either off the line in this space-time—"

"Or they have made the entire universe imaginary," Æther stomps his staff, "I can feel the myself at odds with this reality. Which is it?"

"< You'll never know! >" replies the Elb of Tropical Convergence as it creates a dimensional rift, a doorway linking the Three Kingdoms to the main hall within the Hand of Ice. "< Dispel your fears, trial of strength is now—this way. >" The Elb stops next to the giant automatons. "< These two, your heavy hitters as you so proudly call them... why are they here? >"

"They may be required to compel testimony," Ansebe steps forward, "as litigator I deem them relevant." The Elb glows an emerald green, as if in deliberation.

"< They are not welcome. >"

"No!" Ansebe stands firm and unwavering, "We all go, all of our party including our tetras, the Fy and the xylographitet."

"< All are not required. >"

"All of us or none!" Ansebe gambles on his shamanic insight, "If the all-powerful Elb are flawless, why would they find our full party to be distracting—unless they themselves have some inadequacies?"

"< We are beyond such concepts—all may attend. >"

Ansebe gives a sigh of relief, for only he knows of possible future outcomes foretold to him by Kyubi-K.

And so, through the doorway they all pass, with one step they leave the Three Kingdoms and with the other they step into the Hand of Ice. The Elb leads everyone to the bridge, whereby they find themselves inside the Hall of the Celestial Witnesses. An ominous place, with ill-lit areas, shadows in the darkness at contrast with the unusual rainbow-coloured crystalline floor. Over a large circular platform the Elb moves, showing the place on which they all must stand.

"< All are now present at the second trial of strength. The Judgement of the Terrans. Note this, the paradox of lies and truth may not be used a second time as a defence—we are outside such concepts—the tribunal is now in session. >"

The opening ceremony of the trial of strength begins, whereby three of the Elb use their arcane abilities to bring forth three Astras. The Metal Elb creates a huge arrow made of iron, so large that all present could stand on its tip. Next, the Elb of Fire and Fusion creates an arrow of pure energy, vibrant like the stars. And last, the Elb of Earthly Presence creates an arrow made of pure granite, shaped as smooth as silk. The three Elb spin around each other and as they do, the three Astras rise in the air, levitating ominously overhead.

"The Three Infallible Arrows," Æther whispers to Zara. "Now they're just showing off."

"What do they do?" Zara stares at the gargantuan arrowheads, having to move her head to view the giant fletchings at the end of the shafts.

"With the first arrow, they mark all that they wish to destroy. With the second arrow all they wish to save, and when the third arrow is used, it will extinguish all things chosen for destruction."

"Where's the bow?"

"Think of them as concepts rather than real arrows."

Without warning the three arrows all drop to the floor with a colossal crash, the noise of which explodes outwards throughout the giant hall—creating a wave of misplaced air. Zara shields her eyes as the gust of wind hits, and as it falls silent she gives a sharp exhale, preparing for what my come. And so, the trial of strength begins.

The Elb of Tropical Convergence faces the circular platform, addresses the court.

"< To the envoy of the Eyt Ree-Juhns, this Trial shall be governed by the square and the circle. >"

A circle of pure plasma appears above them, Lady Devanagari reaches out to touch it, but Master Antariksha pulls her hand away. Then a second line of plasma, this time a square within the circle. "< Overseeing your actions, the sacred lines-of-force be in attendance. The squareness interrogates your minds with logic. Where you seek to avoid a straight answer, pursue discharge due to unforeseen occurrences or petition the denial of free-will-argument—this energy is called roundness—and may not be used. >" Ansebe tries to speak, to object, but as he does something strange occurs. His words do not appear. "< When this energy of roundness is detected the circular lines-of-force may be used to mute your argument—or even the more so—make it so that the origins of such evidence never even existed. >" The Elb shines an emerald hue, unaware that it has an aura of arrogance about it. All of which does not go unnoticed by Ansebe; what if they suffer from hubris he thinks, such an excessive pride which could prove their downfall. Giving a wry smile he shakes his head, which infuriates the Elb of Tropical Convergence. A deafening sound reverberates as the Elb adds with a piercing-tone.

"< Do you understand? >"

"No, we do not." Ansebe replies, able to speak.

"< Not? >"

"We do not understand."

"< This is using roundness to avoid the logic of squareness. >"

"How would I know?"

"< We ask again. Do you understand the premise of this trial? In that there can be only one logical conclusion? >"

"I say we do not!"

"< On what basis? Answer! >"

"I request that this court allows Fez-Pyan—the Serpent That Shines—to answer."

"< You may continue. >"

"Serpent That Shines," Ansebe begins his first cross-examination, "can you only ever know and only know this squareness—without roundness—can you ever use logic without resorting to base trickery?"

"I can't say that I can," Fez squints on feeling an unusual sensation in his head, he drums his fingers against his temple.

"Please expand on this." Unsure what to say next, the holo-memory implant triggers one of the thousands of possibilities buried in his head. His mind kicks into gear.

"It's not in my nature!"

"He states it is not in his nature," Ansebe paces a circle, faces the Elb, "not in his nature." He raises a finger, "But what nature is it he refers to? The course of nature? The nature of the beast? Good nature or the nature that abhors a vacuum? Furthermore, can the court even differentiate between these idioms?"

"< You are treading on dangerous ground, litigator. >" The Elb moves in to face Fez. "< On your so-called nature, clarify! >"

"In short, I ignore the sheer scale of what is roundness and whatever squareness is and treat them as irrelevant. It's not in my nature to do otherwise."

"< Why is your nature outside of such things? >"

"Because it's in everyone's nature to have a personality. Some are logical, few are wise, some are calm, many are fearful, the bad are sneaky and even the brave can be sinister. As our character traits are different, our actions shall be also." A moment of sudden insight from Fez, he laughs, "I have an unyielding determination borne from many personalities folded into one—how could I ever know this roundness or squareness of yours?"

The Elb of Tropical Convergence retreats to confer with the court and after a brief respite it returns.

"< This Trial shall proceed without any restrictions on roundness. >"

Ansebe's shoulders drop with a sigh of relief, but this is just the first hurdle. If you think you know what happens next, keep wondering. It is just getting started.

Chapter Twenty-Eight
The Trial of Strength

With the trial of strength underway the five elemental Elb read their charges to the court, muting any argument from Ansebe, who once again finds he has no words. One by one they confront the envoy before them. The Elb of Tropical Convergence takes the floor and begins the opening arguments.

"< This Elb has an affinity with the wood Gods and forest spirits of Terra, the songs they sing tell of how the Terrans have failed Gaia. My energy bleeds at their wanton destruction of rain-forests. Heed our warnings they have not... they cannot change. I say convince me otherwise. >"

Next up the Water Elb moves forward. Its transparent shell a myriad mirror of oceans from countless worlds apart, morphing from one oceanic view to the next as it speaks.

"< This Elb is one with all the worlds of water, the plentiful abundance of life giving sustenance is my abode. >" The Water Elb flows over the Three Infallible Arrows and as it does it transmutes the three arrows into a titanic three-pronged spear. It is the Trident, destroyer of worlds. "< See before you the Earth shaker, harbinger of tidal ferocity, tsunamis and maelstroms. >" The Water Elb levitates the vast weapon and demonstrates a tiny iota of its power. It turns the giant structure on its axis, the three prongs begin to turn in a drilling motion which increases to a spin so fast that the immense structure vibrates the very space they stand in—destructive potential of such a force that the very air rings with an ear-piercing tone. "< A weapon that tears this one apart to use, and yet its eventual use I fear, for the Terrans' crimes against water anger this one so. Rivers polluted beyond redemption, seas made bad, a terrible dumping ground, catastrophes of oil and over-consumption of the creatures of the sea. Moreover, Terrans do not share this abundant bounty. Water apartheid is a terrible sin. None need die of thirst when humanity chooses to be an oasis where the compassion of water be found. >"

Again, Ansebe tries to speak but cannot do so. Then a sudden change in the air, a scent of fire and brimstone as the Elb of Earthly Presence looms in front of them. Its aura is the diabolic oncoming of darkness. A shroud of blackness falls, whereupon the only visible light is a fiery red which radiates from the Elb's translucent shell. A window into a volcanic world. As it advances it transmutes into a raw diamond, a divine light shepherded by the sullen smell of death. "< I can be a scintillating precious thing that cuts deep—tainted minds, hearts and souls are the price men gladly pay to obtain me. Pride, greed, lust, envy, wrath, gluttony and sloth go where I go and do not discriminate in breaking the wanton lives of men. >" The darkness is replaced with a sea of mist, under which a constellation of lights shines from beginning to end. A sudden wind reveals a terrible sight—a deluge of bodies sleeping in a lake of blood. There they lie, from the very young to the old all frozen, each one clutching a ball of light shining like sun-beams through their fingers. "< Look closer! >" The Elb says with an ominous change to its acidic appearance, whereupon revealed before them are raw diamonds in the hands of the dead. A sea of blood diamonds, the apparition becomes. "< The darkest hours of men cast their shadows before you, stains of conflict washed clean, polished and shaped as a love-tokens. >"

Another disclosure begins, this time the Elb of Earthly Presence transmutes into a replica of the Earth weaving a visible magneto-sphere from pole to pole, animating the magnetic fields in shades of red and yellow.

"< The Terrans rely on fossil fuels, slowly destroying their ecosystems—when they have electromagnetism at their disposal—enough perpetual energy to make such fuels obsolete. But, the evils of the petro-dollar industry corrupt the son with the sins of the father—and with that the assassination of clean-energy ideals. I say man is done for, time to let other species prosper. >"

Ansebe remains unable to defend the accused, to speak out, as do the others when Sub-Rohza slips next to Zara, nudging her, "This is a Kangaroo Court! Why don't you speak out? You're way stronger than you realise." With an upsurge of emotion, she does just that.

"I'm sorry, but I need to speak up for those who can't speak for themselves... find justice for those about to be crushed."

"< It speaks! >" The Elb all shout out simultaneously.

"Damn right I do!" Zara shouts, her eyebrows rise, "This is all wrong, you're just picking on our bad sides, there are two sides to the Terrans' nature."

"< The Terran speaks... how is this so? >"

"What's the matter, am I not supposed to?" The Elb of Earthly Presence moves closer to face Zara. It tries to mute her speech, but something prevents it from doing so.

"< This one senses something, not often seen... >" A recognition dawns on the Elb, it transforms into the likeness of an ice-planet, "< Anticipated this is not, we have a symbol before us... a chrysalis no less. >" And with a convulsive shiver the Elb retreats, as if wary of something.

Out of the blue the Metal Elb materializes to face Zara, having plucked two old English knights out of their time-line and into the Hall of the Celestial Witnesses. They fight a wager of battle, mace against battle-axe. In the melee shields clash and with their weapons they try to smite each other. In a berserk rage they fight to the bitter end, unaware of their surroundings, for seared into their eyes is the illusion of where they were only seconds before. A deciding blow hits. The scales of life and death tipped by the cold weight of metal, and with the battle decided the two knights fade away as wraithlike entities returned to whence they just come.

"< I have seen the ages of man find terrible means to wreak havoc, with cold things cast of metal for the letting of blood. My beautiful elements used wrongly so, such is man's use of metal, of whom I wish gone. >"

"No!" Zara shouts, her eyes ablaze with righteous indignation, "I won't have it, we've used metal to build great structures and wonders—we haven't just used this element to create weapons of war."

"< Great structures? >" A giant belt-fed machine gun falls to the floor, miraculously landing on its tripod. Its size colossal. Its belt-fed bullets seem to trail off into infinity. As silence falls it triggers, and with each round fired a terrible crash of thunder. It is of such an intensity that Zara jumps back, covering her ears. It stops suddenly, leaving behind a clamour of echoes. "< For every remarkable thing made from metal, the Terrans have made something far worse. This Elb only mentions the sins of iron, there are many more. I say rid Gaia of the hostility of men. >"

Next up is the Elb of Fire and Fusion, it phases in front of them. Its entrance is impressive, for under its translucent shell an orbital symmetry, as one by one it mimics the atoms of the heavy elements. A surreal animation. "< This Elb has only one sin to list, the greatest of them all—nuclear annihilation. Behold the future winds of change. >" The set changes to a view from the international space-station, the entire crew looking through the window at the beauty of Gaia, but something amiss can be seen in their expressions. A grave seriousness that something is aloof, foreboding. "< I give you mutually assured destruction. As you can witness… >" From the space-station the planet Earth is viewed. A serene blue marble, peaceful, passive, when one of the crew points to a white spot, then another. More follow, leading to a chain-reaction, as the blue planet appears to twinkle in space. The whiteness hails the day of reckoning. "< This is the possibility which man makes certain. What say you Zara Hanson, seeing this glimpse of man's future? >"

"I say we can change. The future takes many paths, like forks in the road, we just need to choose the right one. Stay on the right track."

The Elb of Tropical Convergence returns to take centre stage. "< These are our charges. We are part decided on the Terrans' destiny—convince us otherwise. Litigator Ansebe, you may state your defence. >"

A release of air from Ansebe, at last he can speak. He paces back and forth, hands behind his back, his skin turns a golden hue. It is one of illumination.

"The defence shall cross-examine Zara Hanson," he beckons her forward. "Would you tell the court how long we have known each other?"

"Well…" taken aback, she ponders how best to answer, "you could say days, but then again you could say several lifetimes. It feels like I've known you my whole life."

"And in this time, would you say you trust my judgement?"

Unsure where this is going, she gives a terse reply.

"I've no reason not to."

"I ask that you trust my defence and do not draw any forgone conclusions."

"Okay?" Zara nods, her brow knits together with a look of curiosity. What's he up to?

"Zara Hanson, what is love?"

"Well, you won't find it anywhere near these jelly-beans," she looks at the Elb.

"Please, tell us what love is—not that which it is not."

"What is love?" Zara raises an eyebrow and smiles, "It is something indescribable, to categorise it would do its power a disservice."

"And yet categorise it we must." Ansebe's skin changes its tone, pigments diversify a hypnotic effect, influencing her emotions, "Please—what is love?"

"Love… universal love, such as the inexplicable bond between mother and child is like an inseparable tether. This type of love cannot be severed, because a part of each is within each other. This love transcends death. It remains strong, even if mother and child are separated at birth."

"And you never knew your mother, did you?" Zara's eyes glaze over.

"You know I didn't."

"As you see, you can sense," Ansebe faces the Elb, "hide this love, she doesn't." The Elb remain silent, at which point Ansebe thinks on his feet, choosing his next question.

"Zara, that type of love is a given. In fact, we could even argue it is nothing but evolutionary instinct," he smiles, and as he does his skin glows golden. "Tell us what Terrans say about that which is hard to find, this thing called true love."

"Love, true love is so rare because it is misunderstood—everyone has self-love, people love themselves and consume things that taste good to them, but when lovers engage in this manner it's an untrue love that only sustains self-absorbed needs. It rarely lasts, but true love is not about what you get—it's created on what you give."

"Really, how is this so?"

"By giving to those who you love, you invest a part of yourself in them, and as you love yourself, you cannot help loving that part of you which is in others. Truth is, love is only found within—this is true love, it transcends the sands of time."

"Is love a necessity to live?"

"I believe where there is life…" Zara looks at the Elb, "there is the possibility for love."

"Tell me, can this love bring about the future non-arising of evil?"

"When one loves all living things, one cannot be without compassion."

"Without compassion?" Ansebe asks, with a satisfied nod as if to say it's going quite well.

"What we call compassion arises from the selfless act to alleviate suffering in all its forms—it's freely given, without the need for reward."

"Do you believe Terrans can overcome their inadequacies with love and compassion?"

"I would say so, with a little wisdom—which usually accompanies enlightenment."

"What is the combined result of these aspects?"

"I would say consciousness, from which we find the questions. When we look for the answers, this leads to evolution and understanding the eternal reality, where we fit in—when present on a global scale, it can awaken real change."

"What questions are found?"

"Well… for starters, humanity may start to ask what is the purpose of life? How are we are connected to our universe?"

"Do you wish such a global change to avert the future evils of man?"

"I do."

"Thank you, Zara Hanson." Ansebe turns to the Elb.

"It is said the wish is father to the thought, and success has many fathers. I ask that the Elb show compassion and open the path to the higher-self in all Terrans."

The Elb all reply in unison.

"< We could open this path, this is true. Zara Hanson, you have awakened us to this thing called compassion—we realize the compassionate thing to do is stop mankind's suffering. Make good their wretched existence. It shall be like they never existed, this is true benevolence, is it not? No pain, no suffering, no fear.

226

We shall extinguish humanity and return stability to the universe. >"

"No!" Zara yells, "No, you've misinterpreted—"

"Stop…" Ansebe looks to the floor, recalls the message given to him by Kyubi-K in the Shangari Temple. "Defend humanity I can no more," he closes his eyes. "The Elb are correct." Zara runs to face Ansebe, she looks into his eyes and with a scowl of horror realises the ultimate betrayal. Her lip quivers, she shakes her head.

"No… no, no, no, you're not real, this isn't real," she lunges at Ansebe, slapping him on the arms and chest. "Why do you say this… why?"

Ansebe ignores her blows and turns to face the Elb, with a heavy heart he says, "On behalf of the Eyt we withdraw any and all defence."

"< So be it… do you have any final observations? >"

"I ask you dispense judgement after Zara has had a chance to say goodbye." Zara drops to her knees, shell-shocked, her eyes well up and her shoulders begin to tremble.

In the drama Æther, Fez, Gnash-Byte and the eight Fy are nowhere to be seen—minutes earlier the holo-memory implanted by Kyubi-K activated, subconsciously directing Fez like a catatonic puppet. On seeing Fez leave, Æther followed him. For some reason the Elb were far too preoccupied with Zara to notice them gone. We join them, behind the bridge where the five crystalline shards meet in a place known as the Hallway of Unlimited Potential. A nexus point, one that allows the Elb's Celestial Witness to use their powers in this dimension. They stand upon a rainbow-hued floor, under which tens of thousands of critters glow like bioluminescent plankton. It is the power-source. Fez tilts his head to one side, looking at the floor, just then the holo-memory speaks inside his mind. It is the voice of Kyubi-K:

"< You must break the floor, break the floor diminish the Elb's power! >"

"I must break the floor, diminish the Elb's… what the frak is this?" Fez snaps out of his trance, looks at the floor, then to his side at Æther, "Is this your doing?"

"It is not." Æther stomps his staff, "Quickly, what is it you have to do?"

"I've gotta break the floor, it's an engine—powers the Elb."

"Allow me," Æther drives his infamous staff, the eight-way-emergence into the rainbow-hued material. It whirs, unfolding into a drilling platform and begins to bore into the ground, but makes a terrible screeching noise. "That's odd," Æther clicks his fingers, whereby the uncanny tech returns to a normal staff, they inspect the floor only to find it remains undamaged.

"Here, let me try this," Fez guides Æther out of the way and waving his ass-bone in the air, drops to the ground, swinging the weapon like an axe. It hits with such a force that the critters underneath disperse as if evading a predator, multicoloured waves of force expand under the floor like a ripple effect. The floor stays firm; frustrated, he tries again but to no avail. Losing his temper, he hammers the floor again and again with the ass-bone. "No!" Fez screams, "Force-field protecting it," and in an outburst of fury, he throws his golden shawl to the ground, but when the fleece hits the floor, the multicoloured material turns a weakened shade of grey.

"The Nan-arcons?" Fez exclaims.

"Fate has been drawn." Æther shouts, "Quickly, strike the fleece with the bone."

"Oh yeh…" lifting the ass-bone high, Fez prepares to strike.

"< Wait! >" Sub-Rohza mind-links, "< Ansebe has just shared Kyubi-K's message—timing is crucial, hit it at my command. >"

Fez gazes at Æther, who nods in agreement.

"Hurry up!" Fez's metallic face shimmers red with impatience.

In the meantime, Ansebe leans down to comfort Zara, he whispers in her ear, "I said trust my defence, do not draw any forgone conclusions. We try." A sudden skip in her heartbeat at hearing the tone of his voice, and in between the heartbeat there is hope. Ansebe looks at Zara, "Stand up child, take a deep-breath, for with your own eyes the end-game draws to a close." With that said she stands, calms—hope is all.

Ansebe faces the Elb, "I ask that you now pass judgement."

"< So be it. >"

And with that said the Elb begin to change their form—on seeing this Ansebe closes his eyes, remembers the words whispered to him by Kyubi-K in the Shangari Temple:

'To win a trial of strength, ask for immediate judgement. In doing so the Elb must devolve to their original nature, and this is when they are weak. Remember, victory is only reserved for those prepared to pay its price.'

A deep breath taken, a moment of reflection as Ansebe opens his eyes to see all five Elb returned to their original nature, transformed into giant automatons. The five elemental Elb gaze at their hands and then at each other as they adjust to the new forms. Their appearance is not unlike Master Antariksha and Lady Devanagari, except for far colder faceless features, along with individual transparent shells holding their respective elements of Fire, Metal, Wood, Earth and Water. The Elb of Tropical Convergence calls out to Devanagari then Antariksha.

"< Mother… Father, are you surprised so? >" The two automatons look at their descendants with disdain, a recognition of the abomination which they long since disowned, perhaps since the very dawn of time itself. On seeing this, Ansebe's mouth drops, his ears twitch. This was not foreseen. He shouts to the two automatons, gesticulating frantically, "Antariksha, Devanagari go attack… destroy."

At that very instance, Sub-Rohza mind-links to Fez, who stands waiting over the engine of the Hand of Ice, his ass-bone held high.

"< Fez, do it now. Hit the Golden Fleece with the ass-bone. >"

Fez shouts, "Payback time bizatches!" and screams, "Kaya!" dropping to the ground, swinging the bone like an axe. It hits the fleece, which sparkles golden and then a terrible creaking noise from underneath. The floor breaks. "It's split? I've cracked it…" A look of disbelief from Fez turns to a lopsided grin. And with that the intra-dimensional critters die, but more begin to phase into the engine from the unknown dimension they came from. An eerie cry from the Hand of Ice, its engine out of fuel and with no fuel there is no unlimited potential with which to route the Elb's power into this plane of reality. And with no power, there can be no judgement.

"Time is of the essence," Æther says, looking at the floor, "it won't take long before this self-healing organism is repaired. Quick, to the bridge."

At the same time, in the Hall of Celestial Witnesses Antariksha and Devanagari confront the five Elb, this time something different in the two automatons. A change in their body language, something that will not be conquered or overcome. With the battle about to begin, Antariksha waves Rohza, Ansebe and Zara to get behind him. They run behind the giant automatons, meeting Fez and Æther near the entrance to the hallway, who both stand, gawping at the titanic clash about to begin. "What the frak is going on?" Fez asks, looking up in disbelief.

Chapter Twenty-Nine
The Heavy Hitters

Seven colossal automatons stand ready for battle, five extraordinary immortals against the two primordial deities—unfathomable odds—and yet Lady Devanagari has a trick or two to teach her offspring. In her path the Elb stand outraged, incensed that their power source has been damaged.

"< With our infinite potential severed, trapped in our original forms we stand before you—prepare to face our wrath! >"

She does not speak, her complexion mirrors that of the red-planet, for today Devanagari is the goddess of divine retribution. The giant deity charges into battle, her footsteps echo like the sound of hammer hitting anvil—she stops—stands ready in a low horse-riding stance, one arm outstretched, palm open, the other pulled back as if drawing an invisible bow. The five Elb cautiously advance. Time seems to standstill. Then in the blink of an eye she slaps her palms together, jumps a three-hundred-sixty-degree turn high into the air; as she spins, in her arms appears an Astra created at will. It is the Polestar-Meteor—two deadly weights, spheres of solid light connected by a chain of pure energy. A surprise weapon which she wields without mercy—landing on one foot she spins around, swinging the weights at phenomenal speed and lets loose one of the crushing projectiles. The meteor finds its first target, hitting the Metal Elb with a side-splitting clang, then the second hammer follows through, smashing into the Elb of Earthly Presence, the resulting force cracking the floor on which they stand. They fall hard.

A second later, Devanagari swings the hammer around her body, before releasing it in the direction of the Water Elb. Her target jumps back, tries to flank her, but she lifts her foot up, catching the chain, and pulls back reversing its direction and velocity, second time around the hammer finds its mark. Unable to withstand such raw power, the Elb collapses on impact. Then without warning the Elb of Fire and Fusion attacks from behind with a rear choke. Undaunted, Devanagari clamps down on his elbow tightly and turns, reversing the choke into an arm-lock. Quickly wrapping the chain around its neck, she spins around—with such a force and intensity that the Elb is sent crashing into the Elb of Tropical Convergence. The impact releases such a noise that Zara takes a step back for fear, standing behind her brothers. As the dust settles, the last two Elb lay poleaxed, defeated.

"That's new," Æther says, stomping his staff in admiration. "The Polestar-Meteor, never thought I'd live to see it used." With five Elb defeated, Devanagari drops her weapon, which fades to nothing, and walks away brushing her palms together.

Next up is Antariksha who turns a primordial shade of oblivion as he strides up to the five fallen Elb. He opens his hand, palm facing the Elb and summons his arcane power—photons of light exude from his fingers as he generates enough force to finish the job. To destroy the Elb. Then, at that very moment before he can unleash his arcane power, the Elb of Tropical Convergence taps a finger four times on the floor. "< Behold our deliverance—a hidden Astra! >" The hidden Astra appears, a multi-pointed crystalline lattice of jagged light, turning everywhere a shade of sapphire blue.

"The Divine Mace!" Æther shouts, "Get down." Out of the blue, from the mace a ripple of pure energy expands outward, a horizontal ring of white light which passes high over everyone except Antariksha and Devanagari—the light sears through their bodies and off into the distance. With the light gone, the two automatons turn to face each other, a look shared, each knowing what happens next. In a flash the ring of light returns through them and back into the Astra. Its power instantaneously sends the two deities comatose, they drop to their knees, incapacitated.

Thereafter, the Elb begin to recover, and as they stand they look for Ansebe. On seeing him, the air fills with the odious smell of their pent-up fury. All five Elb point at Ansebe.

"Brother," Fez whispers, "quick, take one of the tetras, and phase out of here."

"That I cannot do," he sighs, "my destiny is already written." Ansebe, looks at the others, at Zara, "I wish I could explain."

"Explain what?" Before she can get an answer, the Elb charge forward in such a frenzy of rage that the great hallway fractures beneath their feet.

"< Ansebe must die! >"

"Oh no…" panic and fear in Zara's eyes at hearing the Elb's words, but Ansebe already sprints to the dimensional rift, back to the Three Kingdoms. Fez goes to follow, to fight, but Æther fights to hold him back. Just before Ansebe steps through the rift, he turns and shouts.

"Say you'll cry for me, sister."

"I'll cry…" Zara yells, placing a hand over her mouth overcome with shock—she goes after him, "No, no… I'm coming…" but Æther holds out his staff, blocking the way, his eyes ablaze with a yellow tinge as he looks into her eyes.

"Zara… have you lost faith in Ansebe? In the prophesy of Kyubi-K?"

"He needs our help!"

"We can help him by not committing suicide."

"They'll kill him! What do we do?"

"What can we do? We wait…" and with that said Æther kneels and closes his eyes. Fez sighs and sits down to meditate alongside with Gnash by his side. He looks up, "Sister, please… sit." Zara shakes her head, and with a heavy sigh sits cross-legged. Just then, the two automatons recover from the short-lived effect of the divine mace and walk to stand aside them. Devanagari ever so gently leans down and cups Zara's back with her giant-hand.

In the meantime, inside the Three Kingdoms Ansebe runs into the cargo bay, and shouts, "Emergency Evac!" From the floor a holo-craft boots up, a one-manned space-shuttle. The five Elb arrive, just as Ansebe jumps into the cockpit. The cargo doors open and with a flash of light the shuttle shoots out into space, almost crashing into the Water Elb as it tries to block his escape. Inside the shuttle Ansebe operates the remote console and creating a hologram of himself inside the Three Kingdoms, transmits a message. The holographic projection taunts the Elb raising a fist in the air, it calls out, "The great Celestial Witness, once able to snatch lightening from the very air—now next to nothing!"

Anger is a human emotion, but the Elb's hubris sees them succumb to it. The Metal Elb stamps on the hologram, but still it appears projected onto its foot. Such provocation plays havoc with their reasoning, and in their devolved state of rage, they blindly follow the shuttle.

Still left with some of their supernatural abilities, in their automaton forms they effortlessly travel in space, gaining on Ansebe—but there is a catch—he is heading into the super massive black-hole.

Off he falls toward oblivion, the five elemental Elb in blind rage follow, unaware they approach the event-horizon, the point of no return. Ansebe switches to auto-pilot, draws a deep breath and places a finger to the side of his head.

"< Rohza, can you hear me? >"

On the Hand of Ice, Rohza lights up, levitates from side to side, "< Yes boss, I can hear you. >"

Ansebe smiles, "< Patch me through to the others. >"

"< Everyone, it's Ansebe on mind-link! >"

"< Ansebe, are you okay? >" Zara asks.

"< Yes, I am—now listen. I am in a shuttle heading into the black hole, the Elb are following— this was my backup-plan, when I realised the trial was unwinnable. >"

"< Why didn't you tell me… this was your plan all along? >" She tries not to cry.

"< It was… >"

"< But you'll die! >" Zara's hands begin to shake, her lips tremble.

"< And humanity will live. >"

"< No… there must be something we can do. >"

"< I was created to serve, to protect others. >"

"< But you're too good to die. >"

"< Zara, the concept is transient. >"

"< It's unfair! Not you… why? >"

"< In but a short time you have shown me the virtues of humanity and compassion. If this is not good for everyone… it is no good at all. >"

"< What shall I do without you? >" Zara asks, her eyes now welled up.

"< Yes, brother, >" Fez adds, tears rolling down his metallic face, "< what shall we do? >"

"< I want you all to gain from my loss, gain from loss of wrath, loss of regret and future concerns, always be in the present moment, and I shall always be with you. >"

"< I'll never forget you… >" Zara shakes her head, her chin trembles.

"< It is the sacrifice for this age… >" Ansebe draws a deep breath, "< Zara, Fez, Æther and not forgetting my loyal Sub-Rohza… my time is almost upon me, know that I love you all. >"

"< Ansebe, I… I… >" Fez cannot get his thoughts together.

"< Don't say it brother, I know. >"

"< Oh God… no! >" Zara's shoulders shudder.

"< Zara, remember that the soul is neither birth nor death, it never ceases to be and once having been, it is eternal and ever-existing… it is not slain when the body is slain. >"

"< Ansebe… answer me… >"

"< …. >"

"< No! No! No… he's not answering. >"

"< He's gone, Zara. >" Sub-Rohza breaks off the mind-link, and in doing so her bright light withers as a torch does losing power.

"Oh God no… I can't feel his presence, his breath. He's not breathing!" Zara cries out, sobbing uncontrollably. Unable to speak Fez stands, walks in a circle, clutching his head. Rohza is the most severely affected, her light begins to fade. The quantum-field that once resonated so strongly with Ansebe is no more and without a master, a Sub-Rohza does not live long. It is Æther who is still calm, with senses tuned into the very fabric of time he experiences a flash-forward, his eyes flicker momentarily.

"Zara, the Urumi… look!" From her side-satchel a glow, her eyes widen, she reaches in. On contact, the elephant's eyes on the hilt of the Urumi sparkle, inlaid gemstones glisten and once again Zara bolts upright, externally catatonic. Internally, she falls through space and time arriving at a vague but familiar location. Shades, images, at first blurred, but then her senses sharpen, return to clarity.

Once again Zara is Princess Rani—she turns to see Prince Fanishwar running, axes held high he shouts, "I have killed many assassins, shan't, can't ever beat the Serpent That Shines!"

Again, Fanishwar stops dead in his tracks, seeing Prince Achuta dead and drops both his axes in shock. Princess Rani once again drops to ground, kowtowing to the Gods, sobbing uncontrollably. There she stays sobbing, praying to the Gods—unable to leave she repeats the same words, over and over, "Krishna, please bring back my brother Prince Achuta and I shall serve you a thousand lifetimes!" After some time, her voice goes hoarse, she cannot speak when an eerie silence falls. Ganesha the elephant taps her on the shoulder with its trunk. She turns but falls back to the ground, shielding her face, scared to look. Ganesha tugs at her arm, she slowly moves it and as she does, her eyes widen on seeing the divine beings Antariksha and Devanagari. Prince Fanishwar runs to the deities and kowtows—unable to speak. Then, no sooner had they appeared, they disappear.

"They are gone?" Princes Rani releases her breath, having been entranced by the very Gods themselves. Then a voice is heard, "Rani," it speaks again, "I had the strangest dream." The princess smiles, she spins around to see Prince Achuta alive, upon which tears of joy roll down her face. "Is it so? It is so! Our prince he lives… he lives!"

Once more Zara kicks back into consciousness with a vengeance, overwhelmed by intense emotions she takes a few seconds to adjust, then she figures it all out.

"I see it now. It's you… always has been." Zara kowtows before Master Antariksha, "You have the power to save him. The Ultimate Salvation—it's not just a lineage, it's a conduit to higher realms… save him, I beg you." Alas, Antariksha shakes his head, crosses his arms and turns his back on her. "Why? Why won't you save him?" Tears begin to stream down Zara's face, but the giant deity stands aloof, indifferent, blind to her pleas. Lady Devanagari on the other hand is overcome with empathy and places a hand on his shoulder, to persuade him otherwise, but he shrugs her touch. Devanagari turns to console Zara, only to notice something unique in her eyes—a gift so unique she clasps her hands with delight. The goddess kneels and with her forefinger brushes a teardrop off Zara's face. With the minute tear on her giant fingertip, she stands and raises her finger over Antariksha's shoulder, so that the teardrop falls. As it lands, an unusual effect in Antariksha occurs as the very stars under his translucent skin appear to go nova, shining bright. And with that change, the giant deity that is in some way part of the universe yields—shakes his head—as if the tear had somehow found a way into the very makeup of his being.

"The Painted Symbol be opened," Æther whispers, his eyes widen. "Look—it influences the deities."

Master Antariksha places his hands on Lady Devanagari's shoulders and facing her rests his forehead on top of hers—a rare moment of unity between the two. Then he turns to face Zara and the others. His familiar non-natural voice echoes loudly…

"Antariksha is space, is everywhere in time. One avatar of my innumerable incarnations stands before you, the smallest spec of my totality is but an abstract material creation. All that is Ansebe remains on the boundary of the gateway before us. Of my avatar, I ask to retrieve his being—of this I ask my higher self to assist."

The one that is the stars begins. Antariksha reaches inside and pulls from out of his body a holographic universe in the palm of his hand. With a flick of his wrist the universe is thrown into the air, with a wave of his hands he expands it into what appears to be a simulation. He places his hand into it and unwinds the cosmic web with his arcane powers. In seconds, he sieves through a sea of innumerable galaxies, and finding the one he wants pulls it out. It is the Milky Way galaxy. Holding it steady in the palms of his hands, he throws both arms wide open, upon which the galaxy expands outwards to every corner of the Hall of Celestial Witnesses. Having opened the galaxy, Antariksha places a finger and thumb to chin, contemplating his next move, and once decided, his voice booms from nowhere, everywhere…

"Information is life!"

And with that said he raises one hand high, one low and claps them together—coordinated with his motion the Milky Way becomes flat. The entire galaxy turned into a two-dimensional disc of glass, hanging in mid-air. Antariksha reaches up and pulls on one end, whereby the entire structure swings on its axis until it touches the floor. He gently places a foot on the end and transfers his weight, whereupon the vast sheet drops to the floor. As it hits it transmutes into a sea of stars encased in what seems to be an infinity-pool of water.

"With but one droplet of the causal ocean, infinity becomes finite," Æther says, with a look of awe glowing in his eyes. The others gaze on mesmerised, just what is the space-deity going to do next they wonder. Time is not left wanting. Antariksha marches to the centre of the infinity-pool, stopping at the mirror-image of the super massive black hole. He kneels, reaches into the water, at the point of the singularity—the centre of the galaxy. His non-natural voice echoes.

"Higher self and lower self. Avatar and Host are one!"

As his hand submerges into the infinity-pool, water ripples move outwards across the surface—at the same time shock-waves hit the Hand of Ice from outside. The giant vessel shakes.

Outside the ship all that is Antariksha's higher dimensional self appears—an enormous hand, unfathomable to behold emerges—like a giant hand reaching into a pond, ripples in space flow outward as the hand breaches the lower dimension. A hand made up of the very fabric of space-time—a universe reaching into another—dimensions merge as the giant-hand ever so carefully closes around the singularity at the centre of the galaxy. Inside the Hand of Ice, a terrible creaking noise as the vessel tries to compensate for the supernatural variations in space-time. Then silence. Time seems to stop as the two hands unify. Outside the unfathomable hand pulls away from the black hole, and with it held information retrieved from the event horizon. Inside the Hand of Ice, Antariksha pulls his hand out of the infinity-pool, grasping that which should be ungraspable. Information at the quantum level. And with that done he stamps his foot, whereby a ripple flows outwards, dissolving the waters into nothingness. His voice echoes once again.

"Reality is information. Ansebe is information."

Master Antariksha walks to the others and opens his hand, showing it especially to Zara. "It's empty?" she says, taken aback but still curious. The giant automaton kneels, shaking his head, and places his giant hand over the floor. At first nothing. Seconds pass, still nothing. Then under his skin a myriad of stars and galaxies group together. His hand turns nova-bright.

At first, billions of atoms, quantum fluctuations take place in front of them. A fine mist reveals an impression, a trace of what once was.

Next, skeletal features, veins, muscles and eyes form.

Then Antariksha's body turns bright white, releasing unknown forms of energy. Thereafter a body, covered in acupoints appears.

Followed by glistening rainbow hues of skin colouration. The finishing touch returns the same clothes he wore before.

"Behold a temporary material creation... returned is Ansebe."

Unglued from the event-horizon he lies before them. Zara rushes to Ansebe's side, she looks at him, "Is he alive?" His body appears still, unmoving, unsure she places a hand on his chest. "He... he's breathing!" tears of joy roll down her face. Lady Devanagari clasps her hands, her empathic senses pleased to feel joyousness in the air.

Ansebe slowly opens his eyes, to see everyone standing over him and as he does Rohza's light returns, burning brightly. He sits up, and rubbing the back of his neck, speaks.

"It has worked?"

"It would appear so," Zara says, wiping her tears—she bites her lip for a brief second, then smiles, her whole face turns a radiant glow of happiness. Helping Ansebe to his feet, she adds, "You know, the people of Earth should be told about this one day."

"Perhaps... in a way you never thought possible," Ansebe says, "but for now let us leave for home," at which point everyone gathers to embrace him.

"Now that I can dig," Fez says, wrapping one arm around his brother's shoulder. As they leave he asks, "So, the universe can do that?"

"It can! It has! It does," Æther says, stomping his staff.

"It is... was, quite stimulating. We try?" Ansebe says, whereupon they all look at one another and burst into laughter.

Just then Rohza reports, "Oh dear! Sub-space transmission. Urgent mission received. Danger-level alpha. Its code-name—"

"Don't say it," Zara cuts in, and as she speaks a multi-coloured geometric symbol radiates under the skin around her right eye, "I already know where we're going, I'm the Painted Symbol. It's going to be awesome!"

THE BEGINNING OF THE END

Epilogue

The past affects the future, the future affects the past. It is sometime in the future, the brothers Ansebe and Fez have arrived unannounced at the Alcazar of the Lords Temporal. In the distance Master Antariksha and Lady Devanagari stand guard at the outer entrance to the Wheel of the Five Phases. As they approach, the brothers nod to one another.

"Are you ready, brother?" Ansebe asks.

"Hold on, I just need to lose my senses... yeh, now I'm ready."

"You sure?"

"Don't worry, I'll deliver."

As they stop before the giant automatons, Antariksha holds his hand up, barring the way forward. His unnatural voice echoes.

"Welcome Ansebe and Fez-Pyan, the Sage Lords have no message of your arrival. Master Antariksha and Lady Devanagari do not grant safe passage."

Fez looks up at the one who is the stars, undoes his shoulder shawl, "Antariksha, after all we've been through? You gonna give me your famous cold shoulder?" As Fez nears the giant-automaton, the shard of the Golden Fleece begins to sparkle. He raises a metallic-eyebrow, "Did I ever tell you the Terrans' story of Achilles?" Lady Devanagari shakes her head, "Would you like to hear it?" she nods enthusiastically.

"Well, his mother Thetis was so concerned about her baby son's mortality that she dunked him into the River Styx. You see, its magical waters had the power to endow one with the invulnerability of the Gods. Alas, Thetis held him too tight by the foot as she dipped him into the river, that the magical water never wet his heel. Thus, Achilles was invulnerable everywhere but there. Why she never swung him around and dunked him feet first as well, I don't know," he shrugs, "but there would be no story if she gone done that. Anyhow, thanks to this story I got this krayzee idea."

Antariksha leans his head to one side, his curiosity peaked. When without warning, Fez sprints forward and as Antariksha goes to grab him, he drops on his side, sliding between the giant's legs to stand up behind him. Before he can move, Fez whips the automaton's heel with the fleece, and holding the ass-bone in hand, spins around to strike the ankle. The giant foot turns jet black, whereupon the one who is the stars drops to one knee. Although meant to be a secondary wall of defence, Lady Devanagari stops to help her partner. At this moment Ansebe slips past them, into the Hall of Heads. "Good luck, brother," Fez shouts, making good his own escape.

As he makes for the entrance, Ansebe throws his quantum dice into the air, unlocking the main doors. Upon entering, force-field doors close and with a wave of his hand the quantum dice stay in place levitating, re-scrambling the access codes. A moment later he arrives at the Wheel of the Five Phases. Within the inner temple he finds a pentagram etched in the floor and sits cross-legged inside the midpoint of the five-pointed star. It begins with meditation; his skin glistens a golden hue as he chants an echo-like incantation. One word, a word that resonates, it is universal.

"Aum… Aum…"

The pentagram begins to glow. He chants louder. "Aum… Aum…"

The pentagram resonates with the chants, when from nowhere a circle of golden plasma envelops Ansebe. It emits a fearsome hum. The frequencies turn otherworldly, and as it reaches a crescendo, Ansebe closes his eyes. Time, sound, sensations all seem to stop. With the opening of his eyes, a metaphysical worm-hole whirls inside his pupils, transporting his astral-essence into an alternate dimension.

He finds himself standing alone at the gateway to the domain of the Elb. It is known as the Kaleidoscope of the Higher Self. A look from side to side then up. It is a place of wonder, one that warps his very senses, so wide it stretches off into infinity—so high that height is a meaningless concept in this place. As far as he can see are myriad patterns, holograms which disperse into dazzling shapes, morphing into technology of extreme complexity, a library of limitless knowledge. Majestic colours of purple, gold and sapphire shine brightly before him, only to fade, revealing a lone figure.

In front of him sits a man on his own with his back to him. An unusual fellow, a humanoid of aboriginal appearance. With a backward glance at Ansebe, he says, "What are you doing here?" A miffed look from Ansebe, he sees just a man—not an Elb in sight, have his thoughts betrayed him? The hermit speaks a second time inside his head, "< Try a little less looking, clear your thoughts and simply conceive. >" Just then the hermit transmutes, transforms into an Elb, which splits into two, the two into four and so on, until in no time at all their numbers are innumerable. A lone Elb approaches Ansebe, a pinpoint particle at first it grows to dwarf him.

"< Who is this that stands before I? The King of Elbs, the One Elb. >"

"I am Ansebe, I come to you with the whereabouts of the Elb mothership the Hand of Ice and where you can retrieve its occupants, your so-called Celestial Witness."

"< What is it you require in return? You would not risk coming here without gaining something in return. Do you wish us to weave a powerful life for you? Affect a life? What is it you wish? >"

"I need nothing for myself, it is for a sibling. I wish an amnesty for the Terrans."

"< It is done. They shall no longer be judged. >"

"One other thing. A tale of recent events I wish to be told on Terra, a story dyed in the colours of her interpretation—she feels people need to be told. Alas, it is forbidden under our laws. On this I mused, then it hit me—an ambiguity in the law, one that allows a way."

"< We know your thoughts, the story you wish told. It is done, six Elb shall be sent. >"

"One more request, O'great One Elb. I ask that you sow the seeds of this story in the past. So, that the word is spread sooner than later."

"< We have a covenant with the Ternion. No Elb shall use their abilities to enter past or future time streams. You are now going to tell me you have a solution? >"

"What if I could give you access to the space-time location of a newborn superpositioning tetra? The one called New-Pyan."

"< Then we could influence its superpositioning abilities, travel through time without breaking our pledge with the Ternion. >"

"You promise its safe return?"

"< We do. Our agreement is done. Six Elb shall be dispatched by the Elb that Rings the Changes, the Elb of Paradoxes shall be overlord of this task. >"

"You shall find the Hand of Ice outside Sagittarius A-star, and your Celestial Witness within."

"< We know. >"

Ansebe raises an eyebrow, if they already knew why make the deal, but before he can ask he finds his eyes closed for him, and on opening them finds himself back in his body, inside the pentagram within the Wheel of the Five Phases. He touches his face, shakes his head and makes his leave. On the way out, the one who is the stars stands aloof, gazing at the palm of his hand, upon which Ansebe makes his getaway. On leaving he smiles, having tricked the deity to gain access to the temple and travel to the dimension of the Elb—but a closer look at Antariksha's palm would reveal the bridge between realities and even closer still Ansebe visiting the Elb's domain! For the farthest reaches of space have been Antariksha's fingers all along, and Ansebe had never left his hand.

Earth, sometime in the not-too-distant past. It is an early summer's evening in England. In the sky Elb comb the land in trans-dimensional transit. In a garden they find the one they search for. Of all the quantum possibilities, something prompts him to look up at three luminal orbs passing high above, followed by three more. At first, he dismisses the sight as an anomaly, an aerial phenomenon. Unbeknown to him six Elb have passed on high, looking for a subject. The first three which pass are the Order Elb, Chaos Elb and the Elb of the Third Eye followed by the Elb of Hidden Insight, Five-Ghosts Elb and the Three-Rays Elb.

"< We agree. It is to be him, he shall be the one that does the telling. >"

"< The Chaos Elb begs to differ. His mind may not endure our guidance. >"

"< The Elb of the Third Eye and the Order Elb shall assist in his endeavours. >"

"< It is decided then, it is to be this one. >"

A week later, an irresistible urge to write as the capricious whims of the Elb come to pass.

Their chosen muse sits pen in hand, words mysteriously appear inside his thoughts. He writes them down, in capital letters:

THE MYSTERY OF THE PAINTED SYMBOL